ABOMINATIONS

17 Spine-tingling Tales of Horrific Creatures and Murderous Monsters

READ ORDER

7	35	11	145
119	59	171	209
73	99		
111	133		
49	195		
79			
89			
123			

EDITED BY
TIM DEAL

SP
Shroud
Publishing

A SHROUD PUBLISHING
ANTHOLOGY
WWW.SHROUDPUBLISHING.COM

ABOMINATIONS
The Second Anthology From
Shroud Publishing

You are holding a limited edition small press anthology in your hands. This book is a result of hard work and creative effort. Enjoy it and celebrate the possibility of all things.

Designed and Printed in the USA

SP
Shroud
Publishing

First Edition
First Printing June 30, 2008
Copyright 2008 Shroud Publishing
All Rights Reserved

Cover Art by Bart Willard
http://www.bartwillard.com/

Line editing by Christa M. Miller

ISBN: 978-0-9801870-1-4

Shroud Publishing LLC
121 Mason Road
Milton, NH 03851
www.shroudmagazine.com

TABLE OF CONTENTS

To my son Calvin, a person who has taught me the joy of creating something from nothing...

-TD

INTRODUCTION
Tim Deal

Welcome to Shroud Publishing's second anthology, Abominations. If you have not had the opportunity to enjoy our inaugural anthology, *Beneath The Surface*, I highly suggest you beg, borrow or buy a copy in order to enjoy the critically acclaimed writing within.

I'd like to start by offering a few words on short fiction and anthologies. Short fiction outside of speculative genres rarely gets the attention it deserves, though its very construction would seemingly make it a popular form of entertainment in the "mainstream." Short stories allow us to sample small tastes of rich characters and intriguing story lines without having to commit several days to a novel. It allows us, as readers, to dive into a story in a relatively short time and then quickly divest ourselves of the content in order to be ready for the next. The anthology serves as our vehicle to do just that.

I like to use the buffet analogy, as simplistic as it might be. I like buffets not for the *quantity* of food, but for the *variety* of food. At a buffet, I can sample a distinct variety of food types regardless of their lack of connection of relevance to each other. I can mix a plate of Fettuccini Alfredo with fried chicken and tacos if I so desire because I am not forced to assemble a completely cohesive theme. The beauty of anthologies is the ability to have that sampler plate made for you so that you can just sit back and enjoy the variety of unrelated tastes, and, perhaps more importantly, enjoy those tastes at your leisure. In that regard, I absolutely love the job of selecting those individual tastes for you.

With Abominations, I wanted to select those tastes that possessed one common core element. I wanted to assemble stories that featured inhuman entities as their primary antagonists. The challenge for me was reading hundreds of outstanding stories from a myriad of talented writers, and only selecting thirteen to publish. Yes, you read that correctly, I said *thirteen*. When I first started the Shroud anthology series it was my goal to feature thirteen stories in each because I felt it would be more manageable and because who can ignore the complete lack of irony in employing the symbolic number thirteen? However, we are only into the second anthology when I realized that thirteen stories were just not enough! As a result I upped the number to seventeen and decided not to be hamstrung by silly number references or limitations.

So back to the challenge. My challenge was to select only a relative few stories out of many submissions. I mitigated this issue by trying to find new, exciting, and unique visions of creatures from the pile of submissions. This meant reaching beyond some of the more common vampire, werewolf, and zombie stories and find examples of whole new creature types or those traditional creatures employed in non-traditional ways.

I think I succeeded. I am especially proud of this selection of monster stories and I am certain that you will be as well.

What lies before you is a good-sized sampler plate of exotic tastes and spicy dishes from the far-reaches of the known world. Here you will find the reptilian, the scaled, the anthropomorphic and the amorphous, and literally *everything* in between. I suggest that you consume this slowly and savor the uniqueness of each offering to its absolute fullest. While I am confident you will find the variety quite satisfying, I am equally confident that at least one taste will catch your palate entirely off guard. Enjoy!

-Tim Deal, *June, 2008.*

SPOILED PICNIC
by Rhonda Parrish

Mandy lay on the checkered blanket and stared up at the sky. The wind stirred the clouds, directing a celestial play solely for her while simultaneously keeping the temperature from becoming to warm. She smiled and studied a shape in the sky created of cloud a wind. A bird, she decided, it definitely looked like a bird. With the grip on her lips, Mandy turned to get a sandwich from the lunch she'd p that morning. However, instead of seeing a wicker basket, Mand' herself staring into the unblinking eyes of a nightmare.

She crab-walked backward on the blanket, eyes fastened on th before her. It looked like a giant ant. Its red armored body, a feet long, reflected the sunlight like a car after being waxed, . eyes stared at her, flat and dead. They were the eyes of a pred feared she was meant to be its prey. The ant watched her sile head to one side. Its antennae waved through the air slowl ture's entire posture spoke of curiosity, and a lack of con'

The wind picked up and Mandy shivered. It no lor friendly, but cold and unfeeling. Maybe all of nature i* me, she thought, half-hysterically.

Stop it, Mandy! she chastised herself. You've crushed millions of ants in your life; surely you're not going to let yourself be intimidated by this one, no matter how big it is. She felt a laugh bubble up to her throat as she imagined the size of shoe she'd need to step on this particular ant, but she suppressed it.

As she shifted her position, preparing to stand and run, the ant pounced. It was incredibly strong, and before she could do more than utter the very genesis of a scream, it was upon her. It held her down with two of its legs and bit her thigh. She felt a stab of pain, and then nothing.

When she woke she was in a tomb-like cavern. The walls, ceiling, and floor were all soft, damp earth. The air was stale, unmoving, and smelled like mold. She strained her ears but could hear nothing. Nothing but the sound of her heart beating in her chest. Strange lichen clung to the round-ed corners where the walls and ceiling met and cast a creepy yellowish light over everything. It was so disorienting that Mandy thought she might almost prefer darkness. Almost.

She tried to sit up and realized she couldn't move. She was lying on her side, bent in a U shape and completely paralyzed. Her chest rose and fell, he was breathing, and she could blink, but no matter how hard she tried, ther movement seemed impossible. She tried to scream, but only a angled noise emerged from her closed-off throat.

dress, once bright and pretty, was filthy and bunched up over thighs and waist. She could see where the ant had bitten r knee. The bite marks were inflamed and swollen, but ve poisoned me, she thought in horror and struggled she'd ever heard about ants and their prey to sort her.

with questions when the ant returned. It scuttled rd her. She tried to scream and failed. Again, the impotent and a pitiful murmur escaped her lips lped, though, for her to hear something human,

lting its head in the same way it had out in the ed together obscenely and its antennae turned receiving information from sources Mandy ally, after it studied her for what seemed like more than a couple minutes, the ant turned bbed against the walls and sent a shower of dirt balls skittering to the floor as it maneuvered in the crowded cave and meandered back out of the room.

Mandy struggled to overcome the terror that clawed at her brain. She knew if she gave in she would descend into madness, or worse. She couldn't let that happen. She had to stay in control of herself if she wanted to escape.

She sobbed, and when the sound reached her ears it was recognizable. She tried, again, to move and found she could wiggle her fingers, ever so slightly. The venom was wearing off!

Her resolution to stay in control and find a way out of her hellish situation strengthened, and Mandy gritted her teeth and began to wriggle her fingers.

The pain struck her the instant she moved, like hot wires being forced through her veins. She didn't know if it was an effect of the poison, or the lack of movement for however long she'd been down here, and it didn't matter. It was agony. After many minutes of struggling, gasping, and crying, her voice appeared to be working, but she hadn't managed to move any more than her hands. Worst of all, the ant was back.

It watched her from the doorway with its head tilted at the now familiar angle. After a moment it ventured into the room, picking its way across the floor with a twisted sort of grace that sent cold shivers down Mandy's spine. I won't scream, she decided, and swallowed back the shriek she felt growing in her belly. I won't scream.

The ant drew nearer. With its deep scarlet face just a foot from hers, Mandy could see every bump, dent and scar upon its surface. It was fascinating, and disgusting.

It never blinked.

It never paused.

It slowly made its way to her as she lay curled up and helpless. Its unyielding leg reached out to her; each little hair on it stuck to her flesh, then pulled away with a sickening ripping sound. She closed her eyes in mortification and felt it touch her face, her hair.

It climbed atop her, balancing with two legs still on the ground. Its sickly underbelly rubbed against her cheek while it made its way up, up until all its weight pressed down on her, making it difficult to breath. She struggled as much as the fading venom allowed, but Mandy knew she didn't have a chance. She could barely move, and the ant seemed equipped with an iron will and infinite strength.

Mandy could see, out of the corner of her eye, the insect tilting its head to look down at her. What does it want? she wondered again, feeling herself teetering on the edge of panic. I won't scream, she thought, no matter what it does. I won't scream because if I start I won't stop. I won't stop and I'll go insane.

The ant shifted its weight and suddenly her question was answered. Suddenly she knew, without a doubt, what the ant wanted.

Her earthen prison devoured her screams.

Rhonda Parrish *has had her work accepted by over two dozen publications over the past year, including Mount Zion Speculative Review, Sorcerous Signals and Burst. In addition, she was honored to have her short story,* **"Sister Margaret"** *be chosen as the cover story for the December 2007 issue of Pantechnicon. To learn more about Rhonda and her writing, check out her website at http://www.rhondaparrish.com.*

DEVOURED BY HER ENIGMATIC SMILE

by Gerard Houarner

B eneath all the other names and the lies that went with them, she was Seda.

In the morning sunlight warming her back, flooding East 67th Street and setting red and golden swaths on fire in the tree canopy ahead of her, she was just Seda, a young woman crossing Fifth Avenue with her heart racing, as if she was six years old again beating boys in schoolyard races. She was Seda, unmasked, innocent, free of the burdens of terror, heading home to mommy and daddy instead of her sub-lease on the West Side. Before kids her age raced ahead to play games she didn't understand and left her behind, before daddy died and reality hurt, somewhere in a land of dreams where words and feelings weren't so complicated, she was always Seda: the true echo of all the other names she used, all the stolen lives through which she lived.

A chill passed through her. The river breeze, making its way across the city, she thought. A front moving through, though the sky was a clear, young dawn's blue. The wind from the traffic racing down the Avenue to make the next light. Anything but oblivion's kiss, always ready to take what was Seda, naked and vulnerable behind all the masks she wore, to a dead, dreamless land of silence and dread.

She brushed away bangs of black hair from her eyes and scurried into Central Park, pulling the sweatshirt hood over her head and zipping up her leather jacket. Gloom thickened on the path she followed under the trees, where the air was cool and crisp and rich with the night's decay, and dawn was still an unspoken answer to mystery. Preschoolers had not yet invaded the playground to her right, and the gates to the zoo down a path on her left were still shut. Birds chirped and sang for dawn. Squirrels, and perhaps rats, made the brush rustle. Seda slowed her pace, breathed deeply, relaxed. The sound of cars speeding by on the transverse road ahead and Fifth Avenue to the rear provided a comforting backdrop: the world was passing her by, ignoring her. She was safe.

Palms sweating, she opened the cloth paratrooper satchel hanging from her shoulder, took out the envelope she had picked up from one of her contacts, a young college student who filled in for hotel night clerk shifts. Inside, she found the makings of another mask: copies of credit card receipts, Social Security card and driver's license for Dorothy Branduit, twenty six, from Chicago, making pre-wedding family and shopping rounds in New York. Rich enough to avoid staying with relatives, to afford New York designers and stores, and plan a wedding without having to worry about a job. Somehow, Seda's supplier had secured the SSN and birth date, charging extra for the risk. The information was good enough for at least a few months of expenses while billing discrepancies, new credit lines and checking accounts went unnoticed. Placed in rotation with other financial identities, Ms. Branduit might last much longer. And they were close enough in age for Seda to live nearer to the surface of Ms. Branduit's life, going to the same type of restaurants and clubs once the original left town, tasting however sparingly, briefly, the rich stew of how real people lived. She caught herself smiling, and did not stop herself.

Under the alert gaze of the statue of the old hero dog Balto overlooking the path, Seda tucked the precious find deep in the bag. That kind of identity was hard to come by, lately, with wealth and busy young female executives with travel schedules vanishing in the post-terrorist economy. The prize deserved to be celebrated. As of now, she decided, excitement bubbling inside her like an active volcano, she was on vacation.

Seda laughed, and the sound of her voice skipped ahead, surprising her with its joy. She sounded like Maureen Siewotz, the Columbia University undergrad whose mom had taken away her credit cards because of Seda's abuse. But Seda still liked to play in her life, every now and then. What would Maureen do? Go with the moment, be spontaneous. Cut class. Go shopping, just for herself. Hang out in a bar where no one knew her, make friends with the bartender, and flirt with strangers. Let go of responsibility.

That meant no identity trolling through trash bins or negotiating with her network of medical clinic and store clerks, cleaning service workers, and prisoners working for catalog order processing companies today. No checking buy lists from her other set of contacts who paid discounted prices for her charged purchases. No bad checks to write, mailing addresses to change, credit lines to open. As of now, she was Maureen. After a quick change to jeans and leather jacket, she might even start believing she was a transplanted Californian having fun being young in the city.

Not even the thought of her mother shaking her head and tsking in wordless immigrant judgment from her Jersey suburb condo could dampen her elation. And why should it? That person belonged to Seda, not Maureen. And right now, Maureen didn't care about mommies or daddies or classes or consequences, because nothing could really touch her.

The path dipped, heading toward an underpass. Cars sped over the bridge in a steady beat of quickly moving traffic, the wind from their passage an exhalation. Leaves gyrated in the air like drunken butterflies, scattered before her in a frenzied dance. She hummed a tune she'd heard on MTV.

"Better not to listen too closely to the true echo," a voice said, feminine, coming from all around Seda, and from right beside her. "You might hear the scream." A gentle, teasing laughter followed, faded.

Seda stopped, body tensed, feet apart ready to kick or run. One hand was in the sweatshirt pocket, fingering the can of Mace; the other was in the satchel, on the stun gun. When she saw the woman, dark-skinned with short-cropped hair, in a sleeveless, iridescent top stained at the neckline, looking down at her from the overpass, Seda jumped back half a step. Police. She'd been caught in a sting. She glanced at the brush on either side of the path, looking for backup units closing in.

"Glittering in darkness, dull at day," said the woman, with the slightest of smiles on her lips, "there is a hole at its center where the answer to this riddle resides."

Seda took another step back, still searching for the police. Maybe she'd run into a set-up by a rival ring of identity thieves, eager to thin the competition. She wished she had a gun. Shock turned to fear looking for a reason to be.

"What do you want?" Seda asked. Maureen was gone. Marguerite, the tough office manager who had become a programming consultant, one of the oldest of Seda's alternate identities, had taken her place. She'd only used the woman's financial information once, and nearly ignored the life she led because it lacked glamour and excitement. But after catching Marguerite handle the city's street people, commuters, sales clerks, waiters, taxi drivers and all the other frequently irritating and sometimes dangerous strangers, Seda had decided to keep the woman in her repertoire of selves. As Marguerite dropped in every now and then to pick up new or reinforce old behaviors for coping with situations, Seda remained impressed by her ability to negotiate her way through many levels of city life. Though lacking the immediate pleasures and satisfactions Seda's other selves provided, Marguerite was the personality she could count on in a crisis.

The woman's gaze locked on Seda. Her arms appeared, bare and smooth, glistening like polished stone in the sunlight breaking through the tree cover, as she placed long-fingered hands on the bridge's stone wall. A scent, both sweet and musky, drifted on the breeze, overpowering the smell of car exhaust. "An answer," she said, in an accent Seda could not place. This time, the voice came from above, as it should have the first time.

"To what?" Seda said, her own accent turning, thickening, to mimic Marguerite's Dominican heritage as she sank deeper into the role of a street-wise, self-confident woman.

"The riddle."

"What the fuck are you talking about?"

"Answer the riddle, or forfeit your life."

"You're threatening me? You want to come down here and say that, bitch?" Seda took a step forward, stun gun in hand though still in the satchel. This wasn't a police action, and it didn't have the feel of a gang ambush. What she saw was all there appeared to be: a lone black woman, early twenties, possibly African by her accent, her tone and bearing announcing she had more than a street veneer of sophistication. Seda searched for signs of a pocketbook.

The woman leapt up on to the stone ledge, sat on her haunches, elbows on knees, fingers hanging claw-like before her. The move startled Seda, and she found the woman's demonstration of limberness and grace intimidating. Her fingers ached clutching the stun gun, even as she wished the dog at her back was more than a statue. She wondered what it would be like to look at the world through such a woman's eyes.

"This is a different age," the stranger said, sitting bird-like overlooking the path. "Your people move so much faster than they did in older days. More threads are woven into your lives, so many more roads are open to you, and you travel on them all at once. The noise in your minds is deafening. I find the answers to my riddles are not as they were in ancient times. But the penalty has not changed. Some things do not change. We will speak again." She jumped backwards off the ledge and was gone.

Seda watched either end of the bridge, but the woman must have crossed the road and escaped from the other side. If she raced through the underpass tunnel, she might catch a glimpse of the mysterious woman. Follow and confront her. Or at least find out more about who she was, and why she talked nonsense to strangers.

But Seda's feet stayed rooted to the ground. Marguerite did not chase trouble. The other masks Seda lived with enjoyed adventure, which was why they lived inside her. But like identities on which she based them, they never took foolish risks. She never let them.

The wind gusted, raising a susurrus among swinging, swaying branches. The birds, she noted, were silent.

Her vacation, hardly started, was over.

* * *

Seda became nervous when the cashier asked her to wait while she called the store manager. Seda was Gabrielle this morning, a Portuguese NYU student, daughter of European jet-setters, who spent most of her waking hours clubbing. She had not been able to master Gabrielle's accent after listening to her gossip one day at a student lounge, but she didn't think anyone in the upper East Side jewelry store would know any better. Her black hair and faintly exotic complexion and features, when coupled with the right look and sound, allowed her to pass for a number of ethnic groups, and she was usually able to use her appearance and friendly manner to disarm suspicion. She had not worked this neighborhood in six months, and the last time she came through she had assumed the appearance of a young, light-skinned Southern black woman. There was no reason she could see for the store manager to speak to her about the credit card.

Seda took a last look at the seven thousand dollar necklace that would have taken care of the week's expenses. She suddenly felt naked under the surveillance camera positioned near the ceiling, looking down on the counter. She turned away from the camera, drifted to another display case. When a new customer walked in, she escaped.

Outside, the sun was fighting its way through overcast skies. A harsh, cold wind blew through the city's concrete valleys, whistling winter's coming. The frigid blast took Seda's breath away, and she fought to keep walking, get away, before anyone came out looking for her.

She crossed the street, headed for the Park. Remembered yesterday's encounter with the strange woman. She looked over her shoulder for a taxi heading west towards Fifth Avenue.

The woman was two steps behind her, in heels and a dark, mid-calf skirt, topped by a leather and fur waist jacket and a leather beret. A few flecks of dried matter on her cheek ruined the beautiful but startling and distinctive symmetry of the angles of her face. Her eyes blazed, lit by the fire from an unearthly lantern.

Seda tripped, staggered towards the street, fell against a parked car. Her hand fumbled for the latch to the designer purse she wore for today's work.

"Glittering in darkness, dull at day," the woman said, walking past Seda, still managing to look down at her, the beginnings of a smile at the corners of her mouth, "there is a hole at its center where the answer to this riddle resides." The woman moved on, paused, looked back. "The threads are untangling, the roads are falling away. When there is only one, I'll have you and you will answer. Or die."

Seda's body flinched as if struck in the gut. Her vision blurred, and she doubled over, taking deep breaths. When her head was clear, the stranger was gone.

This time, she took a taxi across the Park.

* * *

The woman's words circled each other incessantly inside Seda's head. She couldn't quite string them together. They refused to make sense.

Seda shook her head, violently, trying to loosen clogged thoughts, jammed insights. Trying to chase away the annoying buzz of dangerous possibilities. The true part that was Seda and nothing else told her to pay attention to those possibilities.

She continued packing, driven by that true self, choosing pieces useful to several different personas, keeping to basics. Nothing else that belonged to her in the apartment was important to her survival. She had to be ready to leave instantly. Her lives were reduced to what could fit in a back pack and rolling duffel bag.

A soap opera flickered on the TV: overblown dialogue delivered by unbelievable actors using melodramatic gestures and staging. The people were nothing like the real people she had filed away in her mind. They were hollow, offensive, reminding her of a time before she filled her head with other identities, when her life was pale and simple and dull, when she lived with loneliness and a dread of dying before she ever had a chance to experience joy, exhilaration, pleasure. The television was usually an irritating source of distraction for Seda.

But the strange woman's voice, direct but seductive, sang behind the words dancing disjointedly in Seda's head. The subtle song, like a wind turning and twisting through an underground maze of caverns and tunnels, added to her confusion. Seda had a hard time focusing on the things that made her feel better: fantasies about Jocelyn and her harem of boyfriends, Sylvie's street-art performances, Amy's budding theater career. The actors hamming their way across the screen were shadows of the glittering fantasies of otherness that filled and fed Seda. But watching shadows, listening to noise, was better than devoting all her attention to struggling with what a stalker had planted in her mind.

The telephone rang. Again. Seda's hands jumped at the sound. Every few minutes someone tried to reach her, but did not leave a message. Seda was afraid of who might be at the other end. Police. Creditors. The woman. She didn't want to talk to any of them. She carried her friends in her head. Her family had no idea where she was, or what she was doing. For an instant, she imagined her mother calling, her thick alien accent ready to squash English words. What could she ask of a daughter who left home at eighteen and never called back, never visited? What news would she convey: grandmom is dead; your father isn't dead after all, he just ran away and fooled everyone; we lied, you did have a brother, we just got rid of him when you came along, just like we'd have done with you if your father hadn't wasted his seed in other women.

The knock on the door, sharp, short, threw all the words and songs from her mind. She was empty, a vessel waiting to be filled. Terrified of the emptiness.

The knock came again. "Ms. Gammick? It's the super. Hello? We need to see you about your staying in this apartment. Hello?"

For a third time, a strong hand drove hard knuckles against the door. Seda exhaled slowly. Her body felt as if it was about to collapse in on itself. She held on to the duffle bag, but still her hands shook. Reaching the fire escape required making noise opening the safety latches and the window. Would the man break in to stop her?

Someone spoke from further down the hallway: "I told you I saw her leaving a little while ago."

The man at the door said, "She left her TV on."

Silence followed. For half an hour, Seda stood frozen in place, until her back and legs ached, and her entire body shook. Her tampon needed changing. She was about to throw up. Finally, she sat down on a sofa chair and stared at the door. The telephone continued to ring. Cramps wracked her body.

She found Marguerite. Marguerite wouldn't sit around waiting for someone claiming to be the super to come back and question her about an illegal sublet.

Her bags were packed. She could stay at a cheap motel in the Bronx until she found another place to live. She almost cried at the thought of leaving the city's energy behind. Moving to the outer boroughs was too much like going home to the suburbs. The noise, the mass of people, the anonymity of crowds, were all part of the fuel she needed to survive. She'd been driven out of Manhattan before, when she'd been less careful about her use of other people's credit. Everything she'd done since had been designed to prevent having to leave again. It wasn't fair. No one investigated illegal sublets in New York.

Which left the possibilities of police, or a gang of thieves spooking her out of their territory. The stalking woman's bizarre behavior took on a new context. Someone was playing mind games with her.

Seda checked the door, then the hallway. Satisfied no one was waiting for her, she went to the bathroom, showered, changed. Wearing ankle boots along with pants and a top that hugged her body, pulling her hair back into a tight bun, she assumed the character of the Marguerite she had first met, when she stole her purse in a restaurant: the Marguerite showing her street edge, more than five years ago, before the promotions and the schooling and the added a layer of sophistication.

Feeling stronger, almost whole, Seda shed her latest home life, going down the stairs instead of the elevator, careful to lift the duffel bag to make as little noise as possible as she went down. She was out before anyone stopped her, in the subway without anyone noticing her.

In the rocking cradle of an uptown express, stolen companions rising to fill out the emptiness inside her, Seda gave herself to the comfort of all the lives she could never be on her own.

* * *

The police officer stopped her even before she entered the Queens Center mall from the Boulevard. She had not seen him inside the entrance, and she thought she might have provoked his suspicion by stopping outside on the curb to make minor adjustments to her appearance with make-up, a kerchief, and changing from her leather jacket to a longer, plain rain coat. He asked to see her identification and the backpack, and when he became distracted by loud voices coming from within the mall, she slipped outside. She shed the raincoat, checked the back-up ID and hundred dollar bill in a security pocket inside her dress pants, then walked briskly with a crowd across Queens Boulevard, targeting a hospital on the other side as a place to pick up a cab and make her escape.

She was shivering half way to the other sidewalk, though the late morning sun was warm on her face on the unexpectedly warm fall day. She paused in her sprint to beat the traffic light, stopping before a phalanx of rumbling vehicles waiting to for the signal to charge. She doubled over, trying to contain the lump of gut nausea threatening to shoot up her throat and knock her to her knees. Someone put a hand on her back and asked if she was okay. The touch shocked her into a sprint, and she was across just as the "Don't Walk" sign turned red.

Still moving, she cast a quick glance back to the mall to see if the police were looking for her. Granted, she had been sloppy, but she'd never been questioned before she even entered a store. Too many things were going wrong, and no one inside her had any idea why. All they could suggest was where to go to shop, eat and have fun, or in Marguerite's case, how to fight back. But fighting back her way would only cause more problems. She needed more subtle advice. Perhaps it was time to study her hunters, take on the identity of a security executive or even a police officer to help anticipate their actions against her.

Someone touched Seda on the shoulder again. She jumped to the side, as if an electric current had arced through her.

"Your time is running short," the woman from the park said as she walked by. The hand with which she had touched Seda trailed behind her, fingers extended, pointing. "Nearly as short as the answer to my riddle."

"Leave me alone," Seda screamed. People turned to stare. A few men stopped, searching for someone to fight. "I'll give you anything you want," she continued shouting, shutting her eyes, feeling naked and exposed under the scrutiny. "I'll do anything you want. Just, please, stop interfering. Let me live."

No one answered. She opened her eyes. Pedestrians hurried past, giving her a wide clearance. Dressed lightly and obviously distraught, she realized she looked like someone heading for the emergency room in psychiatric distress.

Anger, both sharp and hard-edged, boiled up from deep inside Seda. Marguerite took the restless energy, channeled it into a plan. Follow the woman, find out who she was, and what her game was about.

Seda moved.

Following in the direction she'd last seen the strange woman move, away from the Long Island Expressway cutting across Queens Boulevard, Seda pursued at a brisk walk. From the glimpse she'd caught, she reconstructed what the woman looked like today: brown print ankle-length skirt with matching hat, which was accented with the same soft, black leather from which her hip-length jacket was made. The woman should have been easy to spot on the sparsely populated street. Seda peered as far ahead as she could, across the street, in cars and trucks, the hospital lobby and the small sidewalk stores that followed, but couldn't spot her. Buses accelerated past her, leaving behind a cloud of fumes. Seda slowed, overwhelmed by possible escape routes, and started heading back to the hospital, thinking the woman had ducked inside. She did a double-take after a quick glance down 55th Avenue.

How had that woman managed to get so far away?

More reasonable voices questioned the wisdom of pursuing her tormentor. But the anger flowed, steady, inexorable, ready fuel for Marguerite. You're not looking for trouble, that streetwise voice told her, you're looking for a way out. Seda was glad to be doing something.

She broke into a trot. The street was abandoned, buildings were a blur, silence closed around her. The sound of her own breathing, harsh, raspy, fell into the rhythm of her heartbeat. Her vision of the world narrowed to the strip of concrete beneath her feet.

The sound of her breathing became impossibly loud. A roaring. She broke into a sweat. Someone cried out. Seda slowed. Shivered. Something large, massive, cut across her path. A thick, musky smell made her gag. Fingers gently caressed her face. A woman's voice whispered, "Soon." A familiar near-smile flashed in sudden darkness.

And then she was on her knees, next to a metal garbage bin on wheels, beside a man holding bloody guts in his hands. Red gashes marked his throat where it looked like rough hands had throttled him. His gaze met hers. He frowned.

"What?" she asked, not sure of the question she needed to ask.

"Cer," the man answered. "Sphynx."

"What?" she asked again, crawling away, afraid to get blood on her. She covered her nose and mouth against the stench from the open garbage bin, and the man's torn belly. A crater in his torso exposed ribs snapped off and splintered at the ends and strata of organs and entrails left behind by whatever had torn, or bitten, a chunk of flesh out of the man.

"Didn't know," he answered, beginning to weep. "Didn't know..."

He closed his eyes. His chest struggled to rise and fall. Seda caught the bulge in his back pocket, gingerly lifted his wallet, finding cash and enough ID to start a new identity. She took the keys, money and even the bank receipts and shopping lists from his pockets, and was back on Queens Boulevard heading back to the hospital, checking herself for blood stains, wallet, keys and papers in hand, before she knew she had gotten up and walked away. The smooth, calm Marguerite part of herself called a cab to take her back to her newly rented Astoria apartment on 48th Street, off 28th Avenue, where she had finally settled after fleeing the upper West Side. No train for her today.

She couldn't stop shaking on the ride home.

* * *

Seda recognized the thing sitting on the kitchenette table as her stalker as soon as she walked into her furnished basement apartment . The overhead light was out, the glass and bulb smashed, but the entry fixture illuminated a face that was both familiar and disconcerting in juxtaposition to the other, inhuman, parts of the body attached to the visage.

"Cer," Seda said, the word flowing naturally from her as recognition cascaded through levels of awareness she only dimly perceived. A fleeting instinct to run dissipated under the spell of the creature's primal presence. The new stun gun and mace went untouched in her purse, pathetic in the face of raw power. Seda closed the door, already as exhausted as prey run down on a savanna, aware that her fear of the landlord discovering the thick animal stench permeating the basement was unreasonable, given the circumstances. It was the only reaction her identities, reduced to their barest threads in the face of death's silent howl, could offer. Even Marguerite was silent.

The thing unfolded its feathered wings, and in a flurry of movement Seda identified a snake-like tail whipping the counter top, knocking glasses into the stainless steel sink. Evidence of its restlessness scarred the walls, television, chairs. The rest of its body resembled a lion's, with muscles twitching beneath a tawny mane. There was no doubt the face, eyes painted with kohl, dark skin flecked with malachite and lapis lazuli, belonged to the woman stalking Seda with a riddle. Her penetrating gaze, and the faint, teasing curl of her red ochre-painted lips, hinting of a smile, offered no explanation of what terrible transformation had seized the woman's human body and turned it monstrous.

"Glittering in day, dull at night," the woman said, "there is a hole at its center where the answer to this riddle resides."

"I don't know what you're talking about," Seda said, back pressed against the door. The creature's proximity was a weight leaning on her chest.

"But you know what I am."

Seda's blood sang with the suppressed memories of myth. She remained silent, fighting against the words and images gushing from reservoirs of knowledge that did not belong to her. Speaking would make the truths writhing inside of her real, changing the world. It was not much of a world, but it was hers and she was not ready to give it up.

"Say it."

Seda searched for Marguerite's strength, but that had been stripped away. She called on all that she might have been, had she not relied on the identities of others, but nothing answered. All that she always was had no choice but to answer, in the quavering voice of a child, "Sphynx."

"Your kind recognizes us," Cer said, with a nod of her head. Her tail settled, as did her wings. "Since before the days of Aeschylus, the priests who suckled at the banks of the Nile knew us. Mother Hathor granted us sanctuary. And when the wider world beckoned, and Sirius the Dog-Star guided our flight from Ethiopia to the Greeks, those northern men knew what we were, though their eyes could only translate such power as belonging to men." In claws dyed with henna, she held wild honeycombs between her front paws. Her head dipped, her mouth opened, distending her face and displaying rows of teeth. Eagerly, she consumed the combs with a crackle of brittle hive's heart, and licked her lips when she was done.

"What do you want from me?" Seda asked.

"You know the riddle."

"That man, the other day, you killed him."

"Yes."

"Why?"

"He did not satisfy the riddle's question."

School-book memories mingled with the deeper truths running through her. Confused, she asked, "Will you kill yourself if I solve the riddle?"

"That is the wishful thinking of fabulists."

"But you'll kill me if I answer it wrong."

"Yes."

"Will you leave me alone if I answer it?"

"It depends on how deeply the truth runs in your answer. If the riddle is answered in full, you will be allowed to pass, and the roads you walked before we met will open once more."

Seda slid down the door, crawled along the wall toward a corner of the room, collapsed to the floor under Cer's crushing gaze. "Why?" she wailed, then wept.

"You came to me," the Sphynx answered, then licked a paw. "I'm one of those who wait, in the dark, in moments of blindness. You chose the road that brought you to me, like others of your kind who think they can see in darkness, who believe they are not blind. I plucked the riddle that offered itself from you. I am only a mirror, an echo, of the mystery inside you."

"Are you going to kill me now?" Seda asked, her body coiled, barely able to speak through trembling lips.

Cer stood on the table. Her tail curled and hovered over her head. With a disdainful flick of her head, the Sphynx jumped down, trotted to the door, opened it with her mouth. A hot, roaring wind blew in. The Sphynx turned to Seda and showed her teeth.

Seda could not tell if the creature's expression was a grimace or a grin.

"Not yet," Cer said, and left, her serpent tail high and rattling, exposing her sex.

When Seda finally stood, she discovered a fine coat of sand covered the floor, and her, like a blanket.

* * *

In the last bedroom she'd had as a child, Seda tried to find the answer to the Sphynx's riddle.

Seda knew she should have called her mother. It was at times like these that family reached out to one another, forgiving past sins and transgressions in the face of overwhelming troubles and unrelenting enemies. But what could she have said to turn the years of silence between them into the intimacy that might unlock secrets to satisfy the creature stalking her? Help me, mom, there's a monster who wants to know about a hole in the center and I don't understand, please mommy, I can't find the answer, it's coming after me, it's going to kill me, no, I'm not lying, I swear, it's true, this time, there is such a thing, I know she looks just like any other lady, but I've seen what she looks like, what she's really like inside, and it's scary, mom, and I've seen the dead man and what she did to him, and that's what she's going to do to me if I don't give her what she wants—

No, that wouldn't work. Any more than standing in her old bedroom would magically unleash the secret Cer saw in her. The rest of the apartment had gone through a transformation: a new living room set, different color coat of paint, though the pictures of Dad remained enshrined in their old places. There were a few of her Mom and Dad together, along with Grandmom, cousins, aunts and uncles from the old country. But none of Seda.

Her old room hadn't changed since she left home after graduating high school. Another shrine. Or perhaps a tomb. The part of her that was always Seda stirred, grew strong again in the safety of its old shelter from the world. The bedspread, a motley pattern she had picked herself against her mother's wishes, remained as a tribute to an old, small victory. She remembered the feel and smell of the fake fur on the stuffed animals packing bookcase shelves, and fought against the urge to throw herself on the bed and cover herself with their light, tickling bodies.

The high school yearbook on the dresser table provoked sharper memories: girls and even teachers she'd impersonated, getting drivers licenses and credit cards under their names, shopping and, later, sneaking into clubs under their names. Behind the masks of those first people she pretended to be, the world had opened up for her. She'd stopped being the hollow shell of a child, carrying unspoken burdens of immigrant parents expecting more from themselves than a single, socially-crippled little girl. She'd been liberated from the burdens of her father's death, his lingering reputation as a womanizer, and her mother's random, displaced rage. She'd been set free of the numbing anonymity of her life, drifting untouched through the white heat of adolescent passions and friendships. The terrible pain of seeing, with the crystalline clarity of an infant's hunger and innocence that would not break or mature, all that was happening in, around and to her had lifted as if she'd been injected with the purest of opiates. Impotence no longer choked her with frustration. She did not have to envy others who found their cliques, or who withdrew into drugs, or violence, or committed suicide, or broke down and were shuffled off to institutions. She'd found her alternative to the nothingness stretching out before and behind her, suffocating her with the silence of others discomforted by her uneasy existence.   She was spared oblivion: a lifetime of walking among the living as a ghost, alive but dead to everyone around her, as disconnected from all that was Seda inside her as she was from all who were not Seda surrounding her.

Life had infected her with its possibilities. She embraced the disease, and became the people she could not understand. She lived as she never could on her own. Her life had meaning; the meaning of the masks she took on.

The vision of her life swept her up, became a mask itself, suffused her with the rushing, consummating joy of being in the moment.

The vision burned. Consumed itself. Searched for something within her to sustain its fire. Found only all that was Seda. Dissipated.

The visions left her drained, standing in a room that did not belong to her.

The room tilted, and Seda became dizzy standing in the empty place. She sat on the edge of her old bed. The mattress was too soft. The air was stale, and dust tickled her nose. She wanted to throw up.

There was nothing in the room or in the apartment for her. For the Sphynx. She had wasted her time. Better that she leave, before her mother came home from work and found her, began asking questions, expecting answers that made sense. When the walls, ceiling, floor and her head had settled, she left. Wishing she could leave the Sphynx behind in the apartment, waiting for her mother, she went down the stairs to the small ground floor lobby.

Stopped.

A police cruiser had pulled up next to where she had parked her rental. One officer stood on the car's passenger side, back to her, peering into the front and back seats, while the other officer spoke into a handset. Seda backed away from the door, went out the back door, past where the garbage bags were piled, and dove into the strip of wilderness separating the complex from the strip mall further down the road.

Today she had been Dorothy Branduit, at least financially, able to rent a car to get to Bloomfield, New Jersey, and her mother's condo complex. Though the Sphynx had shattered the illusion of the life of the young, wedding-planning Dorothy with the whole world at her feet, along with all the other identities inside Seda, her credit status should have been secure. The car rental had been Seda's first use of the name. There was no reason for the police to be suspicious of a rental car.

She waited in the brush, hiding as she had when she was younger and trying to escape her mother. The police came around, bumbled through the trees and bushes, withdrew. A tow truck came and took the car. The police left. Dusk fell. The condo apartment lights remained out, announcing that her mother had not yet come home.

The Sphynx rose in her mind with the darkness falling around her. In the crackle of dried leaves underfoot and scrapping against concrete sidewalk, she heard the creature's approach. The same desperation that had driven her to pay a secret visit to her mother's house gnawed at her as she hid in the brush, unwilling to go, but not wanting to stay. Finally, Seda went to the garbage bags and opened them up until she found mail with her family's name. She carefully inspected the refuse and mail, her body shaking, desperate for a clue. Hungry for something to give to the Sphynx. But all she found was old food and discarded catalogs, empty envelopes and bags.

A door opened in the night. A light came on upstairs.
Seda went to the strip mall, called a taxi to the nearest bus stop, and returned to the city. At every stop, she expected Cer to step on board and sit next to her.

* * *

The part of her that was always Seda knew she was dreaming. But not her racing heart. Not her legs, bound in terror, or her arms, heavy with fear. She wanted to run. But she couldn't. The bed she lay on, her first, from the old house before the condo, when Dad was still alive, trapped her in a tangle of damp sheets. Where was Mom? Dad? Didn't they hear the thing coming up the stairs? Each step shook the house, rocked the bed, made her jump. The bed held on. She wanted to scream. A high-pitched sound came out, like a steam kettle forgotten on the fire. In the sound, she heard the name Cer. In the hallway outside her closed bedroom door, the Sphynx walked. Coming nearer. Panting. Scattering pieces of her riddle

before her: "glittering in darkness," "hole at its center," "riddle resides."
Coming for her.

Seda woke, hearing the sound of her keening scream. She stared at the closed door, listened to the late night silence, tried to remember where she was sleeping, who she was supposed to be, why she was frightened.

Not the Sphynx. It was not the Sphynx that frightened her. It was the answer to her riddle. The thing she could not see, that would not come through the door and show itself to her.

* * *

There weren't many rich tourists or wealthy business people on the Lower East Side. Fashion ran from goth to eclectic vintage, with tattoos providing a thread of uniformity. Business was most often done face to face, without credit cards or bank checks. Though many locals hid themselves behind masks, the neighborhood required a kind of honesty that made Seda uneasy. But food could be cheap, the ground floor studio was available for what Seda could afford, and no one asked questions about what she did for a living.

She'd abandoned even the financial skeletons of the precious selves she had adopted over the years. They were bringing her too much attention. Instead, she invented herself as the daughter of the man she had found dead on the Queens side street. She actually felt sorrow over his death, the way she never had for her true father. It was a relief to mourn. The sadness of loss cushioned her feeling of vulnerability, took the edge off of being stalked. The role made it easy to forget, if only for a little while, what had stripped her lives away.

Trying to support herself with the neighborhood's meager resources also diverted her from the feeling of being threatened. Using her petty thieving skills, Seda picked pockets and swept up unattended purses in area bars and clubs, keeping the cash and brokering the occasional viable identity information she found. For many hours in the day, she never thought of the thing that had come to her last apartment.

Settling into a new routine, living a single life closer to survival's fringe than she was accustomed, Seda left the safety of her latest sublet only to conduct the business her continued existence depended on, watching soap operas and movies, vainly trying to live through the shallow characters spilling from other people's imaginations. The identity she had constructed as the dead man's daughter offered her no options for entertainment; it was as empty as its creator. Seda counted the days since she had last seen the Sphynx.

She stopped even counting them when she saw Cer cross First Avenue at Third Street, heading east, in the night's deepest hours on a late November day.

In the night, illuminated by a street lamp and the beams of a passing taxi, Cer was not a monster. The cold and the dark, the rain slick streets and shuttered storefronts made her seem small, delicate, dressed in boots, tight pants, and the familiar leather jacket, with a small, shiny black purse riding her hip, strap slung across the opposite shoulder. Braids swung in rhythm to her stride. For a moment, Seda thought she was mistaken, the woman couldn't possibly be the nemesis that had driven her so far from her preferred living range.

Seda followed, at a half-block distance, keeping to the other side of the street. Across Avenue A they went, heading to B. Then the woman vanished. Seda approached the tenement's shadowy front. Music, grating and metallic, pulsed from the basement. Above, on the third floor, flickering light escaped from partly drawn curtains. There were no other lights on in the adjacent buildings. Seda started for the basement, looked up again. The light flickered wildly. Shadows whirled on a sliver of ceiling. Seda walked up the front steps. The front door was open. A body lay in the vestibule.

Seda froze, nearly cried out. But the figure was only a teenager, empty bottle in hand, passed out. She stepped over him, through a sharp urine stench, and went up the stairs.

The apartment was easy to find. Its door was cracked open. The light flicker had settled into a soft glow warmed by nacarine walls. Faintly sweet incense wafted down the landing, inviting her to enter.

She had not been mistaken. The woman was Cer.

She was still human, though by crouching over a fallen man in the middle of the small, crowded living room, she looked more like a cat protecting its kill from poaching rivals. The pale beads at the ends of her braids clicked as she turned to look at Seda.. She shifted away from the apartment entry, leaned closer to the man's face as she kept her gaze locked on Seda. Murmuring something into the man's ear through barely parted lips, she nearly smiled. His belly, a chalky hill protruding from an open shirt over sweat pants, rose and fell more quickly with her words. His arms rose, fell. Fingers pointed to a row of mounted guitars and records on the wall, or one of the book cases crowded with record albums, audio tapes and CDs, or a pile of magazines and papers on the floor or table or on top of cabinets. One hand settled back to the floor like a wounded bird, another pointed at a framed poster announcing a thirty-year-old rock concert. The group name on the poster matched the one on the displayed records, where one of the young, long-haired teenagers might have grown to be the balding, white-haired man on the floor. Seda flinched at the changes, seeing herself in the future, locked in a deteriorating form, frail, helpless, rundown, options and choices falling away until she had nothing left but a single identity.

A cold sensation sank through her. Cer had already made her the broken figure's kin in most regards.

Candles burned throughout the apartment, small flames steady, nearly frozen, like bright mice waiting for the passing of a dangerous predator. There was no television, but colorful bars and indicators flashed on a complicated stereo system in a corner glass cabinet. Speakers distributed throughout the room remained silent. Even street noise sneaking in through the part in the curtains had been muted. Only the sound the Cer's voice, a faint, almost soothing current of sound running through the quiet, disturbed the peace.

The man lifted his head. Eyes wide, nostrils flaring, his mouth opened and closed several times before he finally said, in a clear, strong voice, "Stones."

Seda gripped the door to the apartment. The man had answered the riddle. Not hers, she realized after a moment of exhilaration, but the one Sphynx had found in him. She let the door go, slumped against the frame. Seething with jealousy.

"That is true," the Sphynx said, settling herself on the man's chest, pinning his arms with the heels of her boots. Still looking at Seda, she said, "But not true enough. What are you?"

The man whimpered, looked to Seda, expression pleading. Violent tremors shook his body. He kept pointing at the poster, as if his former status could save him. But that self was long gone, and it seemed as if nothing had grown to replace it.

"I don't know," he whispered.

Seda took a step back. The cold sensation that had dropped through her floated up again, chilling her more deeply, seeping into bone and tissue. She felt involved in the tableau, as if both participants were waiting for her intervention. She had no answers, for herself or the man. All she wanted to do was run. But time stood still, balanced on the razor's edge of Cer's curled lips. Seda's body would not respond to the instinct of flesh; it was captured by a primordial intuition to stay, to witness terrible wonder.

A low growl vibrated through the sweetly fragrant air, which turned heavier with the scent of musk. The candle flames flickered again as something barely visible whipped through the air. The faint outline of an enormous feline body sitting on the man's chest separated itself from the shifting play of glow and gloom. The walls turned a darker, deeper shade of red. Wings fluttered.

Cer the Sphynx turned her full attention to the man beneath her. Her hands moved to his throat, became paws closing over flesh. The man kicked, bucked, croaked. Cer lowered herself, drew her hands down, talons opening flesh. Blood pumped out, splattering her face. She licked her lips, cocked her head one way, then the other, before darting down. Her mouth yawned, impossibly large, a distended orifice lined with teeth. A short, gurgling cry escaped the man, and then he sagged as the Sphynx took a bite of neck and shoulder, raised her head, shuffled back, buried her face in his chest, tearing, ripping. Bones snapped. Her head reared back, blood arcing through the air following a storm of braids, a sucking sound accompanying the slap of fluid on wall and wood.

Cer ignored Seda at the door, threw herself back into the still carcass, gouging a deeper hole. The monster form took on solid mass; the human shape faded to a faint blur. Before she took another bite, she paused over the man's remains, spoke into the cavern she had dug between his ribs in a rumbling voice, "Your turn will come."

Seda turned to leave, released from the spell of death's mystery. She saw Cer's purse on the floor, took a step toward the stairs, stopped. Again, she wanted to run, but the purse, and its possible contents, held her. Tempted her with possibilities.

Who was Cer, besides the Sphynx?

Feeding sounds filled the apartment. Candles sputtered out. The stereo system was dead.

Seda ran back inside, blind, holding in the vomit rising in response to the stench from open entrails. She reached for the purse on the floor from memory, found a strap, pulled. The purse leapt into her hands. She bolted, finally free, the thrill of escape lending power to her legs and lungs. As she flew down the stairs, she wondered where the courage to steal the Sphynx's property had come from. Had there been enough Marguerite, or someone else, left to inspire her? Or had the vestigial part of herself, the part that was always Seda, suddenly come into its own?

Before she could consider the implications of such an awakening, Cer's laughter chased her down the stairs. She clutched the purse to her chest and burst out of the building, fled into the deepness of night.

* * *

There was nothing in the purse. No money or credit cards, or scraps of paper with names and telephone numbers, passwords scribbled in corners, directions, addresses. Not even pictures of relatives. Seda almost laughed at the last thought: what would Cer's family look like? Women with snakes growing from their heads? Men with torsos like bulls?

Just dust. And bits of rock. Not rock. Something like the beads in Cer's hair.

Bone.

Seda dropped the purse, wished she could throw it out. But she didn't want to open the door, which she had just shut and locked. The street, raw and naked, lay on the other side. Along with the Sphynx, somewhere close. Feeding. The sounds of the monster consuming the meat of a man, and her laughter, still chilled the back of Seda's neck.

Who was Cer? Bone and dust. Hunger and riddles. Questions without answers. A thing out of time, stalking tangential roads through life, picking off loners, broken heroes and lost adventurers, stragglers from the herd, the exiled and the mad: anyone searching for what they were missing, and what they could never get.

Who was the Sphynx? A mask. An image from another age, an illusion, a face in a pond, a reflection. She felt the chance to escape the Sphynx slipping away. There was nothing inside the creature for Seda to hang on to, to pattern herself after.

The creature was like a reflection: cold, remote, empty. Untouchable. Like the people Seda used to prop up her life.

The Sphynx's riddle teased Seda: glittering in darkness? The image resolved itself for the first time in her mind, inspired by the resonance of Cer's presence: stars. The engines of creation, sparkling in the night, producing light to fill the emptiness. But the emptiness was still there, between and behind the glitter. Dull in day? Stars made invisible, drowned out by the nearest star, the Sun, whose light also masked the emptiness beyond clouds. A hole at its center? What lay beneath, behind, between the mask of stars and sun, in the heart of the night? Emptiness. Where the answer resides?

Behind the mask. Behind what Seda pretended to be, past all the identities she lived through. At the source of the true echo of her self, in depths beneath the reflection she saw in mirrors. What she always was when she was Seda: like the purse she had stolen from the Sphynx.

Empty. Nothing.

Her self.

Was the answer as simple as that? What glittered in darkness, was dull in day, had a hole at its center where the answer resided: her self?

The stunted thing that took such profound joy from simple victories, that had grown stronger in the domain that had nurtured its pain, mewled in protest. All that was Seda, the wounded child stuck inside her like a fly in amber, that had driven her to seek other identities in the first place, that always knew she was Seda and nothing more, but still managed to provoke a final purse snatching in a desperate, instinctual spasm of self-preservation, protested the riddle's answer. Not me, it seemed to want to say. But it offered no words of rebuttal, no other answer.

This was what she was when she was Seda, the true echo of all the other names she used; what she was in the land of dreams, before the struggle with reality began.

The infant inside her screamed. Seda held herself, missing the memory of anyone holding her tightly, giving her comfort.

Someone knocked on her door.

Seda jumped back, two steps away from the entrance. She looked to the curtained window, expecting an explosion of glass, a mass of muscular flesh leaping in.

Laughter, soft again, penetrated the steel door. Seda withdrew to the loft bed, sank into the shelter of the miniature office beneath the sleeping platform, kneeled on the thin, worn carpet.

The knocking grew louder, raising dust around the door. Hinges popped. Metal ground, squeaked. The door fell in with a crash.

The upstairs neighbor cursed. Silence followed.

Cer walked in, framed by night made deeper by the broken street lamp outside, blood smeared across her face, sauntering like a model vamping for the front row of buyers, her braids clicking. As the distance between them shortened, Cer became something else, something more, taking from the apartment's shadows, filling the tiny space, knocking over the small dinette table and a couple of chairs. She became the Sphynx, still recognizable by Cer's visage.

A paw swiped at Seda, knocking her to the floor. The same paw dragged her to the middle of the studio. The Sphynx settled on Seda, the weight of the monster pushing air from her lungs, keeping her from catching her breath. Cer whispered the riddle in her ear.

"My self," Seda offered, her voice thin and high and tremulous, like the distant wail of widow discovering her husband had been lost at sea.

"That is true, but not true enough," the Sphynx said. She stared deeply into Seda's eyes, not afraid to peer too closely at the heart of what was Seda, and licked her lips. "Who are you?"

Seda opened her mouth to answer, but found no words. The emptiness would not speak.

The Sphynx lowered her head, whispered in a tongue that made no sense to Seda. The creature's voice drowned her in a warm, soothing bath of sound, draining her strength, loosening will from body, flesh from bone. After a while, the Sphynx stopped speaking. She looked down on Seda, lips curled slightly again in a smile that was always coming, but never arrived.

Her face grew larger in Seda's vision, filling it to overflowing. Her breath was hot on Seda's skin, and stank of rancid meat. The heart of the beast beat louder, faster, than Seda's, pulsing against her ribs. Fur tickled her nose. A snake wrapped itself around an exposed calf, and squeezed. Wings stretched, scrapped against the ceiling.

And as the Sphynx became all that Seda could see, could imagine, the creature's near smile parted with her lips to reveal rows of hard, sharp teeth bordering a bottomless maw.

Smiling her enigmatic smile, the Sphynx came nearer still.

Waiting for Seda's answer.

But already, Seda felt as if she had been devoured, and she gave herself to that smile, aching with a terrible and forlorn hunger to belong to, and be, the thing that teased such riddles from the soul, and consumed the lost with such fearsome, piercing teeth.

Gerard Houarner *is a product of the NYC school system who lives in the Bronx, was married at a New Orleans Voodoo Temple, and works at a psychiatric institution. He's had over 250 short stories, a four novels and four story collections, as well as a few anthologies published, all dark. To find out about the latest, visit www.gerardhouarner.com.*

B.E.K.S
by Richard Farnsworth

The special agent's body lay gray and tattered, half covered by the sheet on the stainless steel table. Morales nodded slowly. "Yeah, that's Mamatez." He meant to cover his nose at the wet, ruined-meat smell, but stopped to scratch his face self-consciously.

The pathologist across the autopsy table gave a solemn nod and pulled the sheet back up over the body. Air-conditioning kicked in loudly, ensuring the room stayed meat-locker-cold.

"Most of him anyway. Crabs do that to him after he got dumped? I heard about how that can happen," Morales said.

An uneven stencil, proclaiming it the medical examiner's property, settled over what had been the agent's face. Like they wanted to make sure nobody walked off with a sheet from the morgue. Morales had had his fill of morgues lately, morgues and courtrooms both. The body's smell subsided and the sharp disinfectant didn't seem that unpleasant after all.

"No, I don't think so. I've only done the prelim, but the wounds all appear to have been inflicted while he was alive. We called your office as soon as we ID'd."

Light reflected off the pathologist's round lenses, and for an instant the eyes looked as if they were covered with silver coins. Morales thought of the ferryman's toll for the dead and the other's he'd known who'd paid that fare.

"Those are some nasty tears. Dogs maybe?" That was a difficult thought. Mick was a good man. Had been a good man.

"I'm not sure. I emailed digital images and measurements to the FBI's forensic lab. The technician I spoke to couldn't say."

Morales stood quietly, running a hand through his dark hair. He sighed through his whole body, but didn't speak.

After a brief, awkward pause the pathologist excused himself to leave Morales alone with the body.

He didn't get any time, though. Before the stainless steel door stopped swinging, Supervisory Agent Daniels lumbered in. Another man followed closely, sharply contrasting with the older agent. With his close-cropped hair, crisp dress, and rigid military bearing, the new guy carried a cheap briefcase and a whole lot of attitude.

Daniels glanced unwillingly at the autopsy table, then looked at Morales. "Frank, real sorry about Mick." Daniels had that I'm-going-to-tell-you-something-you-don't-want-to-hear look, fidgeting there with this other guy standing close.

Morales waited.

Daniels opened his mouth to speak again as the other man pulled latex gloves from the box on the little rolling table, then snapped on a pair and reached for the sheet.

Morales grabbed the man's wrist and said, "The hell you think you're doing?"

The new guy tensed but didn't react immediately. Then a smile tugged at his mouth and he snapped his wrist free.

The confidence and the way this new guy was put together made Frank Morales pause for the first time in a long time, unsure if he could take him. Taller than Morales' five-eleven, and just a little broader in the chest, the guy was hard.

Daniels stepped forward and between the two men, crowding Morales away. With his ruddy complexion a little redder, he smiled nervously, shaking his bulbous gin-nose like a pal.

"Special Agent Morales, Major Rogers. He's investigating the circumstances surrounding Mamatez's death." Daniels' speech sounded too rehearsed.

The major reached out a hand to shake. "Call me John."

Morales looked down at the gloved, outstretched hand but didn't take it. "Major John, hunh. What? State police?"

"No." The Major didn't elaborate. He dropped his hand and turned his attention from Morales back to the body.

Daniels took a few steps back, guiding Morales with him across the stained linoleum. "Frank, he's is from the DOD. Army-something, I don't know what. He's investigating Nick's death in relation to an ongoing operation."

Morales frowned. He didn't like this. No respect coming in here like that while he was attending to the remains of an agent killed on duty. One of his men. What could be so damn important?

"Don't make trouble," Daniels said quietly, hand on Morales. "I know things been hard for you since little Frank-"

Morales flicked the comforting hand away and said between clenched teeth, "That's none of your damn business."

Daniels held the hand up, patting the air, placating, not meeting Morales' intense expression.

Morales saw the hurt in his supervisor's eyes, knowing he had snapped too quickly. With a softer tone, a little sarcasm to appease the man, he asked, "This guy want to know what happened, or just ogle the body?"

Daniels barked a little laugh. Conspiratorially he said, "Didn't say one way or the other. I got called into the field office at six o'clock in the frigging morning and he's there waiting for me. On a Sunday for Christ's sake."

Rogers covered the dead man's face with the sheet, cleared his throat and said, "Special Agent Morales, I'd like to have a word,"

"Yeah, I got a word for you."

"Frank, no screwing around." Daniels stabbed his hand at Morales and then waved it open-fingered. "Cooperate. Fully. You understand?"

Rogers stooped to pick up the case from where he'd left it on the floor, then stepped over.

"What do you want? I just lost a good man," Morales said.

"I'm sorry. I know that can be hard."

"Do you?" As soon as he asked it, Morales could see in the man's eyes that he did.

"I need to know the story. What he was involved with." Rogers had the kind of eyes you'd use words like piercing and gunmetal grey to describe. They stared, unblinking, at Morales from a weather-roughened face.

Morales outlined the undercover operation they'd been working since he came back to the job. He explained how his team was infiltrating the organization of a Haitian cocaine dealer, gaining his confidence, and how his agent had posed as a dealer. He explained how his friend and colleague had disappeared two days ago, and been found late the night before, snagged on the lip of a culvert that emptied into the Baltimore harbor.

"So, you believe his last known whereabouts were with this dealer?" Rogers asked.

"He was supposed to make a drop for Petite Louis, the Haitian. Mick reported he left, but never made it to his destination. His disappearance wasn't enough to float a warrant to search, and we worried about blowing the investigation. But now..."

"Now?" Rogers asked.

"With the body, I don't think we'll have a problem with a warrant," Daniels interrupted.

They both looked at the man as if they just realized he was still there.

"Anything unusual about this Louis?" Rogers asked.

"Nope. Piece-of-trash drug dealer. A medium-big fish. We want the next level up."

"And this house. Anything unusual there?"

"A row-house on Rosemont. Like, maybe a hundred other crack houses in the city," Morales said, shaking his head.

"The people that live there, you ever see them yourself?"

"Ask me what question you're hinting at." Morales didn't like to beat around bushes.

The corner of Rogers' mouth pulled back in a half smile. He looked like the kind that would rather torch a bush than beat around it. "Any children on the drug dealer's premises?"

"Kids in and out all the time. Lots of these guys use children to deal. So, yeah. I guess." Kids dealing had been background noise to Morales, before it touched his own world so completely.

Rogers opened his military issue briefcase and pulled out a manila folder. He laid it open on the empty stainless steel table so that Morales could see the close-up photo of a preteen boy. "Ever see one that looked like this?"

Morales studied it for an instant and said, "He looks like a kid. Maybe, what, ten? Twelve?"

"Really? Look at his eyes." Rogers didn't look at the picture; he studied Morales.

Morales examined the photo. "Yeah, he's got eyes. Dark."

"How about the sclera?"

The way Rogers was spooling it out frustrated Morales a little, but he looked again. "What's sclera?"

"The whites. Can you see the whites of his eyes?"

Morales couldn't. The eyes were solid black, like the kid was wearing some kind of opaque contact lenses.

"That's freaky-looking." He looked up to catch Rogers' half grin.

"We call them BEKs."

"Like the beer?"

"Like B-E-K. For Black-Eyed-Kids."

It pissed Morales off when Rogers wouldn't explain more. It really pissed him off when Rogers told him soldiers were going on the DEA raid to the crack house. And Daniels standing there in his cheap suit nodding, the guy that could intercede, didn't say a thing.

* * *

Morales made his way through the urban effluvia to the crack house with the entry team. Half the agents would go in the front with him while the other half went through the back. The embroidered yellow letters D.E.A. stood out on the black fabric front and back of his body armor, all that over blue jeans and athletic shocs.

They had met Rogers in an alley down the street, and he and his men filed in behind Morales. The soldiers carried Heckler and Koch MP-5s on short slings, with body armor under pixellated camouflage. Morales felt his team looked a little shabby in comparison.

After the final equipment check in the assembly area, Morales went over the plan. He explained entry procedures, fire discipline, rules of engagement and several times reminded everyone that the soldiers had no authority to interfere with law enforcement operations under the Posse Comitatus Act. Rogers watched with an almost amused expression as Morales drove home the point that he, Morales, and not the Army, was in charge.

When it was Rogers' turn, he explained the high points of what he was there to do. He talked about the special ammunition, the communications plan, and then told the agents to watch out, call when they saw kids and not to look the BEKs in the eyes, and no, BEKs didn't mean beer.

As they started out Morales asked what Rogers meant about his special ammo. The soldier popped a round from a spare clip. "Teflon bean-bag filled with a silver nitrate solution," he'd said.

"I don't think those rounds are NATO-approved."

"Our targets aren't members."

"Maybe for werewolves or something?" Morales asked it as a joke.

"Something."

Now the sun cast a faint red glow over the rooftops to the east. Morales intended to enter before the Haitians woke up. Drug dealers weren't usually morning people.

The crack house had been grand once, but now it was on the verge of being condemned. Urban settlers hadn't made it far enough into the city to start the gentrification of this neighborhood.

"If they're making so much money, why are these guys living in such a dump?" Rogers asked softly.

"Bales of cash are hard to spend. Louis walks in somewhere with a wheelbarrow full of hundreds and we can put him down for tax evasion. As it is he has to limit purchases to less than ten grand."

At the front of the house Morales motioned to the two men that would go in first. Both wore bomb-squad vests with Plexiglas shields bolted to their helmets. One carried the Halligan tool, a device with a mallet on one end and a crowbar on the other, for breaking down the most stubborn of doors. The other carried a short-barreled shotgun with a rotary cylinder that looked like an old Tommy gun on steroids.

All in place, Morales said, "Now," on the common frequency.

The door smashed in one practiced movement. The special agent with the tool flattened against the doorjamb and the rest crowded behind the one with the shotgun. Crouching into a tight mass, they poured in. "DEA!" Those at the back door were doing the same.

The front foyer emptied into a long dirty hall, stairs and a big room to the left. A shirtless man on the couch, his dreads pulled into a loose pony-tail, held up his hands and whimpered. On his face, they zip-cuffed him. The agents flowed out through the room as Rogers and his team entered.

Radio calls indicated the agents had come into the back through a kitchen. They found the basement door and part of the team went down as planned. The rest secured the back of the house while the front entry team went up the stairs.

Rogers nodded to Morales like he was impressed. "I'd have come down through the roof and flushed the targets out the front to snipers, but this works too. Different agenda's, I don't need my targets alive."

Shouts and loud thumps from up stairs, but no gunfire. An all clear call from the basement. Morales had been right. The druggies wouldn't be trouble.

He let go a raspy post-adrenalin sigh, knowing this was a clean take down. He smiled at Rogers, gave him a modest "that's how it's done" shrug.

Then he heard the single shot fired from the basement. This followed by a short, staccato burst.

"Doughtery, what're you doing?" a disembodied voice said through the receiver. Dougherty had been tasked with the basement.

"We need to help them. They're scared, can't you see?" Another voice, followed by two more bursts of automatic fire and a confusion of calls.

"Shit, they found one," Rogers said. He signaled to his team and the five men fell into line, trotting toward the rear of the house. "Morales, I'm a go for the basement. Get your men out of there, now!"

Morales said on the common freq, "Dougherty, what's going on?"

Rogers spoke over Morales, "All law enforcement agents, this is Major Rogers. Get out of the basement. Now!"

They stopped in the kitchen, Rogers telling Morales if he was going, to stay in the back and not get in the way.

The Special Forces team moved like five fingers of the same hand. Through the hall and down the stairs. Two moving three on watch. Then three moving and two on watch. They leapfrogged down into the darkness, their boots heavy on the wooden stairs.

Morales tried to keep up without getting in the way; he wasn't going to leave his men down there.

At the bottom of the stairs Rogers hand-signaled and stepped over a dead agent on the landing. Multiple gunshot wounds, all above the vest's neckline. As the soldiers filed past and fanned out in the basement, Morales bent and found no pulse. The face obscured in a pool of meat and blood. He pushed down the panicky feeling at losing another agent. Compartmentalize and focus on the job.

Another narcotics officer lay just beyond him on the rough concrete floor, twitching out the last bit of life. There should be two more.

Grey light from the small casement windows illuminated the cramped basement. Old brick walls and pillars with a hundred years of peeling paint cut the space into a gloomy rabbit warren of interlocking rooms.

Rogers hand-signaled straight ahead. Morales saw the outline of Dougherty in a doorway, just past them, crouching to listen to a preteen boy.

The boy turned and Morales caught the unmistakable eyes from fifteen feet away. Rogers squeezed a short MP-5 burst. Three rounds tore through the grey Old Navy hoodie, lifting the boy into the air, propelling him backward. A split second later the squibs in the silver nitrate rounds went off and the liquid exploded outward.

Morales had his pistol out now, confused at seeing the big soldier spray a kid with automatic fire.

He heard Rogers' voice over the radio saying, "My favorite part."

Holes burned from the inside out as the little body immolated there on the floor. The burning chemical smell caught in Morales throat more than the cordite.

Satisfied, Rogers turned his attention to Dougherty. The agent stood confused, looking to where the BEK had been.

"He isn't released so there have to be more," Rogers whispered into the mike.

Sergeant Douglas disarmed Dougherty and left him unconscious. Morales wanted to say something, but it happened so quickly. Douglas dropped the clip from the agent's carbine, one-handed, and tossed the gun toward the stairs. Never leave a loaded weapon unattended.

The five continued through the little doorway and stayed close to the wall. Old furniture, mildewed boxes of tattered magazines and things not easily identified in the gloom didn't slow their steady progress.

Douglas stopped in front of Morales while the rest continued, bending to peer into a pile of trash. The soldier stood slack, his weapon pointing at nothing.

Morales called over the freq, "Soldier, what's wrong."

No answer. Morales flinched as Rogers fired a quick burst into the trash heap.

The little monster in there screamed over the echo of the shots and then Morales saw the burnout between the boxes.

Douglas shook his head and gave a thumb's up. He mumbled, "Mary had a little lamb..."

"What?" Morales asked.

Douglas said, "The mantra interferes with the mind control."

All the soldiers repeated it together now. Familiar repetitive words helping to clear the mind as they continued their sweep. Two rooms down.

Morales went through a low doorway, and bumped into Douglas. All the soldiers stood quiet, weapons lowered.

Morales started to say something and then he heard the voices.

"Mary," someone said on the radio.

The calm, pleading voices. They just needed help.

"...had..." someone mumbled.

A good guy would help these kids.

The clatter, as his pistol dropped to the concrete, didn't even register.

Three kids stood around him, one talking softly. Morales couldn't understand what was being said. While looking into the bottomless wells of its eyes he saw his son, little Frank in them.

His son was caught in a gangland crossfire, dead three months; a drive-by victim because he stood in the wrong place eating an ice cream after a little league game. But now little Frank was here asking for help.

"Will it be okay, Poppa?" That's what little Frank seemed to say.

"Sure, miho," Morales said.

He reached out to hold the little guy's hand. The sharp nails with blood on the fingers made him freeze. Someone made gurgling sounds. Like blowing bubbles through a straw into a milkshake.

"It's okay, Pop," little Frank said.

Morales' hand was stuck in midair. Douglas dropped to his knees. Thick, oxygen-rich blood from his opened throat blurred the muted greens and grays of the pixellated camouflage into a dark brown bib.

Rogers, beyond Douglas, raised an MP-5 to his shoulder as if to fire, and lowered it. Up. Back down. Up, then back down.

A kid stood beside the soldier, talking to him, and Morales wondered how that man had looked into the BEK's eyes, because you had to make eye contact for the mind control to work.

His own arm wouldn't move. Little Frank was there and then he wasn't, like his son was coming in and out of focus. One minute the little boy he loved more than anything, then something ugly was there instead. It kept talking, faster now.

Morales focused on the floor. A pool of blood spread into his field of view over the pock-marked concrete.

He saw his hand lowering. He willed it to draw his pistol, but the weapon was on the floor. He concentrated hard on gaining control of his own body.

"Poppa, you really need to help us."

Morales did. He really needed to. Some part of his brain knew he didn't, but the voices were so persuasive. His son's voice. He missed the boy so much and now they were together again. He meant to wipe the tear from his eye, but the arm wouldn't work for that either.

He needed to break this hold or he was dead.

A BEK held Rogers by the elbow as he walked stiff-legged and continued to raise the weapon up and down. Up and down. Then he raised the weapon at Morales.

"Frank, we have to get these kids back to their Momma. They're lost and need our help."

Morales nodded. His arm still wouldn't move. Beads of sweat coated him. His breath was labored, like he'd been running all morning.

The MP-5 came up level with Morales face and he looked sidelong. If he held his head just so, the radiant image of his son stayed and the ugly thing was gone.

Rogers' weapon lowered a few inches this time. He wasn't getting a full drop now. The next time it just dipped, and came back immediately.

Rogers sweating, looking confused. The index finger came out of the trigger guard and flexed in a pulling motion. Morales could see that some part of Rogers knew what was going on.

Morales had been shot before and knew the impact of those big forty caliber bullets would suck. Would the bullets ripping into him be worse than the little explosions though? Teflon and silver nitrate tearing through your body. What was that like?

Little Frank, and at the same time not, beside him touched his elbow. "It's almost over, Poppa."

And it was. They were all dead, just like his son. It was just a matter of playing out the hand.

Rogers' weapon pointed at Morales head. "It's for the best, right?" Rogers asked.

Morales' head nodded on it's own. All he could see was the gun now, no more than a foot away. The muzzle was a black eye staring at his mortality.

He looked back down to say goodbye to his son again. The two images were superimposed now. Little Frank smiled a mouthful of pointy little teeth. Frank focused on them. He was able to see the teeth that didn't belong to his son. The mouth and the noses that didn't belong together came apart. He pulled the image of the BEK from that of his son with his mind and the two came apart like Velcro. Little Frank's face there beside the other but distinct, it smiled at his father and then was gone.

As Rogers' willpower gave out, Morales pushed the MP-5 pointed at his head to the little monster that had tried to impersonate his son. A spray of bullets and the hot muzzle flash deafened and burned Morales as the rounds tore past his face and through the BEK beside him.

Still holding the wildly firing machine pistol, Morales drew Rogers' nine-millimeter Beretta from its shoulder holster. He flicked the safety off with his thumb and squeezed rounds into the BEK to Rogers' left, the one controlling the soldier.

A spray of thick blood and the little monster went down. Rogers released the MP-5 trigger immediately and blinked at Morales.

The other BEK broke for cover. Morales dropped into a two-handed Weaver stance and put two bullets into one little beast as Rogers took careful aim at another.

Sergeant Jepson got up from his knees and found his weapon. He started up with the nursery rhyme again and put three to five controlled bursts into everything that moved. The three of them hunted the remaining BEKs through the refuse, through crowded little rooms to the back of the basement. An old coal grate, the wrought iron cover pulled to the side, showed where the last BEK had escaped into the morning.

Now Morales could hear the radio traffic over the beginnings of a migraine. Funny how it had been mute before.

"Major Rogers, over here, sir," Jepson called.

The two of them, tense, followed the voice to a pile of carpet fragments. There, covered with newspaper, were three cantaloupe-sized pods. Sweaty and pulsing, Rogers blew each one apart with well-placed rounds.

"Intel was right, this was a nest," he said to Morales.

* * *

"I said, tell me what's going on, or I am gonna beat your ass," Morales said, his voice rising even though he was trying hard to keep it cool pointing his finger at this stone-faced soldier. Hard to do with the post-adrenaline shakes, the splitting headache and this new crop of Gestapo bastards he found on the main floor after they stomped the nest.

The hard young soldier didn't rise to the bait. Right hand on the pistol grip of his MP-5, the other hand was held palm forward and even with Morales' chest. "Major Rogers will be with you shortly, now please just have a seat and be patient."

There were five or six of them, dressed like Rogers' team, keeping Morales and his agents sequestered in the front room of the row house. Others, dressed in tan, one-piece outfits, had gone down into the basement.

"Frank, I said for you to cooperate." It was Daniels' voice; Morales hadn't seen him enter. But now that he saw the man, the pissed-off agent readied a barrage.

"These Army types have the area secured, and they'll be done soon," Daniels said. He nodded a smile to the soldier, who didn't respond.

"I come up from a shoot-out with those little monsters in the basement and these guys up here, say they have the scene." Morales gestured over his shoulder to the other agents all cooling their heels. "It's like we're prisoners at our own bust."

Through the tattered drapes covering the front window, Morales could see shiny black Suburbans blocking off the road. A few residents were milling around outside of the cordoned-off area.

"They say they just need the scene for a few more minutes and then they'll turn it back over," Daniels said. He was standing just inside the threshold to the room now. Crowding past the soldier that held Morales in check, another one just behind Daniels.

"To hell with that. Where'd they take the druggies?"

Daniels tried that patting motion again and started another set of excuses, but was cut off by the squeaking of three gurneys being wheeled down the central hall past them. Thick, grey-green neoprene fabric covered the man-sized bundles. Rogers was coming up behind the last gurney.

Morales, red in the face, wanted to draw his pistol. Instead he jabbed his finger. "And you, you son of a bitch, where you draggin' my men to in those body bags-"

Rogers cut him off. "Human remains pouches."

"What?"

"You stuff garbage in a bag; you put a man in an HRP."

That stopped Morales. He blinked for a second, trying to work his indignation back up.

"Listen--we have a protocol to follow when we take down a nest. We'll process the bodies for forensic evidence off-site and get them to the morgue, no later than seventeen hundred. You have my word."

Morales, looked from Daniels, who wasn't helping, back to Rogers.

"And the Haitians?"

"They'll be interrogated off-site and delivered to you at the federal building. Also no later than seventeen hundred."

Morales let out a heavy sigh, not sure where to go with this. He had jurisdiction, but thought the only way he could enforce it with these guys was by drawing down.

"That was a close one today. Thanks for saving my ass." This with a sincerity that Morales wouldn't have expected. Rogers reached out his hand.

Morales took it grudgingly and said, "You gonna tell me what those things were?"

Rogers shook his head. "I wish I could."

"Classified?"

"Not that. I really don't know. We've had the BEKs looked at by forensics guys and university eggheads. No one can tell me what they are exactly."

Morales shook his head in disbelief.

"Seriously. I've heard Amazonian primate, old Nazi genetic experiments, and alien hybrids. We stumbled on these little monsters in counter-narcotics operations in Columbia back in ninety-six. Been finding them a little further north every year since."

"So now what?"

"Well, I find the next nest and stomp it. Then clean up the mess and move on."

Morales nodded again.

"You know, all the people I've worked with, no one ever broke a hold like that."

Morales guessed the memory of his dead son had a stronger hold on him.

Rogers passed over a business card and said, "Might be able to find a place for you on the team, if you're interested."

Without looking, Morales took it from Rogers and then tucked it in one of the straps holding the soldier's body armor tight. With the cheap white card standing out against the pixellated grays and greens, Morales snapped, "I'm interested in you calling off your dogs and giving me back my crime scene."

Rogers nodded with a tight expression. "Well, watch yourself. These little monsters can hold a grudge, and your performance today was certainly grudge-worthy."

Morales didn't respond, and Rogers gave the agent another appraising glance. He passed orders to his men and they stood together, not talking.

The soldiers took another ten minutes to clear the scene. On his way out, Rogers pulled the card from where Morales tucked it and left it on a grimy little table beside the front door.

"In case you change your mind," Rogers said.

Morales didn't respond, just gave the man a get-out-of-here jerk with his head.

When the soldiers were gone, the DEA agents went back to work, securing their scene with low comments and plenty of headshaking. None of these guys had been in the basement. The federal investigation teams, now allowed access, came in and started their own forensic investigation.

Morales waved his boss's excuses away and went to the front door. Standing there, he slipped the card off the table and read the name and email address, all that were printed on the card. Then something caught at the periphery of his vision, and he looked up from the card and out the open front door.

There, in the milling crowd of rubber-neckers across the street, stood a kid dressed street. The look of hate in the coal black eyes was unmistakable, but the little monster was gone before Morales could get to it.

Standing on the buckled concrete sidewalk with all the lookie-lou's, he gazed down at the card again.

"Yeah, Rogers, maybe I will," he said, and then went back to work.

Richard Farnsworth *has published stories in Atomjack (June 07) and Thuglit (Jan 08). He also has two stories accepted, one in Nossa Morte and one the Graveside Tales anthology. He is a research scientist and in this capacity has published numerous technical articles. In addition, Richard is a U.S. Army officer.*

WORM-SACKS AND DIRT-BACKS

by Lee Clark Zumpe

The sanitary world around Dr. Kenneth Sprague had rotted away, revealing its rancid underbelly.

"Who are we kidding? Reconstituted disinterred entities? The formerly expired? The prematurely lamented?" Sprague had used his last euphemism. Frustration and fatigue finally stripped him of his last ounce of professional prudence as he bickered with the chief of staff at Arnesville Regional Hospital. Surrounding the two men, the dead huddled in a once spotless hallway, many clustered in familial groups, whimpering and trembling. They had spilled into the corridors from an overcrowded and understaffed emergency room. Outside, they shambled through the parking lot, gazed despondently at their reflections in car windows and picked at their own putrescent flesh. Sprague continued, "They're walking corpses. How am I supposed to treat walking corpses?"

"Just do your job, Dr. Sprague." Dr. Zephram Ames responded to Sprague's outburst with a cold stare and an unsympathetic tone. The 50-something physician ran the hospital with an iron fist in the best of times. The current crisis had transformed him into a fascist despot devoid of compassion for his colleagues. "I expect you to treat each one like any other patient: Examine their symptoms, manage their pain and monitor their progress. It's all that we can do until a treatment or a cure is developed."

"There won't be a treatment or a cure," Sprague said, his tone growing more insubordinate as his discontent and resentment mounted. Those who required and deserved legitimate health care were being turned away from the hospital because of the extraordinary circumstances. Sprague had not worked his way through medical school to spend the rest of his life dealing with an endless parade of moldering patients. "This isn't a disease. It's an aberration of nature."

"We have our orders." Ames referred to strict government directives outlined in a hastily drafted Presidential Executive Order shortly after the onset of the epidemic. "Our hands are tied. The law dictates our actions. I won't risk my career over this."

"And I won't waste mine medicating things that by all rights should be destroyed."

Sprague turned his back and walked down the grim corridor, navigating the ghastly tangle of lurid flesh and moaning cadavers. He longed for fresh air, untainted by the fetid stench of the dead. At the end of the hallway, he hesitated in front of a service entrance, wishing he could leave it all behind him; wishing he could ignore his conscience and go home and wait it out.

He could not help but feel beguiled by the bliss of seclusion, the promise of total tranquility as could only be achieved in complete isolation. At the same time, he feared what might become of the city – of the world – in his absence. What today manifested itself as a plague of the dead could tomorrow become a scourge of the living. He had an obligation to stay alert, to stay focused, to watch for signs of mutation.

After a moment's deliberation, he turned toward the stairwell and headed for the roof. Though he had no weather reports, he could tell a cold front was pushing through the mountains. He hoped the arctic winds would offer a temporary reprieve from the stomach-turning aroma saturating the hospital's lower levels.

Down there, everything smelled like the grave.

He had examined dozens of reconstituted disinterred entities over the last few weeks, poked and prodded them, even gathered specimens to be forwarded to the USAMRIID task force facility located on the outskirts of the city. He continually questioned the military's unprecedented utilization of civilian medical personnel to act as first responders in the outbreak; he criticized Army scientists for distancing themselves from the hot zone.

Nothing about the epidemic made sense. The government's initial reaction had been to quarantine the city, a feat made feasible thanks to the area's rugged topography. Set in the Appalachian Mountains in far western North Carolina, Arnesville could be cut off from the rest of the region relatively easily with the closure of four state highways and a 20-mile stretch of the interstate system. State police simply rerouted traffic through nearby Canton and Waynesville.

A media blackout quickly followed. All television, radio and newspaper services terminated with swift and shocking efficiency. The military apparently deployed some form of equipment that jammed external radio signals and made satellite dishes ineffective. All phones, both land-line and cellular, ceased to function. Postal deliveries were halted.

Not a single journalist entered the city after the implementation of the quarantine.

Then, instead of inserting troops to round up the infected corpses, the military positioned itself along the quarantine perimeter and set about patrolling the back country in Black Hawk choppers. No epidemiologists arrived to relieve the overtaxed medical community. No FEMA workers appeared to assess the conditions and provide logistical support. No government representatives visited to address the concerns of local residents, to offer reassurances or provide explanations and chart strategies.

Finally, word came down that the president had extended limited Constitutional rights to those affected – and that the "killing" of any such entity constituted a federal offense punishable by, ironically, death.

Unlike those in Washington D.C., Sprague had no misconceptions about the state of the "corporeal undead," the term employed to describe the entities in the official document. The dead rarely spoke, exhibited no emotion other than chronic depression, and appeared to have only limited fine motor skills. He saw no spark of intelligence in their eyes, no flicker of remembrance and no internal motivation to survive. Left to their own devices, they might well waste away into nothingness; they ate nothing, drank nothing and, aside from wandering aimlessly and groaning unremittingly, they did nothing.

Admittedly, some of Ames' closest associates had achieved some success with experimental therapy. His team worked in secrecy in the upper levels of the hospital, selecting trial candidates through a careful screening process. From the notes he had shared with other staff members, the things could be nourished intravenously, taught to perform simple skills, prompted into speech.

That Ames sanctioned such trials repulsed Sprague. Those responsible for the research argued that their work was a logical extension of their scientific background. They considered themselves medical revolutionaries exploring cutting-edge rehabilitation techniques.

Sprague likened them to grave-robbers bent on harvesting the dead for their own selfish professional purposes.

"Fed up with the working conditions down there, Dr. Sprague?" Arriving on the roof, the physician found a congregation of expatriated interns smoking and sharing a bottle of Jack Daniels beneath the ruddy evening skies. "Or have you come to collect us and usher us back down to our stations?" Randy Donne had apparently been elected as the group's provisional spokesperson. The other greenhorns lacked the courage to voice their antipathy and aversion to dealing with the dead. "If that's the case, I'm afraid that we'll have to decline the invitation."

"No," Sprague said, "I'm here for some fresh air."

"Not much to go around." Donne flicked his cigarette butt over the side of the building, followed its descent with his gaze. The street in front of the hospital teemed with squirmy corpses. "There's so many of them now you can smell 'em all the way up here."

"Damn worm-sacks and dirt-backs," Freddie Julian said, downing a swig from the bottle. Sprague had heard both expressions in recent days, counted them among the more evocative inventions in an evolving lexicon. Worm-sacks referred to corpses over six months old, dug up by optimistic relatives and subsequently abandoned due to their advanced state of decomposition. Dirt-backs were the recent dead, in most cases spontaneously reawakened in the midst of their own burial. "Someone should be corralling them, herding them toward a crematorium or something."

"That's not the will of the government," Sprague said with a hint of sarcasm. Black Hawks hovered over the distant horizon, combing the countryside. Occasional weapons fire had been heard over the last few days, suggesting that some citizens had attempted escape. "For whatever reason, they want to keep them intact for the time being."

"Probably want to register them for November's general election." Donne glanced at the stars emerging in the twilight between wispy bands of clouds. To the west, a line of storms crawled along the Appalachian crest. "Why do you think they've all come here, to the hospital? Why not go to their homes, their families?"

"They're suffering physical pain," Sprague answered. "That much we know. Assuming they retain some memories of life, they associate the hospital with feeling better."

"I guess we should be thankful they aren't flesh-eating zombies." Julian – not a particularly squeamish individual – visibly shuddered at the thought of how much worse things could be if the dead had awoken with a ravenous appetite. "I mean, that's what you expect the undead to do, right? Feast on the living?"

"I don't really know what to expect them to do, Julian." Sprague looked down upon the crowds, wondered how many had passed through the hospital doors previously on their way to the burial ground. How had the gardens of rest been transformed into the gardens of the restless? Julian's gratitude that they did not more closely resemble their cinematic representation led Sprague down another disquieting avenue of thought: With so many variables at work, so many mysteries as yet unanswered, no one could really be certain that they might not all rise up and start gorging themselves on the living. "Honestly, I don't think they know what is expected of them, either."

* * *

The meat wagons began to arrive the following day just after sunrise.

Dr. Sprague had spent the night on the roof with Donne and several other interns, waiting for a squall line that regrettably stalled over the highlands. The first indication the day would be different came with the appearance of dozens of Chinooks, sweeping in from the south and flying low over the Pisgah National Forest. Like impatient buzzards they circled the distant Arnesville International Airport, waiting for clearance.

"It's about time," Donne said, his upturned palm eclipsing the morning sun as he followed the helicopters' flight. He imagined the transport copters filled with anxious National Guardsmen, ready to take all the dead into custody and convey them out of the city. Simultaneously, a column of black panel trucks maneuvered a maze of side streets and convened along Avery Boulevard. Escorted by local police, the caravan carefully approached the hospital. Some shell-shocked residents stumbled from their homes along the thoroughfare to watch the grim procession. "Maybe they've come to their senses."

"Maybe," Sprague said. "I'd better find Ames – see if I'm still employed." Before returning to the stairwell, the doctor peered over the ledge as paramilitary guardsmen escorted the first of the corpses into the backs of the meat wagons. The dead went without any hint of resistance. They moved like cattle, without deliberation or reflection. "You all should get downstairs, see if you can help. When this mess is finally swept under the carpet, people will need our help again. That's why you're here. That's why you'll stay."

* * *

Sprague found Ames on the 10th floor. He had appropriated an entire wing for his team of researchers, ostensibly to investigate how best to treat the dead. Where uniformed security guards had restricted access yesterday, this morning Sprague found no obstacles.

"Dr. Ames," he called out, catching sight of the doctor down the hall. A tall, gaunt man with greasy hair and an expensive, tailored business suit conversed with Ames in front of a shadowed alcove at the far end of the corridor. From the man's emphatic gesticulations and boisterous tone, Sprague inferred a considerable degree of conceit. As he approached the pair, Ames lifted a hand to curtail their tête-à-tête.

"Dr. Sprague, a pleasure to meet you," the man said, turning to face him. He contrived a disingenuous smile that unfolded across his pallid countenance like a serpent uncoiling itself to strike at some unwitting rodent. "I'm Bernard Chesterton, CEO of Therst Weber Pharmaceuticals." He began to extend his hand to cement the greeting, but pulled back reflexively as if concerned about potential contagions. "I was just expressing my gratitude to Dr. Ames for his handling of this situation."

"I'm sorry," Sprague said, looking back and forth between the two men. "This seems like an odd time to be hawking new drug treatment options, doesn't it, Dr. Ames?"

"Actually, Dr. Sprague, Mr. Chesterton is here to take guardianship of our corporeal undead. His company has taken full responsibility for the situation." Everyone knew Ames received kickbacks from the major pharmaceutical companies. His zealous support of their products resulted in endless perks and enabled him to build his palatial 5-bedroom mansion on a ridge overlooking the city while paying alimony to two ex-wives. In addition to pushing unessential prescriptions on patients through hospital staff and local doctors, Ames regularly advocated and approved clinical trials for dubious medications. "Because of its culpability, the company has made arrangements to oversee the re-education process."

"I beg your pardon?" Sprague needed no clarification. As he had suspected from the onset, someone behind the scenes had orchestrated the whole depraved enterprise – and Ames had played a pivotal role. The worm-sacks and dirt-backs had been intentionally revived. "So, you aren't going to destroy them? You're going to treat those things?"

"That's right, Dr. Sprague. It's no fault of theirs that they've been reanimated. Following a treatment regime developed and tested in part by Dr. Ames here, they will be reintegrated into society. Properly medicated, they'll continue to serve as active members of the community indefinitely."

"As what? Doorstops?"

"Come with us, Dr. Sprague," Ames said, placing a firm grasp on his shoulder as if to rein him in. "We were about to tour my makeshift recovery ward. I think you'll be surprised at the progress we've made."

Behind the guarded doors, air fresheners masked the stench of decomposing flesh. The revivified dead rested comfortably in hospital beds meant for the living. Unlike their kith and kin downstairs, these pampered examples had regained some semblance of color in their skin. They demonstrated a diverse range of palpable, though imperfect, expressions and displayed rudimentary emotions. Their arms and legs did not quiver and their fingers did not fidget. They exhibited a sense of purpose and identity.

"What have you done to them?" Sprague looked over the dead patients, flinching at their two-dimensional personalities, their deceptively sterilized appearance, their vacant stares. "You can pump them full of chemicals, but they'll never be the same – don't you see that? The spark is gone. Their time is already up. Science can't alter the processes of nature."

"Kenneth ... Sprague," a familiar voice called from out across the room. "Kenny, is ... that ... you?" Sprague went from bed to bed, searching for the speaker. He found him in the far corner, a copy of the Bible lying spread-eagled on his dinner tray. "It's ... good ... to see ... you ... Kenny."

"Uncle Howard?" Sprague's uncle had been dead for two years. The cancer that claimed him had resisted every form of treatment available at the time. Dozens of mourners had attended his funeral, watched as he was laid to rest in the mausoleum at Serenity Gardens. "This isn't possible."

"I ... can't ... explain," he said, his words punctuated by uncomfortably long gaps. Sprague stared at him wordlessly, studied the glowing flesh that should be withered and wasting away. The corners of his mouth twitched as he strained to smile. His fingers remained rigid, his arms fixed at his sides. His eyelids drooped but he never blinked. "How ... long?"

"Two years," Sprague answered, realizing instinctively what his uncle wanted to know. "It's been two years."

"Why ... am ... I ... here?" Each word, each movement had to be meticulously calculated and judiciously executed. Even with the treatment, the body processes lacked the fluid animation of life. They had degraded into clumsy mechanics, driven by an awkward automaton mimicking vitality. "Why ... was ... I ... brought ... back?"

"I'm sorry, Uncle Howard," Sprague said, trying to repress both his grief and anger. "I don't know why." Sprague swallowed the heartache he had relinquished years earlier, reminding himself that the thing in the hospital bed could only be a shadow of the man he had known. "Those men can tell you why," he said, turning toward Ames and Chesterton. "Those men did this to you – to all of you."

Around the room, Ames' subjects exhibited a collective flash of recognition. Their medically-sustained solemnity deteriorated rapidly as the revelation gripped them. At once, all their misery and anguish and restiveness resurfaced. Something else emerged, too – an emotion thankfully absent until that critical epiphany washed over them. With newfound hatred, the corporeal undead struggled with the restraints confining them to their beds. They fought so violently that the adjacent skin tattered and turned a macabre shade of purple. Their glassy eyes bulged from their sockets.

Sprague recognized in their hostility a thirst for retribution, for justice and, maybe, for blood.

"Damn it, Sprague," Ames said, beckoning his private staff of assistants. Aides swarmed into the room, prepared to sedate the rebellious dead. Chesterton, savvy enough to appreciate a bad situation that might get even worse, quietly slipped out the door. "Get out of my ward, Sprague. Get out of my hospital."

Downstairs, lines of dead had formed in the corridors. They stretched through the emergency room, across the parking lot, and down the sidewalk bordering Avery Boulevard. Troops crammed them into the backs of the black panel trucks, which ferried them to the airport. There, more troops loaded them onto Chinooks. When filled to capacity, the helicopters lifted from the tarmac, heading east to some unknown destination.

Sprague, now unemployed, joined in the crowd of spectators watching the dead depart.

* * *

Later that evening, Sprague rested on his sofa nursing a bottle of imported Irish stout. Cable service had not yet been re-established, but local television stations had begun broadcasting live reports from Arnesville that afternoon.

Officially, an unnamed pharmaceutical company had been to blame for the epidemic. An allegedly unsanctioned five-year study of a drug said to promote longevity had gone horribly wrong. Ten towns across North America had been affected, including Arnesville. Exposure rates which should have been limited to 10 percent of the population had exceeded 80 percent. Though the root cause had been determined, the catalyst that actually triggered the reanimation of the dead had yet to be discovered.

Government troops had begun overseeing an evacuation of all corporeal dead entities from the stricken municipalities. Remote camps had been established to help treat and reintegrate the victims back into society.

At 8 p.m., the president addressed both houses of Congress. Sprague, on the verge of sleep, roused himself to watch the historic broadcast.

"Everything," the president said, "Will be ... all right." Sprague sat up and perched on the edge of the cushion. He upset the bottle as he hunted for the remote control. "My friends at FEMA ... are working with ... the military," he continued. His speeches had always suffered from his sluggish tone and staggered delivery. Tonight, though, Sprague paid closer attention to his cadence and inflection. "We welcome ... these people ... with open arms," he said, his eyes oddly unblinking. His rosy cheeks seemed too red, like someone might have applied blush just before he went on the air. "And I ... am willing ... to ask my colleagues ... in Congress," he stammered. His hands rested on the sides of the podium, completely motionless. "To grant full citizenship ... to the victims ... in return for ... five years of ... service to our country ... in the United States Armed Forces."

The camera panned across the floor of Congress. Representatives and Senators applauded with mechanical synchronicity, their expressions lacking any emotional subtext. Sprague spilled onto the floor, crawled over to the screen as he scanned the audience. Though some of the older members seemed a bit disheveled, most projected at least the semblance of life. A few, though, had only just begun the treatment. Their ashen faces, their sunken eyes, their leathery flesh betrayed their lingering putrescence. Tonight, the dead governed the living. Tomorrow, the world would know no better.

Regardless of the morning's setback, unflustered by potential impediments, Bernard Chesterton, CEO of Therst Weber Pharmaceuticals, stood among the powerbrokers, contented with his coup.

Lee Clark Zumpe, *entertainment columnist with Tampa Bay Newspapers, earned his bachelor's in English at the University of South Florida. His nights are consumed with the invocation of ancient nightmares, dutifully bound in fiction and poetry. His work has been seen in magazines such as Weird Tales and Dark Wisdom, and in anthologies including Horrors Beyond, Corpse Blossoms, Arkham Tales, High Seas Cthulhu and Frontier Cthulhu. Visit www.freewebs.com/leeclarkzumpe.*

WHEN IT RAINS

by Mark Tullius

D el followed his co-workers onto the covered balcony of the second floor and took the chair next to Taylor, the one closest to the kitchen door. If they wanted to get wet, that was fine with him, but he was staying by the door. This wasn't just a mild September shower, a thunderstorm to be laughed at. On a night like this, there was no telling when you'd need to retreat inside.

"Holy crap," Martin said as lightning flashed, illuminating the entire property. From his spot at the far end of the balcony, he pointed toward the rushing river some twenty yards down the grassy slope. "You see that water? Look at that. Amazing, isn't it?"

Del obliged and looked at the overflowing river, keeping his comments to himself. The torrential rains had transformed the usually quiet creek, upsetting the balance of things. Martin wanted someone to agree with him, tell him it was a beautiful sight, but Del figured he'd leave that to the other ass-kissers who'd say that grass was orange and pumpkins were green if their boss said it was so.

Martin must have noticed Del's indifference because he was quick to ask, in his Swiss-accented, slightly mixed-up English, "Does this all the time happen? The crazy weather like this?"

Taylor took a swig of his drink. Del could see the clown wearing his flashy jewelry and trendy clothes, sitting in a bar in Hollywood and downing his cute little orange drinks, but not out here. If the guy ever ordered that in one of the local bars, he'd be laughed out of town. Taylor wiped his mouth and asked Del, "Yeah, what the hell's up with this place? It was nice as shit earlier today, all warm and sunny like L.A."

Del was tempted to mention the grey clouds that had been on the horizon all afternoon, but thought better of it. Instead, he took a chug of his Bud Light and said, "The only difference was the lack of smog, huh? Remember, just last week you couldn't stop raving about how great the clean air was?"

Taylor didn't look away from the storm. "Yeah, too bad the freaking pollen count's so high. I've never sneezed so much in my life."

"Seriously, Del," Martin asked in his slightly mixed-up English, "the weather gets horrible all the time like this here?"

"Over in Ashford and up in Heaven, they get downpours like this pretty often, but not so much down here. Every once in awhile it'll come down real hard like this, but it's usually just quick showers."

Billy, who'd been unusually quiet most of the night, chuckled and polished off the rest of his Jack and Coke. "Heaven. I can't believe you guys got a town called Heaven."

"Welcome to the Bible Belt," Del said.

Martin asked, "What does that mean? This Bible Belt? Some kind of religion clothing?"

Billy hacked a wad of phlegm into his empty plastic cup and tossed it onto the floor just a few inches from the burning candle by Taylor's feet. "It means there's a goddamn church on every corner and one in between them."

"And what the hell's up with not being able to get booze on Sundays?" Taylor asked.

"Yeah, I thought that whole wine being blood bullshit made alcohol okay," Billy said, the disgust dripping off his words like the snot oozing out of his discarded cup.

Del inched his chair toward the kitchen just in case the lightning found its way onto the balcony. "People out here like to pray. Most of them got good reasons."

Instead of letting it go, Billy continued, "The whole God thing's bullshit if you ask me."

The balcony shook as a thunderclap broke above the house. Martin, the smart one in the group, said, "Maybe you shouldn't be so quick to say such things. Who do you think makes the rain?"

Billy pushed out of his seat and headed toward Del. Del scooted his chair out of his way as the muscle-bound bully stomped into the kitchen, mumbling under his breath.

Del leaned toward the group and told them, "I don't think it's too good an idea to crack those kinds of jokes. Not on a night like this."

"I agree," Martin said. "Needs to be more understanding of other people's beliefs, that guy."

Taylor took a sip of his drink. "Thing is, he's not joking. Guy's got a serious problem."

"Was he never an altar boy?" Martin asked, seemingly surprised when everyone burst into laughter.

"What the hell's so funny?" Billy asked as he came stumbling back onto the balcony, a fresh drink in his hand.

"It was nothing," Taylor said. "Just chill and enjoy."

"This shit's miserable. You know how dirty the Escalade's gonna be tomorrow? We live on a goddamn dirt road."

Another burst of lightning exploded above them. Taylor pointed to the driveway below. "You might want to move it, Billy. If the water keeps rising, you're gonna need to get it detailed. Your rims are gonna be a mess."

Billy turned to Del as he pulled a ring of keys from his pocket. "Go throw it in the garage for me."

"I'm not going out there."

"You afraid of a little rain?" Billy asked before he took another drink.

"Nope, but I'm still not going out there."

"Come on. Earn your keep. You don't pay rent."

"Yeah, and neither do you. Plus, I'm only here during the week."

"What if I turn on the outside lights for you? Maybe Taylor can hold your hand."

Del was tempted to tell Billy where he could go, but it would only make matters worse. Instead, he shook his head and sat back in his chair, staring out into the darkness.

Billy stuffed the keys back into his pocket. "Fine. No big deal," he told the group, although his tone said it was. "I can afford to get it washed."

The storm picked up in intensity and rain came streaming against the side of the house. Martin got out of his chair and asked everyone to scoot over. For someone who claimed to be an outdoorsman, he sure didn't like to get wet.

"It ain't gonna melt you none," Del said.

"Yeah, Martin, it's just a little rain," Taylor added. "So guys," he said, changing the subject, "are we gonna head out or what? I need to get laid."

"You want to go out?" Del asked, making sure he'd heard correctly.

Taylor said, "Hell yeah. Tonight's college night down at Frank's. The place sucks, but I bet there'll be some easy women out there."

"I doubt it," Del said. "Not in this weather."

"Stop being such a pussy," Billy said.

"Go ahead and go out there. I ain't going."

Billy finished his drink and dropped his empty cup next to his first one. "The storm will be over in ten minutes."

"I bet my house it won't."

"Shit, Del, are you gonna drive it over here and drop it off in my driveway when you lose? I don't want to go all the way over to your trailer park to pick it up."

Taylor snickered then quickly told Billy, "That's not funny, dude."

"You laughed."

"I was thinking about something else. Don't pay attention to him, Del."

"I never do," Del said, wishing Billy would go jump in the river.

Billy leaned forward in his chair and turned toward Del. "What's your problem with me, country boy? You jealous or what?"

Del was afraid of what he might say if he opened his mouth. Martin attempted to break the tension and suggested, "Now, now, fellas, let's be quiet and enjoy this."

"I'm going to head on in," Del said as he rose from his chair. "Gotta get up early." He reached for the kitchen door. When lightning flashed suddenly, Taylor yelled and nearly fell out of his chair.

"What's your problem, Taylor?" Billy asked.

"Did you guys see that?" Taylor stammered, pointing toward the river. "Holy shit, did you see it?"

"See what?" Billy asked, sounding bored.

"Look, look!" Taylor screamed. "Down there in the shadows."

Del peered into the darkness. He couldn't see anything, but he was afraid he knew what Taylor saw. Straining to keep the fear from his voice, he asked, "What'd it look like?"

"Leave the little girl alone," Billy said. "Spooked by a deer or some shit."

Taylor got to his feet and retreated until his back touched the wall. "That was no deer. Keep looking down there. I'm not fucking around. Something's out there."

Martin was starting to say that he couldn't see anything, when the lightning struck again, illuminating the sky. No one said a word, but they all saw it.

Everyone got to their feet. Billy got closer to the edge of the balcony and stared into the black of the backyard. Martin turned to Del and asked him what the creature was.

"A lurker."

All of a sudden Del became the center of attention. Bombarded with questions and accusations, Del tried to explain without sounding scared. "I've never seen one before, but that's what it's gotta be."

"You knew about these things?" Billy shouted.

"I told y'all. Y'all didn't listen to me. Never do."

Martin nearly shrieked. "What do we do? Who do we call?"

"It's all right," Del said, trying to calm down everyone, including himself. "Just leave it alone and it'll leave us alone. Let's go inside. I don't think it likes to be watched."

Billy returned to his chair. "Screw that. I'm gonna sit right here and watch where it goes. I'm not letting it sneak around until it finds a way into the house. Hell no, I'm not."

After Martin ran into the kitchen to get the phone, Del said, "I said you guys were crazy for living so close to the river. No one with any sense has a house near the water."

Lightning flashed and lit the backyard. The yellowish creature, the size of a large man, reminded Del of a lump of his nephew's Play-Doh-- but covered in mud and algae, slowly climbing the embankment, the rising river at its feet.

Taylor pointed at it. "It's getting closer. You didn't say a word about those things."

"I said there were probably lurkers in the river. That's why I said not to go down there."

"I thought that was some kind of fish."

"Yeah," Billy agreed, "or a mosquito or some shit."

Martin ran back onto the balcony with the portable phone in his hand.

"No dial tone."

"Storm must've knocked it out. Happens all the time," Del said. When he saw the men reaching for their cell phones, he reminded them they didn't get service at the house.

"Goddamn it," Taylor said as he stuffed his phone back into his pocket. "I always gotta go at least ten feet from the house to make a call."

"So go do it," Billy ordered.

"Fuck you. You go do it."

Del said, "It won't do no good no how. Police won't do nothing."

"Why the hell not?" Taylor shouted. "There's a monster down there!"

"Relax," Del said as he turned to go inside. "They won't bother you as long as you don't bother them. Just stay inside."

"Absolutely," Martin said. "We stay inside."

"And I'd lock the doors and windows," Del said, smiling inside, enjoying that the oh-so-smart city boys were finally paying heed to what he said. "Just to be safe."

"Where are you going?" Martin asked as a thunderclap shook the house.

"To my room." He could tell they were impressed with his couldn't-care-less attitude and he wasn't about to blow it by telling them he was going for his Glock. If the stories were true, the lurker wouldn't come after them unprovoked, but this was the first time he'd seen one of the ungodly creatures and he didn't want to risk being wrong.

Del paused before descending the staircase to the lower levels and flipped on the light. He reached the bottom and headed for his room, disappointed at himself for being frightened. Nothing was in the house. The lurker wouldn't bother them. It would rummage around the river until it found a dog or cat or some unfortunate creature and then it would return to its home under the river.

After entering his room and pulling his .357 out from under the mattress, Del stretched out on his bed and waited, listening to the battling storm. Twice he thought the loud bang outside his bedroom window might have been something other than thunder, but he reassured himself it was nothing but his nerves. Lurkers wouldn't try to get in a house, especially a locked one.

Del studied the window, wondering if he should get up to pull the shade. He decided not to do it. He wasn't afraid. And he'd want to know if a monster was on the other side of the glass. He wouldn't shoot it unless it attacked, but if it did, he was gonna put a hole in that son-of-a-bitch's head.

Someone upstairs shouted; it sounded like Billy. A moment later, everyone yelled.

Del jumped off his bed and ran for the staircase. Bounding up the stairs two at a time, he reached the top and rushed through the kitchen, chambering a round, afraid of what he would find on the balcony. Before he lost his nerve, he kicked open the door, and took aim.

He lowered the gun when he realized the three idiots were unharmed. They were cheering. Billy was holding a bow, and a quiver of arrows rested at his feet.

"He got him!" Taylor shouted. "He got that motherfucker."

"Right in the goddamned eye," Billy said, his voice full of pride.

Martin smiled and clapped Billy on the back. "One heck of a shot, this guy."

Del looked beyond the balcony and spotted the lurker lying flat on its back, the blue bolt of an arrow pointing toward the heavens. He turned to the three men. "Why? Why'd you do that? I told you to leave them be."

"Look how close he got. He was coming for the house," Taylor said defensively.

Del didn't want to agree, but the lurker was only a few yards from the house, its body lying in the square of light shining through the back door window. "You still shouldn't have done that."

Thunder rocked the house and the skies opened, doubling the deluge. The river was lapping at the dead lurker's webbed foot. If the thunderstorm didn't let up, water would be seeping into the house within minutes.

"Another one!" Taylor shouted, pointing over the railing just beyond the slain creature.

Del followed the direction of Taylor's trembling hand, straining to see through the sheet of pounding rain. A shapeless yellow figure was emerging from the roaring river, extending an arm toward its dead brethren.

Billy nocked an arrow and told Taylor to get out of his way. Taylor stepped away from the railing and Billy and took aim.

Before Billy could shoot, Del grabbed hold of the arrow. "Not again! Don't do it!"

"Look at it!" Billy yelled, his arms trembling as he kept the bow taut. "Let me shoot it!"

Keeping his hand on the arrow, half expecting it to fly and rip the skin off his palm, Del glanced over the railing. The creature was kneeling in the muck next to its fallen kin. It looked from the arrow to the balcony. Its expressionless eyes, black as sin, studied each of the men. Then it lifted its head to the sky. A horrifying howl pierced the night, louder than the rain, the thunder, the pounding of Del's heart.

"Goddamn it! Let me shoot it!" Billy screamed as Taylor and Martin both shouted for Del to let go of the arrow.

Although he held the gun and could call the shots if he desired, Del wasn't ready for that responsibility. He'd been taught to leave the lurkers alone, but what if that was wrong? And they'd already shot one. This wasn't up to him anymore. They were all grown men. All he could do was tell them what he knew.

As everyone yelled for him to let go of the arrow, a loud sucking pop, like the top being pulled off a can of potted meat, drew their attention down below. The lurker held the arrow, a slimy black mass trailing from the tip, in his hand. The body from which the arrow had been pulled began to deflate, large pieces of its mottled skin sloughing off and dissolving in the rising water that had already reached its chest.

Del released the arrow and turned toward the kitchen. Just as he crossed the threshold, a loud twang sliced through the air, followed by a series of cheers and slapping high fives.

The weight of the gun was reassuring, but for the first time in his ten years of owning it, he wasn't comfortable with only fifteen rounds in the magazine. There had never been a need for it before, but he wished to God he had brought along his extra boxes of ammo that were collecting dust back in his home in California.

Del knew they probably wouldn't listen, but he shouted anyway, "Now blow out that candle and get inside!"

Only Billy responded and it wasn't polite, so Del continued toward his room. He was passing the fridge when Taylor yelled, "There's another one!"

"There, too!" Martin shouted.

Billy said, "I see four of them!"

Lurkers weren't supposed to travel in packs. Del ran for the near wall and flipped the switches, turning on the outside lights. When he made it to the balcony, he counted six of the strange beasts. Three were sloshing through the river toward the dissolving heap of yellow by the back door. The other three were already on the driveway.

"The Escalade! Fuck no!" Billy shrieked, nocking an arrow and taking aim. He released the arrow and it zipped past the nearest lurker, piercing the Escalade's driver side door.

"They're too far away," Taylor said. "Get the ones near the house."

Martin agreed with him and told Billy to get the ones by the back door.

Billy turned on Del. "I'll take care of these. Get the ones out there."

"Screw you."

A series of thuds came from the driveway. Though not appearing very solid, the lurkers sure packed a punch. In a matter of seconds, the Escalade was crumpled with giant dents. "That's a seventy-thousand dollar vehicle!" Billy cried.

"It's already ruined. You've got insurance," Del reminded him.

"Give me your gun, then."

Del shook his head. The sound of smashing glass and crunching metal mixed with the roaring river and thundering sky.

"Come on, you pussy," Billy said. "If you're not gonna use the gun, give it to me."

"I'll shoot them if they come in the house. We don't need to piss them off any more then we already have."

Another loud howl tore through the night. Billy said, "They're taunting us."

"Let them. I'm going inside and getting my Bible. I suggest you guys do the same," Del said as he turned his back on them.

"Fuck you and fuck your Bible," Billy said.

Del heard an arrow being drawn. He spun toward Billy and shoved the barrel of the.357 at the bastard. "Draw a weapon on me again and I'll put a bullet between your eyes, you son bitch."

Billy glared at Del, but the Glock's barrel must have been too intimidating, because he let the arrow fall to the ground.

Still aiming at Billy's forehead, tempted to pull the trigger, Del said, "Do what you want, but you're not touching this gun."

Billy snatched the quiver off the floor, keeping eye contact with Del. "I'm not scared of them. Not like you."

"Yeah, and I'm not drunk or stupid like you."

After slinging the quiver onto his back, Billy brushed past Del and ran for the front door. Once Del heard the door open and close, he turned his attention back outside where the lurkers were reducing the Escalade to a hunk of scrap metal.

"Hurry up, Del," Taylor urged, peering over the railing. "They're right below us."

"Back up and be quiet. Both of you." From the look on Martin's face, it was obvious that Martin didn't like being told what to do, so Del added, "Trust me on this."

Martin nodded and stepped away from the railing just as a loud twang came from the driveway. The lurker who'd been caving in the rear of the Cadillac fell to its knees, the blue tip of the arrow sticking out the back of its head. Billy rushed onto the scene, the bow stretched to its limit with an arrow ready to fly. He swiveled at the lurker on the passenger side and let the arrow loose. It flew several feet to the side, glancing off the demolished vehicle.

With the unnatural speed of a tsunami, the lurkers crashed down on Billy from either side. Before the bully could do so much as scream, both lurkers were lying on top of him, one ripping through his stomach, throwing heaps of intestines over its shoulder while the other one clamped its massive jaws on Billy's face and began tearing out chunks.

Taylor was yelling something at Del when a giant crash below shook the balcony. Del glanced over the railing, but he didn't see any of the creatures, only the water lapping at the house.

"What was it?" Martin asked, his voice shaking worse than the balcony had.

"The door, I think."

"You think?" Taylor cried. Before Del could tell him to back away, he was on his hands and knees, his head between the railings, peering over the edge. "Holy shit. They knocked down the goddamn door! They're inside!"

"Come on," Del said as he watched the two lurkers in the driveway get up from their victim, leaving an unrecognizable mess where Billy had been only moments before. Both of them staggered toward the Escalade, grabbed hold of the rear bumper and heaved the SUV into the air. As the rear end went higher and higher, the lurkers walking underneath the carriage, Del felt a sense of helplessness at their inhuman strength.

Taylor followed Del's gaze in time to see the Escalade crash onto its roof, its momentum rolling it into the river. "They're damming the river."

Martin's eyes grew wider. "They know what they're doing."

"Taylor, get up," Del ordered. "Both of you follow me. Come on."

Taylor began to stand. Suddenly, a purple tongue the width of Del's wrist, and God knew how long, shot through the air, wrapped around Taylor's neck and slammed him onto the balcony.

Del yelled for Martin to grab Taylor's feet as he ran to the railing and stuck the .357's barrel against the beast's tongue. Taylor gurgled as he tried to pull away from the tongue and the gun just inches from his face. Realizing he had to risk Taylor's hearing or try to save the man's life, Del pulled the trigger. The tongue blew apart, pieces spraying the side of Taylor's face.

Martin yanked Taylor toward him and helped him to his feet. Before Taylor could talk, he tore at the dissolving tissue wrapped around his neck. Clumps fell free and splattered on the ground.

Del held the kitchen door open for them. "Inside! Now!"

This time there was no hesitation. Martin was brushing by Del when Taylor cried out. He had been right behind Martin, but now he was reeling backward, one grotesque tongue gripping his left ankle, another latched onto his right bicep.

Del reached out for Taylor's outstretched hand, but he wasn't fast enough. A loud snap cracked the night as Taylor's low back smashed into the railing, the agony on his face indicating it may have been his back that had snapped and not the railing.

Martin stayed pressed against the wall at the back of the balcony as Del ran to the railing, aiming with his right hand, trying to pull Taylor back with his left. There were five lurkers below; two were pulling with their tongues while the other three waited patiently.

Just as he was about to fire at the lurker latched onto Taylor's ankle, the creature next to it let its own tongue fly. Del swiveled and fired two rounds, both bullets striking the lurker's spongy forehead at the same instant the meaty tongue slapped Del's forearm. Then the tongue fell to the floor.

Del turned back to his original target and fired two more rounds. The creature fell backward, losing its hold on Taylor's leg. Neither Del nor Taylor was prepared for the sudden release of tension. Taylor fell forward, his face bouncing off the floor. Del lost his grip and Taylor was whipped off the balcony, his scream cutting off abruptly when he splashed into the rising water below.

Pulling the trigger as fast as he could, Del killed the lurker that had pulled Taylor down, as well as the one whose teeth were buried in Taylor's neck. Before he could shoot the third, an explosion rocked the house. The lights cut off all at once and the candle at their feet was the only thing between them and complete darkness.

The darkness seemed to amplify the smacking and slurping, screaming and snarling down below. Unable to see, Del backed away from the railing until he bumped into Martin. Del scooped up the candle and stepped into the pitch-black kitchen, bringing Martin with him and closing the door behind them.

"What was that?" Martin whispered.

"The circuit breaker's down there. They took it out, maybe with the propane tank."

"We need to get out of here."

Del was just as scared as Martin, but he didn't like hearing the panic in the man's voice. "You want to try running out the front door? I wouldn't."

"My Porsche. It's in the garage."

Del looked around the dark room, unable to see past the kitchen's center island. "Even if the lurkers haven't gotten into the garage, the water sure as hell has. The car won't start."

"We should try."

Del waited for the booming thunder to finish before he told Martin to go right ahead and try to reach his car.

"We should stick together."

"I think so," Del said. He sniffed the air. "Shit! Something's on fire."

"So we go to the garage?"

"I didn't say that. I'm going upstairs to Billy's room and locking myself in there."

"Okay, but I'll take the gun."

"Hell no. It's mine," Del said, having a difficult time hearing anything over the pounding rain pounding and rushing water outside.

Martin held out his hand. "Del, give me the gun."

"I'm going upstairs. You can follow me if you want."

"Hand over the gun and I'll give you a raise."

Del shook his head and placed the candle in Martin's hand. "Take this and find the flashlight. It's in one of those drawers by the sink. And hurry up,' Del said, aiming the .357 at the kitchen doorway even though he couldn't see past the tip of his gun's fluorescent front-sight.

Martin opened a drawer. "I double your pay."

"I don't care about money. I want to live," Del said as a wave of smoke washed over him, stinging his eyes and burning his throat. "Hurry up. I think it's in the one closest to me."

One drawer slid shut and another opened. "Here it is," Martin said as he clicked the light on.

Del's heart caught in his throat as the lurker's bloated face appeared less than two yards in front of him. He pulled the trigger three times, erasing its twisted smile.

Martin gasped and the flashlight clattered on the floor, its beam shooting past Del's feet. Del spun toward Martin, taking aim at the lurker holding his boss. The monster's arm covered the man's entire face. Before Del could get off a shot, he heard the sound of a tongue being launched from the far corner. The tongue hit its mark and smacked the candle, extinguishing the flame as it sent the candle sailing across the room.

Understanding that Martin was as good as dead whether or not he accidentally shot him in the darkness, Del fired three rounds where he thought the lurker was. It sounded as if two bodies fell to the floor.

Aware that there was at least one more lurker in the room, Del bent over and picked up the flashlight. He brought it up and spun in a circle. A gang of yellow creatures surrounded him, and at least ten sets of empty black eyes glistened in the dim light.

In what was only a split-second, but seemed like forever, Del considered his course of action. His life was over. He had four or five rounds left in the Glock, not enough to kill them all, but more than enough to end this nightmare himself.

The first tongue struck him square in the chest, knocking him into the arms of the lurkers behind him. Another tongue wrapped around his left thigh, a second wrapped his right. He thought of his dead co-workers, wondering where they were. He refused to believe that taking one's life was a mortal sin, grounds for spending an eternity in hell. Not willing to give the lurkers the pleasure of inflicting his painful death, Del pressed the gun to his temple and screwed his eyes shut as he squeezed the trigger.

Mark Tullius *is an exporter that splits his time between California and South Carolina. He was previously a bodyguard, correctional officer, boxer, and no-holds-barred fighter but has given all that up, opting for the much safer occupation of writing where he inflicts pain on paper and his antagonists can't strike back. Mark is excited to begin yet another fun-filled but scary adventure. He and his wife, Jennifer, are about to have their first child.*

MARKED
by Tracie McBride

Hannah knew Silver wasn't right in the head from the moment he first came into the café.

Within seconds of taking his seat, he leaned across the counter and introduced himself to her in a high-pitched, reedy Irish lilt. Not the done thing, thought Hannah. Not the done thing at all. And he smelt funny; he gave off a distinct odour of smoke, with faint undertones of scorched flesh, cinnamon and pond scum. She gave his outstretched hand a perfunctory shake and went back to wiping down the counter. Usually customers would do a double-take at the sight of her face and then let their glance slide away, settling on a point somewhere just over her shoulder, but he stared for a full minute, and then asked without apology or preamble, "How did you get that?"

Oh, please, she thought. Not another creepy middle-aged scar fetishist. Her fingers flickered self-consciously over the thick, ropy red scar that started at her left temple, crossed her cheek, and wound down over her chin and neck before disappearing out of sight under the collar of her shirt.

"Lightning strike," she said. "Are you going to order something or what?"

Silver nodded as if he met lightning strike victims on a daily basis. "I've got a scar too," he said. "Do you want to see it?" Without waiting for an answer, he pulled open the grimy striped scarf around his neck to reveal a pale puckering of skin in the hollow of his throat. "And yes, I'd like a coffee, please. Black. Five sugars. How far down does it go?"

"What?" Hannah frowned and stopped in mid-pour.

"Your scar. How far down does it go?"

"All the way to my right foot. That's why I walk with a limp." He was starting to piss her off now.

"That must have hurt."

"I don't really remember. It happened fifteen years ago. I was only four."

Silver was still staring at her, his eyes glittering in his thin homely face. "Like being touched by the hand of God," he said dreamily. "Can I touch it?" He reached a hand out to her chest.

"No!" she said, slapping his hand away. He sat back in his chair, looking so much like a wounded puppy that she felt an unwelcome pang of guilt. "Here's your coffee," she said, slopping the cup across the counter. "I've got to go — it's the end of my shift."

* * *

He turned up nearly every day after that. He never mentioned Hannah's scar again, but he talked a lot about his own scar, each day telling a different story. One day he said he got it in a motorcycle accident. Another day he said he sustained it from the injuries that ended his career as a professional boxer. Taking in his gangly frame, Hannah greeted this with barely concealed scepticism. Despite his apparent lack of employment, he had an endless supply of bicycles, parking a different colour and model each day outside the café. Hannah suspected that he supported himself through petty thievery, but as long as he paid for his coffee and kept his hands off her stuff, she didn't much care. After a while she became used to his harmless brand of madness, and they settled into a routine of sorts, Silver holding a random one-way conversation between sips of coffee and Hannah doing her best to ignore him.

When he didn't show up for over a week, Hannah started to worry. Although he had told her several different versions of his life story, she realised that she knew virtually nothing about him. If something had happened to him, she didn't know if he had any close friends or family who could help out. And she didn't know his address, his phone number, or even his last name to check on him herself.

So when he stepped out from behind a minivan as she was crossing the deserted car park at the end of a late shift, she didn't know whether to be frightened, angry or relieved.

"Jesus, Silver!" she said, punching him on the arm. "You nearly scared the shit out of me!"

"Hannah," he said, "I've got to show you something." He took hold of her elbow in a surprisingly powerful grip and propelled her towards the shadows of an alleyway on the far side of the car park. His customary loopy smile had disappeared, replaced with a grim frown of concentration that etched deep lines into his face.

Hannah eyed the alleyway ahead. Her heart beat faster in trepidation and she fought in vain to free herself from his grasp. A police siren wailed a few streets away, and Hannah looked around hopefully, but it faded into the distance.

"Are you on something?" she said, struggling to keep up with his long-legged stride. "Come on, Silver, stop mucking around and let me go."

He stopped at the entrance to the alleyway, raised his finger to his lips to indicate silence, and pointed.

Hannah looked and saw a tiny child, clad only in a nappy, rummaging around in the overflow of rubbish from a skip bin. She looked to be barely two years old, with tight blonde curls framing a cherubic face. Silver darted forward and grabbed the girl by the hair, holding her out at arm's length. Hannah tensed in expectation of the scream that was certain to follow, but the girl remained silent, her contorted face the only clue to the pain she must be feeling.

Silver gave the child a vicious shake. "Do you see, Hannah?" he said. The child wriggled and squirmed, tears spilling down her cheeks. "Do you see?"

"What are you talking about, you fucking lunatic," sobbed Hannah. "Let her go!" She grabbed the child and yanked her away from Silver, leaving him standing with a fistful of the little girl's hair.

"Poor little baby," she crooned, hugging the girl close and turning her back on Silver. "I won't let the bad man hurt you."

Hannah looked down at the child in her arms and gasped. Suddenly, she did see. The girl's face had gone slack and expressionless. Beneath her now translucent skin, a dark, grimacing monster pulsed and stirred.

* * *

Silver caught the girl as she fell from Hannah's nerveless arms, bundled her into a sleeping bag, and then slung her over her shoulder like a pig in a sack. Numbly obedient, Hannah followed him down a labyrinth of dimly lit streets to a small workshop in a light industrial area. He unlocked a side door and ushered her in.

The inside of the workshop was immaculate. Blue gingham curtains decorated the windows. A vase full of daisies sat next to a folded newspaper in the centre of a red Formica-topped table. Half a dozen bicycles in various stages of repair rested against one wall. An adjacent wall was taken up with a huge furnace. Its interior was ablaze.

Silver motioned her to sit on a camp stretcher. He dropped the sleeping bag on the floor and kicked it closer to the furnace. He picked up a four foot long metal pike, its tip sheathed in what looked like gold. Despite the oppressive heat in the room, Hannah hugged herself tightly and shivered.

Without warning, Silver opened the furnace door, reached into the bag and pulled out the child by the foot. He flung her into the flames. Hannah screamed. The child's skin blackened and shrivelled almost instantly. Hannah's scream became a whisper of pure distilled terror as the creature within emerged as if from an obscene chrysalis.

It perched toad-like on the lip of the furnace door, its lumpy bruise-purple skin impervious to the heat. Red slanted eyes glared from the sides of its hairless misshapen head. Two vertical slits sufficed as nostrils. Thin crooked fangs crowded its wide lipless mouth. Each bony hand and foot had four digits ending in curved yellow talons.

The creature tensed its haunches as it prepared to spring at Silver. Before it could leap, he skewered it through the chest with the pike. It writhed on the end of the pike for a moment before slumping to the ground. Hannah gagged as it dissolved into a puddle of putrid ooze which rapidly evaporated, leaving behind a cloying smell of cinnamon. Within minutes, there was no trace of either child or monster.

Silver shook off his overcoat, hung it over the back of a chair, and then sat next to Hannah. His hair stuck to his forehead with sweat and he was trembling slightly from his exertions. All the menace that had exuded from him in the alleyway was gone.

"What was that thing?" asked Hannah.

"A Voraku," said Silver. "A manifestation of malevolent energy that takes possession of human form by invading the bodies of very young children. The child that you saw was only a shell. The way I found it wandering around at night alone like that, it must have recently killed its host parents. We've been keeping them at bay for years, but there's been a sudden upswing in their numbers, and we're starting to lose the battle."

"If these monsters are possessing children and killing the parents, how come it isn't all through the news?"

"It is." He picked the newspaper up off the table and tossed it to her. Dozens Dead From Spate of Arsons, the front page headline claimed. "Of course, the cops don't know the truth of it. They'd think we were crazy if we tried to explain it to them."

"They're not the only ones," muttered Hannah.

"There's about twenty of us working as Voraku hunters, but it's not enough. We need to recruit more people who have the ability to see through Voraku disguises. Like you. You're Marked, Hannah." He gestured at her scar, and she flinched away from him. "I'll introduce you to some of the others tomorrow night, and we'll start your training."

"No," said Hannah. She stood and crossed to the door. "No, no, no. I don't care what I've seen, or think I've seen tonight. I am not going to join your little band of loonies to go around bumping off little kids. Stay away from me, or so help me, I'll go to the cops myself." The chill night air blasted her as she opened the door and hobbled away. Silver didn't pursue her, but his parting words stung as he shouted after her.

"But you're Marked, Hannah. You're Marked...."

* * *

Two weeks later, Hannah retraced her steps to Silver's workshop. She knocked on the door. Silver opened it almost immediately and let her in. He looked much smaller by day, almost harmless, thought Hannah. She lowered her backpack to the floor and slumped at the table.

"You bastard, Silver," she said wearily. "Ever since you showed me that thing, I can't stop thinking about it. I can hardly sleep, and when I do, I have nightmares. If I get one more warning at work, I'm going to get fired. And I... I saw another one. I didn't just see another Voraku; I saw it take over a child. It was a little boy, maybe eighteen months old, and he was playing in the park. He chased a ball into some bushes, and this mist rose up and just sort of soaked into him. I don't know how to describe it exactly, but it was as if the mist hollowed him out from the inside." She looked to Silver for confirmation.

"Did you puke?" he said. "I did the first time I saw it."

She gave a small, hysterical giggle. "Yeah, I puked."

"And then what did you do?"

"What else could I do?" She bent and opened the top of her backpack. A dark-haired toddler stared impassively up at them. His face was the only part of him that was clearly visible, the rest being obscured beneath the intricately knotted lengths of rope that encircled his body. "I didn't want him wriggling around in there," Hannah explained. "Lucky his babysitter was too busy sucking face with her boyfriend," she said, sounding anything but lucky, "or I might not have got away with it."

"So does this mean you've decided to join us after all?"

"I suppose so," said Hannah. "And did I mention that you're a bastard?"

Silver smiled and caressed the scar on her cheek. This time she let him.

"Welcome to the club."

Tracie McBride *is a mother of three from New Zealand. She has a diploma in creative writing and is a member of the Wellington-based Phoenix Science Fiction Writers' Group. Her work has appeared and is forthcoming in various electronic, print and podcast publications, including* Pulp Net, Gambara, Electric Velocipede, Bound Off, Bravado *and* T-Zero.

FOR THE GOOD OF THE FLOCK

By Jeff Parish

Our Lady of Victory stood nearly empty this late in the afternoon; the only other soul they had seen so far was an elderly secretary who informed them the priest was in the Adoration Chapel. Most of the lights had been dimmed, and footfalls echoed strangely. Anna felt goosebumps running up and down her arms. Stop that! This is the house of God.

She crossed herself and looked at her husband, who kept tugging at his tie and collar. She smiled; he had listened when she asked him to wear suitable clothing. Her own dress made her look something like a black beach ball, but she had picked the nicest clothing she owned. First impressions were important, as her mother had always said. Anna frowned at the two boys following him. Why couldn't they have listened for once? Stephen wore a sweat-stained track uniform from his old school. His younger brother, Zachary, sauntered in his ripped jeans and red T-shirt, skateboard tucked under one arm. Her scowl deepened at the black ball cap perched backwards on his head. Anna flicked the bill, knocking it to the floor.

"Hey, Mom, how 'bout you just ask me to take it off next time?"

She slapped his cheek. "Don't sass me, young man."

"Yes, ma'am," he replied sullenly and retrieved the offending cap before stepping into the chapel.

The brick-walled chamber was just as gloomy as the rest of the church, with only a spotlight shining on the monstrance in the center. A handsome, dark-skinned man dressed in black sat in the front row, staring at the altar so earnestly Anna felt embarrassed to have intruded. She reached up to tug on Bill's sleeve, and in doing so released the door. It slammed shut.

The man jumped at the sound and turned a glare on them that seemed equal parts murderous rage and guilty shame. Anna hissed in surprise and backed up a step. Then the man approached them, wearing a warm, inviting smile. Anna shook her head. Must have been a trick of the shadows or something.

"¡Bienvenidos!" He spoke softly, but his powerful voice carried easily. Anna found herself toying with a lock of her hair. "Welcome to God's house."

"Howdy!" her husband said. "We just moved here and wanted to come check out the local church. I'm Bill Weidner."

Bill's country accent sounded harsh in the still room. He seized the priest's hand in his own meaty paw. The two were of equal height, but the pastor was leaner than her bull-necked husband. A muscular frame strained against his black suit, and wings of white stood out in his black hair. Mamma would say she could eat him with a spoon. Anna blushed. I don't know that I'd bother with the spoon.

Bill introduced the rest of his family, starting with his wife. Anna heard herself giggle slightly as the priest took her hand and smiled down at her. Her cheeks felt as if they were on fire. Then he moved on, asking Zachary about his skateboard and what tricks he knew. Even the normally sour twelve-year-old was smiling and nodding by the time the priest moved on to Stephen.

Some strange emotion crawled across the pastor's features as he spoke briefly to her oldest son. He leaned in close, nostrils flaring slightly. Her burning face cooled while Stephen talked about his sophomore year and the medals he had won at school. What is he doing? She'd tried to ignore the media attention the Church had received in recent years just because a few bad priests couldn't keep their hands to themselves, but something in the way he looked at her son made her uncomfortable. It reminded her of the way a coyote might stare at a rabbit. She chewed on her bottom lip.

"Welcome to Paris. I am Father Guillermo de los Lobos."

"Los Lobos? That's pretty good." Bill chuckled. "Just like the band, huh?"

Anna winced, but Guillermo simply laughed. "Sí, but please do not ask me for 'La Bamba.' My mother told me I sing like a baying hound." He spread his hands. "What brings you to this far corner of Texas?"

"Company transfer," Bill said. "They moved me out here from Mobile to see what I can do about manufacturing."

"Con mucho gusto. I am happy to have you here. Our parish sees so little young blood these days. Have you found a home yet? Moving for your job can be very hard. There is so much running around, with much to do in a little time."

"We've looked like headless chickens the last few months, but the company took pretty good care of us." Bill laughed again. "We got ourselves a nice two-story house over off Church Street. She's a real beaut. You ought to see it some time."

"I would like that very much. Gracias." He looked at his watch. "Regretfully, not today. I have matters to attend to. It is good to meet you. Please to not hesitate to contact me if you need anything."

"Will do, padre." Bill flapped his hands, shooing them out the door. "We'll see you Sunday."

"Vaya con Dios."

Anna watched the three boys shake hands with Father de los Lobos and file out the door. He followed them out into the hallway and waved as they left. She thought she caught that hungry gleam in his eye once more as she turned away. Surely the diocese wouldn't put someone like that in charge of a parish, not after all that's been in the news. She shook her head and waddled after her family.

A sharp smack echoed down the hallway. Anna turned back. Father de los Lobos waved with one hand; the other held something glittering against his cheek. His smile looked slightly pained. She blinked and headed down the hall, her mind already turning to unpacking and arranging furniture.

* * *

Guillermo let his smile slip as the woman turned a corner and disappeared from sight. He dropped his rosary back into his pocket, careful not to touch it any more than he had to. His cheek and hand burned where he had slapped it against his face. The ache would linger – as well it should – but he could feel the flesh already healing.

Groaning, the priest walked the other way toward his office. *I was doing so well. Why did they have to move here with their young, tempting flesh? Lord, please help your weak servant.*

This small northeast Texas town had seemed an ideal place to send him, home mostly to elderly, wrinkled and above all unappetizing parishioners. There had been...slips in the last couple of years, of course, but the diocese had suggested ways he might distract himself. Guillermo had started to think he might have finally broken free of the hunger. Then this new family arrived. *The fat wife might make an interesting morsel, but it was that boy who grabbed his attention. He looked lean and healthy, and his scent... I'd like to see that one run.*

He halted in the hall before his office. The priest shook himself and growled, wiping a string of drool off his chin. *No! I will not give in again!* He shoved a hand in his pocket, tightening his fist around the silver rosary until his knuckles cracked. *Our Father, who art in Heaven, hollowed be Thy name...* He ran through the prayer while searing pain cleansed his mind. Momentarily free of temptation, he opened the door and walked to his desk. The priest sat and stared at the phone. He had hoped he wouldn't have to make this call again.

Finally, he sighed and grabbed the handset. Guillermo called up an outside line and slowly dialed the number burning his mind as surely as silver. He stared at the angry cruciform indention in his palm while the line rang at the other end. *Please, Lord, let them still be there. I don't know if I have the strength to do this again.* A click and a pleasant female voice answered.

"Hello. Tyler Diocese."

Thank you, Lord. "This is Father Guillermo de los Lobos in Paris. I need to speak with the bishop, if he's in."

"Hello, Father. I think he's here. Please hold."

Music floated down the line. Doubtless they meant to be soothing, but the priest couldn't stop tapping his fingers impatiently on the desk. After what felt like an eternity in Purgatory, the line clicked and a welcome, scratchy voice spoke.

"Hello, Guillermo." Lee Hodo sounded like he might be smiling, which came as no surprise. *The Bishop liked to smile. Too bad I must ruin* that for him today.

"Hello, Excellency."

"Oh? Is this to be a formal call, then?" The voice had taken on a worried tone.

"I am afraid so. I have been having... thoughts about some of my parishioners."

"What sort of thoughts?" All traces of amusement had vanished.

"The same as before, Excellency. Evil, hungry thoughts. A new family has moved to town, and they have a very healthy hijo..."

"Guillermo," the Bishop said like a parent scolding a particularly naughty child. "I'm very disappointed to hear this. You were doing so well. It's been close to a year since we had one of these discussions. I had started to think we were past such setbacks." He sighed. "You understand I'm going to have to report this to Rome. I can't keep this within the diocese this time, not after your previous lapses."

"I understand, Excellency." He paused. "For what it is worth, I am quite ashamed."

"I have no doubt of that, but that will carry very little weight with the Vatican. Not many wanted to give you the chance to enter the clergy, not with all the bad publicity we've been getting. This could sway the few supporters you've had, I'm afraid."

"They could kick me out of the Church?" Guillermo's hand crept to his white collar. "What would I do then?"

"Try to remain calm. I'll do everything I can to keep that from happening. You've done a lot of good work despite your unique temptations. That should count for something." Lee sighed. "I'll make the call tomorrow. They'll probably want to move quickly on this one way or the other; I should have news for you Monday."

"What should I do until then?"

"I would recommend fasting and private time with your rosary. Pray without ceasing. You need to be strong, especially now. This is not a good time for you to weaken, you know. Think of your flock and what is best for them."

"Of course, Excellency. Thank you."

"You're a good man, Guillermo. I hope we can still save that part. Take care, my friend."

"Vaya con Dios, mi amigo."

Tossing the phone into its cradle, Guillermo slumped back in his chair with lips twisted as if he had eaten something sour. I know they watch the calendar, but did he have to be so blunt about it? He glanced at the datebook on his desk. Sunday's block, which showed a pale circle in one corner, had been circled thrice in red. Lead us not into temptation, Lord. He picked the telephone back up and dialed the front desk.

"Barbara? Please call Father Cantrell in Sulphur Springs and ask him to hold Mass here Sunday."

"Why? Are you not feeling well, Father?"

"Just do it, vieja," he barked. Sighing, he softened his tone. "My apologies. You are right, I am not well. Just please call Father Cantrell. He'll understand."

"Of course, Father. You know, I thought you looked a little under the weather this morning. I told myself, 'Barbara, there's a man who should have stayed in bed today...'"

Her stream of words cut off as he slammed the receiver down. The plastic base cracked and the handset broke in half. Foolish old woman. I'd tear her throat out, but I doubt it would shut her up. Guillermo shuddered and closed his eyes; his mouth felt too small for his teeth, his skin too tight. Let go. He growled at the whisper coming from the back of his mind. It always spoke to him in times like this, taunting him with his father's wild voice. He told you: It's your flock. Who cares about a few sheep? Why deprive yourself?

No! He groped in his pocket until his burning fingers told him he had found the rosary. I am not an animal!

Drawing the string of beads out, he balled the rosary in his fist and clenched the searing metal. Pain cut through some of the red fog that had descended, but didn't lift it entirely. His body trembled as his soul fought the transformation threatening to overwhelm him. He opened eyes on a world that had become much sharper. His nose twitched, searching for the scent of prey nearby...

Though I walk through the Valley of the Shadow of Death, I will fear no evil... Thou... art... with... me... Guillermo shoved the rosary in his mouth.

Agony set his brain aflame. He muffled a scream against his arm and beat his fist on the desk. Antique oak cracked and splintered. He trembled on a razor's edge, fighting to regain his balance while damnation waited for him to fall.

Finally, his quivering subsided. The priest spat the silver out with a gout of saliva and blood and collapsed on his desk, panting. He had taken a step over the precipice and somehow managed not to fall. The beast was not gone, however. He could feel it, snarling and looking for an escape from its temporary cage.

Guillermo scrambled to his feet. I have to get out of here. He snatched the rosary from its puddle and put it in his shirt pocket, ignoring the pain in it brought. Walking to the door, he placed one hand on the knob, paused and sniffed the air. No one was nearby. The old woman must not have heard the noise. Barbara liked to take her hearing aid out when she got to reading one of her romance novels. Maybe she's asleep. He stepped through and shut the door behind him. The priest dashed through the halls in near-silence until he burst through the main doors.

Twilight spread across the parking lot. He breathed deeply and smiled. The town stank, as did every other place in this country – was there no place free of all the cars and factories? – but it felt good to be outside, away from the cages humans built for themselves. Here he could run and hunt with nothing but the horizon hemming him in.

Shaking his head, he trotted across the asphalt for a small house set in the corner of the church's property. "Be strong," the Bishop said. I am trying, Lord, but it is hard. Please lend me Your strength. He staggered inside, shut the door and locked the deadbolt. He switched on a lamp and threw himself on the couch. A portrait hung on the far wall, its bushy-haired subject glaring down at him, seemingly rebuking his weakness. Guillermo's lip curled in a challenging snarl.

"Why did you have to have children, Father?" His tongue still ached, and his voice came out as a rasp. "Why could you not be happy keeping this curse to yourself?"

Foolish question, he chided himself. When not terrorizing the countryside around Zacatecas, Rafael de los Lobos loved nothing more than gathering his litter and regaling them with tales of how their kind had once ruled the night. His stories always ended the same way: "The world was as it should be in those days. A man dared not step outside his door at night for fear of the wolves. Then civilization came and drove us into hiding. But what once was will be again!" Then Father would pace the floor until full dark and venture into town to get drunk on tequila or blood, whichever was most readily available. Mother had been a restraining influence, but she had been killed in Mexico City years before. Father's moods and drinking grew worse after that.

As the eldest, Guillermo bore responsibility of caring for his brothers and sisters. He did the cooking and cleaning, made repairs on their run-down house and performed odd jobs for the neighbors to bring in a few more pesos. He made sure the other children attended school. Whatever Father thought, they could not hunt down civilization and tear out its throat. Better they learn to live in the modern world than try to hide or die fighting it. At night, he lit a candle and struggled to learn from their textbooks.

Father spent his days as a guide for turistas who visited the city. On those rare nights not filled with drinking, he took his children by ones and twos to hunt whatever prey they could find. Guillermo loved those moments with his father, particularly when they had men to hunt. Cunning quarry made the kill all the more satisfying, the meat that much sweeter.

Then had come the night Father staggered in the house, declaring it was time for his "pack" to drive men from the city...

The priest shook his head. What am I doing? The Bishop said to pray, not dwell on the past. Yet he found it hard to banish the memories – the thrilling chase, jaws tearing flesh and crushing bone. He growled at the portrait. Why did you do it? You had to know they would kill us all. If I hadn't gone off to find my own meat, I'd be in a silver-lined grave next to you and my brothers and sisters. He dug the rosary from his pocket once more and watched the silver burn his flesh. The priests took me in, even knowing what I was. They helped me cage the beast. And now I seek to repay that kindness with betrayal? He knelt beside the couch and clasped the rosary between folded palms.

Lord, help thy servant. My spirit is truly willing, but I fear my flesh, Lord. It is not weak. He began to whimper from the pain in his hands. My flesh is strong, and it hungers. Lead me not into temptation, but deliver me from evil, I pray. Show me what to do. No answer came, save a building desire.

The boy's mother had been fearful. He could smell it on her, see it in the way she looked at him. She knew he wanted her son for something, that lovely boy who looked as if he could run and run...

Saliva ran down his chin and pattered onto the sofa.

Lord, I have sinned. Please take this cup from me before I drink of it. Blood ran from his hands. His nose twitched. It had been long since his last hunt. Too long, that voice whispered. He quashed it ruthlessly. After his last "lapse," a young blonde woman who worked at a diner downtown, Bishop Hodo had suggested that if he could not banish his desires, Guillermo should sublimate them. It was an agricultural area; why not hunt livestock? The loss of a few cows and horses was better than murder. He had found it a satisfying, if boring, substitution. He shook his head in disgust. Cows were slow and stupid. Horses could run, but they weren't much brighter. Father would laugh at me. *Where is the challenge? What thrill can there be in bringing down a side of beef?*

A passage from Hebrews rose unbidden: "It is not possible that the blood of bulls and of goats should take away sins."

He dropped the rosary. "No," he whispered. "That is no solution. I will not give in." Sweating, Guillermo dropped his head once more. He tried to focus on the rosary, say the proper prayers, but he couldn't focus. *What would you have me do, Lord? I do not know if I can fight this again. I am so weary. I am trying to call upon Your name, but I see no wings, nothing to help me rise above this. Why hast thou made me thus?*

He paused. The question was from the previous week's sermon from *Romans*. Perhaps the answer lay there. The priest reached a dripping hand toward an end table and opened the drawer. He pulled a Bible from inside and opened to the concordance. The passage he sought was in the ninth chapter. He flipped more pages. A trembling finger ran down the text and stopped at verse twenty: "Nay but, O man, who art thou that repliest against God? Shall the thing formed say to him that formed it, why hast thou made me thus?"

Get thee behind me, Satan. I will not listen. The Lord said to feed his sheep, not slaughter them! The Bishop told me to be strong. What did he say? Think of your flock and what is best for them.

Yes, but doesn't a good shepherd cull the flock to make it stronger?

He raised his head. He hadn't thought of that before. Even in his father's voice, it had the ring of truth. *What did Paul say in his letter to the Corinthians? Who feedeth a flock, and eateth not of the milk of the flock?*

Guillermo shook his head and jumped to his feet, pacing back and forth. *What should I do? It sounds wrong, and yet it feels right.* He lashed out in frustration. His arm caught the lamp and sent it crashing to the floor. Darkness enveloped the room.

No. Not complete darkness. Silver light flowed in through the windows, the glow of a nearly full moon high overhead. It sang to him. Not the irresistible pull it would become in a few days, but a strong call nonetheless.

The priest threw back his head and howled. One clawed hand reached for his collar and ripped it free. He tossed it on the couch, where landed on the silver rosary.

"No more," he growled. "I have been made thus. I will not ask why."

Stepping toward the door, Guillermo ripped it free of his hinges and tossed it in the bushes beside the porch. He howled again and grinned. Too long. He ran, a fluid, shifting shadow in the night.

The wolf headed toward Church Street, where his prey waited. The diocese would have questions no doubt, but that was a matter for later.

Tonight he would hunt.

He must.

For the good of the flock.

Jeff Parish *is a 30-something native Texan. He's worked at several papers of varying sizes, but decided to suffocate his newspaper career in its sleep in February 2006. He realized journalism might be a noble profession, but slowly starving his family to death was not. He took a job in internal communications for a helicopter manufacturer in the Fort Worth area, where his primary responsibility is still writing—and editing—an internal newspaper.*

OLD STOOPING LUGH

By Lincoln Crisler

The old cobbler hunched over the counter. Stephen MacKennelly was tempted to pity him. He forced it back; after all, this man owed his kinfolk.

"Ye need to be payin' up, old man." He leaned into the shopkeeper's face. The old man's graying red hair tangled in the gangster's beard as he flinched back. Stephen brushed the tarnished gold from his face and raised his fist.

"Don't try to put the squeeze on me, ye bloody Southie," the cobbler shouted. "Ye know damn well I'm already payin' to the Italians. That's how it works in North Boston."

"Ye owe your allegiance to yer kinfolk, Lugh. Ye pay us for protection, not the Wops." Stephen stalked around to Lugh's side of the counter and grabbed a handful of the old man's shirt.

"I canna afford to pay both o' you, and ye know what the Scortesi gang'll do if I stop kickin' up to them." The shopkeeper's voice scratched its way into Stephen's brain. "I'm putting my grandchildren through school, f'r God's sake."

Stephen remembered his mother taking that tone with the landlord back in the old country, but it was different now. This time, he was the master. "So you think you're better than us, do ya? Me da' was naught but a potato farmer, and yer not much better. Yer kids can go to the same schools as the niggers, kikes and other poor micks. Now, pay up."

"So ye don't want better for yer children than what ye've had; the law of the shillelagh and looking over yer shoulder for the police from dusk 'til dawn? Do yer worst, but I'll not be payin' ye."

Stephen looked over his shoulder at his enforcers and nodded. The two burly youths stepped outside and returned with a pair of metal cans. They ran through the small shop, splashing gasoline on the walls, the workbench, the displays of shoes and piles of raw leather. Lugh's eyes opened wide, but when they met Stephen's, they were cold as ice.

"A curse on ye, Stephen MacKennelly. Yer children will die in their beds and from this day forward, yer family will be less than the worms of the earth." A single tear rolled down Lugh's seamed cheek and hung in his beard like the morning's first dew.

"We'll see about that," Stephen slugged the old cobbler in the stomach, and then struck a match.

* * *

Stephen could still smell it on his clothes when he got home. A few hours laughing it up with the boys, drinking and throwing darts, couldn't wash it away, nor could they eliminate the look on the old man's face when they left him to burn with his shop. He didn't look scared, not one bit. Only angry. And his screams had filled the night air for as long as Stephen had risked staying.

He rolled into bed with his wife and held her close to keep the nightmares at bay. It would be a long night, and the demons were sure to torment him, but it was a small price to pay for his children's future. Old Stooping Lugh might be dead, but the others would fall into line soon enough.

* * *

Stephen was relaxing in his morning bath when he heard his wife screaming. He grabbed a towel and bolted down the hall to his son's room. Grace was kneeling before little Donal's bed. Her hair draped over him like a shroud, and Stephen could see that the boy was not moving. Surely, with all that noise, he'd have awoken.

"He's not breathing, Stephen," his wife murmured. Stephen leaned over his son's still form. The boy's skin was pale, and his lips were blue. His chest was motionless. He lifted Donal's hand and released it; it dropped bonelessly beside him.

"That bastard. That hunching, old, evil bastard!" Stephen was beside himself.

Yer children will die in their beds

How could that old shoemaker know what was going to happen?

A curse on ye, Stephen MacKennelly

No, he had made it happen, somehow. Stephen laid a hand on his wife's shoulder.

"I'll fix this, Grace. He might be gone, but I'll find a way to torment his soul."

* * *

Stephen dressed quickly and drove into town. His crew would be at the butcher shop having coffee. They had a small piece of business over at Lugh's shop; the old man's money had to be in there somewhere, and someone had to take the boss his share. Mickey Rourke didn't need to know the particulars, and he wouldn't care as long as Stephen MacKennelly's crew gave him his taste. This was fine with Stephen; he couldn't see himself telling the boss of the family that Old Stooping Lugh put a curse on his son.

Stephen pulled the car against the curb outside the butcher's. Sure enough, Seamus and Patrick were at a small table outside, sipping coffee. They looked up when Stephen slammed the door.

"Slug it down, lads; we've a spot of work to finish." The boys pounded down their coffee and jogged over to the car. Stephen tossed Seamus the keys and walked around to the passenger side.

A few minutes later they arrived at the cobbler's shop. The police had strung caution tape around the perimeter but Stephen brushed it aside; Mickey had Boston's chief of police firmly in hand. The block was deserted, and Stephen and his crew entered the charred shop without incident. The inside was covered in ash, and Stephen could see the tracks the police had made during the course of their investigation.

Stephen waved Seamus and Patrick ahead of him and walked around to the shopkeeper's side of the ruined counter. As the boys made their way to the rear of the store, Stephen felt around the edges of the countertop. He found what he was looking for, sure enough: the key to the old man's cashbox.

"I found it, lads," he declared. "Get into that office." Patrick wrestled the warped door open and the three mobsters stepped into Lugh's office. It had been untouched by the fire, and the old cobbler's cashbox was centered on the worn but meticulously polished desk.

Stephen inserted the key and opened the box. There was enough money inside to fill his pockets; not only was the old man the only person most of the town would trust with their shoes, but he was known for his thriftiness as well. Seamus and Patrick eagerly accepted their share and headed for the exit.

Stephen took one last look into the lockbox. Removing the old man's savings had uncovered a small leatherbound notebook. It was relatively new, in contrast with many of the old man's belongings. The gangster flipped through it quickly. There were a few pictures tucked inside, and the pages were scribbled with addresses and notes. His family's addresses. Stephen whistled as he left the building.

It appears me luck has changed.

Outside, Seamus and Patrick were leaned against a wall, smoking and whispering to each other. They looked up when Stephen approached.

"You boys have a good time. I need to have a word with the man."

* * *

Stephen MacKennelly had several reasons for not bringing his boys to Rourke's place. Etiquette was a consideration, to be sure; foot soldiers didn't regularly socialize with the commander, after all. More importantly, however, he didn't want the old man to hear Patrick and Seamus' recounting of last night's events. He couldn't afford to have news of the old cobbler's curse get out. That wouldn't help his reputation at all.

By the time Stephen pulled up in front of Mickey's restaurant, his thoughts were collected. His audience with the boss lasted all of five minutes; he gave Rourke his cut of Lugh's money, told him about Donal and accepted his sincere condolences. Then he walked out. For the first time all day, Stephen felt normal. Perhaps Grace would care to join him for lunch before going to the undertaker.

* * *

Stephen felt Grace and he had given Donal a bloody fine wake, all things considered. Shortly before lunch their friends and family arrived, bearing food and condolences. He could have cut the tension with a knife when his 'associates,' led by Mickey Rourke, arrived just as Grace's family was getting in the door, but once the music began and the drink made its rounds, things sorted themselves out rather nicely.

After he had attended to the obligatory niceties, Stephen retired to the washroom and spent a few minutes riffling through the old cobbler's notebook. There were two pictures of small boys; they were labeled Shane and Ethan. A moment of further investigation revealed the locations of the two children. Ethan's family, Lugh's daughter and son-in-law, lived closest and Ethan himself looked a lot like Stephen imagined Donal would have, had he lived a few years more. Stephen spent the rest of his son's wake plotting Ethan's demise.

After a few hours of eating, dancing and playing cards, the hearse arrived to escort Donal's body to the funeral home. Stephen stood rock-solid in front of the gaping earthen maw, thinking dark thoughts as Grace sobbed into his shoulder. When the minister was finished, Stephen bent forward and pitched a handful of earth onto Donal's casket.

May ye choke on this, Lugh, ye bloody demon.

* * *

As the MacKennellys' family and friends left the graveyard, Rourke pulled Stephen aside.

"A few pints'll do ye good, lad." Stephen was in no condition to argue. After spending the whole of his son's funeral killing Lugh's descendant over and over in increasingly brutal mental effigy, he had given himself over to grief. He allowed Rourke to lead him to his car and then to the pub. The mob boss whispered a few words to his driver and then fell silent for the duration of the trip.

The Bronze Spigot was about as far north as the boss of Boston's Irish mob was likely to spend his evenings, and the dim lights revealed a sort of person he'd not be likely to spend his evenings with. Filthy, beer-soaked laborers rolled dice on the sidewalk and frolicked with garishly decorated whores in the alley ways. One such painted tramp laid a finger on Rourke, but a stare from Stephen, tainted with grief and flavored by his thoughts of murder, sent her scurrying away.

"At least we'll have some privacy," Rourke grinned. "Who'd look for us here?" He motioned for the driver to wait. Stephen grabbed the cold, brass door handle and pulled it open. Rourke stepped inside and stalked gracefully around the noisy drunks to a lone, empty corner booth.

"My boy. I wanted so much more for him than I ever had, Mickey." The boss nodded as they sat down and waved a waitress over.

"More than ye have, lad? That would be my job. Ye don't mean anything by that, do ye?"

"Eh. You know what I mean," Stephen paused as Rourke ordered whiskey and stout. "I'm proud to be part of our thing, but I always fancied Donal growin' up to be a doctor or a lawyer. Never thought for a second I'd outlive him."

Mickey pulled a leather case from his coat, extracted two cigars and passed one to Stephen, who in return produced a lighter and lit the older man's.

"You know, I lost me brother when--" Rourke whirled in his seat as the bar's door crashed open. Three men in dark suits opened fire from the doorway. The bar's patrons dove for cover, but Mickey wasn't fast enough. As Stephen slid under the table he saw his boss take three rounds in the chest and one in the face.

"MacKennelly! We're coming for you MacKennelly!" The lead shooter gestured with his gun. "I just seen him," the rough voice noted to his men.

Bloody guineas. Stephen began crawling towards the rear exit, away from the sound of Rourke's killers congratulating themselves. Now he could add the boss of the family to his latest job's body count, in addition to his son and, of course, the demon who started it all, Lugh. His life wouldn't be worth shit if the full story came out.

Yer family will be less than the worms of the earth, Lugh's phantom voice added. Don't forget about them.

"There he is!" The gunman's shout slammed into Stephen's thoughts as gunfire filled the air again. He lurched to his feet and sprinted towards the exit. He hit the door hard. As he stumbled into the cool night air, he heard the Mafiosi flipping over tables in hot pursuit.

"Fuck!" He slammed his fist into the building's brick wall. Rourke's driver was slumped over the steering wheel with a hole in his head. Stephen ran to the car, dumped the man unceremoniously to the ground, slid behind the wheel, and cranked the engine. He peeled out of the parking lot just as the gangsters crashed through the exit.

Gunfire exploded behind him as he squealed into the road. In the mirror he saw one gunman take a knee as the others climbed into their car. Seconds later one of his rear tires burst, and he fought for control of the car.

Damn guido. He pressed the gas pedal to the floor and wrestled the wheel with one hand as he reached into his back pocket. He struggled up with Lugh's address book, which was sticky with blood from his hand. He turned the pages with his thumb as he struggled to keep the car on the road.

168 Lyple Street. If I have to get out of town, by God I'm leaving my mark.

The car struggled through the twists and turns as Stephen made his way to Ethan's neighborhood. With each corner he turned the mobsters got a bit closer. Finally, after what seemed like an eternity, Stephen blew past a street sign reading Lyple, wiped the sweat from his brow, climbed over to the passenger side, threw the door open and jumped.

He landed in thick, dewy grass, clambered to his feet, and ran. As he cut across the nearest yard to Lyple Street he heard Rourke's car hit a fire hydrant, another vehicle, something, and the pursuing car screech to a halt.

Almost there, he screamed inside. 168! 168!

He slowed a bit, jogged down the street, peering into the dark at each house. 168 Lyple Street, home to the fruit of Lugh's seed's seed, hulked in front of him. Stephen sprinted into the bushes.

One room still lit, he mused as he shuffled around the perimeter. It has to be the boy's, that strange parental intuition flashed, he's just the right age to be scared of the dark, still.

Stephen made his way around to the front door and turned the handle tentatively. He met no resistance. The door creaked open and he slipped inside. As he shut the door behind him, he heard a faint sound of music. A harp, perhaps, and some singing. Slowly, he made his way towards the sound, up the staircase. His fingers crawled inside his jacket, wrapped around the handle of a small revolver and brought it up to his eye. Six rounds in the cylinder.

As he reached the top of the stairs, the music came to a twangy, off-key halt. A door was cracked slightly open, and a sliver of flickering light danced in the dark.

Stephen held his breath and slid against the doorjamb. He listened,

listened hard, but heard nothing. He thumbed back the hammer on the revolver and pushed the door open.

"Stephen MacKennelly, I've been expecting ye." Stephen blinked. Sitting beside a bassinet on a rough wooden stool was a man. The dim candlelight glistened in his red hair and beard, and his green eyes were slivers of ice. He sat his instrument, a beautiful mandolin, on the neatly made bed across from him without taking them off Stephen. "Ye'll be dropping that weapon now, boyo. Ye won't be harming anyone here."

"Who are you?" Stephen pulled himself together and focused on holding the gun level.

"A curse on ye, Stephen MacKennelly," the man began. Slowly he rose, leaned over the bed and stroked sleeping Ethan's cheek. "Yer children will die in their beds and from this day forward," he turned and thrust a finger into Stephen's face, "Yer family will be less than the worms of the earth!"

"Ye can't be...." Stephen rubbed his forehead. "We burned you--"

"Aye, you did. Set me to burn, along with most o' what I held dear." He looked back at Ethan. "Most of it. Now ye know how I feel."

"But there's not even a mark on you!"

"Are ye so bloody stupid, MacKennelly?" The man's eyes widened. Quicker than Stephen could think, the young man plucked the gun from his hand and tossed it onto the bed beside the mandolin. "My people held Ireland long before yours ever staggered, rubber-legged from months on the water, filthy and malnourished, onto our shores. We gave over the land freely; took up other pursuits. Ye should have listened to yer da's stories, laddie!"

"You... really are Lugh," Stephen breathed.

"Aye."

"Saints preserve me." Stephen whirled, ran back to the staircase and then leapt over the balcony. He landed on his feet, but the impact knocked him to his knees. He scrambled for the front door and threw it open. He cast a look behind him as he ran back into the night. Lugh was leaping over the railing behind him, wild-eyed.

Somehow he made it to the end of the block. He crouched beside a bush, just outside the wide circle of light cast by a nearby streetlamp. He could see Rourke's car; it had, indeed, impacted with another, and there was a small group of people standing around. He didn't see the Italians anywhere. He peered back the way he had come and saw Lugh stalking down the middle of the street. His hair fanned out behind him like torchlight in the wind.

No way this guy is one of the bloody Tuatha De Danaan. He patted his pockets before remembering that his gun was still in the house, in Ethan's room.

The gun and the wee lad, Stephen mulled it over in his head, both in the same place. A place where Lugh is not. Yes!

He took another look back; Lugh was getting closer still, looking around him as if searching for him. Stephen sprinted down the street and around the next corner. When he came to the corner of Lyple street again, he saw the door to Lugh's house standing wide open.

"This is why ye lose all ye hold dear, ye bloody villain," he muttered as he crept up the driveway. "Ye just don't give any thought to the consequences of your actions."

He poked his head through the door and saw, heard nothing. Trembling with excitement, he took the stairs two at a time and rushed into Ethan's bedroom, already lunging for the bed and his weapon as he crossed the threshold. He realized it was gone even as his hand closed on thin air. He whirled towards the bed.

It was empty.

"Good thing that mick cobbler's paid up," a low voice spoke behind him. Two of the mafiosi from the Bronze Spigot stood in the doorway. One was holding Stephen's revolver and the other, Ethan. The gunman leveled the weapon at Stephen's chest.

Stephen ducked, and the first shot went over his head. He crashed into the two goons, knocking them to the ground. He scooped Ethan up and ran for the stairs. The little boy was screaming in his ear like a banshee. As he hit the ground floor and turned toward the front door he heard another gunshot, and pain exploded in his lower back. Instinctively he held Ethan up as he fell to the ground. Just before he blacked out he saw Lugh step into the house and pluck his grandson from his arms.

Stephen came to in an unbearably bright room. The walls were white and unadorned, and the air smelled of medicine. He heard the rustling of cloth, the rolling of wheels and the soft beeping of machines. He tried to look around him, but he couldn't move.

"See what ye've done now, MacKennelly?" Lugh loomed over him, appearing out of nowhere. Stephen tried to shrink back, but his body wouldn't respond. "I spoke to your doctor. You're paralyzed from the neck down, boyo."

"Where's Grace?" He forced the words out past his thick tongue and dry lips.

"Read this." Lugh pulled a newspaper from his back pocket, unfolded it, and held it in front of Stephen's face.

"Grace MacKennelly of South Boston lost control of her car, hit a tree and died on the way to see her husband in the..." Stephen began. "You demon!" He tried hurling himself forward, but didn't move even an inch. Tears of frustration and loss trickled down his cheeks.

"I'll take my leave of ye now, Stephen MacKennelly. Enjoy what's left of your life." Lugh turned away and was gone the next instant.

Lincoln Crisler *is a horror, fantasy and science fiction writer from Rochester, NY. He has written for Rochester's Northwest Times and Democrat and Chronicle newspapers. He is a veteran of both Operation Iraqi Freedom (04-05) and Operation Enduring Freedom (06-07). He is currently stationed at Fort Bliss, TX. Since July 2006 his fiction has appeared in a variety of print and online venues, to include Twisted Dreams Magazine, The World of Myth, Down in the Cellar and The Late Late Show. Lincoln is a Contributing Writer at The Horror Library, including the Horror Library Blog-O-Rama. His editorial debut, Our Shadows Speak, is available in print and electronic formats, and he is currently accepting submissions for two new anthologies. His first collection of short stories, Despairs and Delights, will be available soon from Arctic Wolf Publishing.*

GRACE'S GARDEN
by Anna M. Lowther

Grace hobbled down her porch steps and made her way to the mailbox. Her cane tapped the fieldstone walk with a steady rhythm, in counterpoint to the heavy drag of the thick orthopedic shoe on her malformed leg.

She was surprised the mail had come so early, but as the truck pulled away she realized it was a new postman. "I suppose he's taking the route in reverse, Amos," she muttered as she leaned down and patted the iron head of her lawn jockey.

She opened the box and took out two envelopes; one was her bank statement, and the other a letter from the bank president. She slid the statement into her apron, but tore the letter in half before adding it to her pocket. "No need to look at it. No matter how many times I tell him I won't sell, he keeps trying. Still, don't you worry one whit. As long as I live, this will be our home. We've been together too many years to part ways now." Grace pulled out her handkerchief and polished the black face of the statue until it sparkled. A ray of morning sun reflected off the iron man's eyes, and for a moment they seemed alive.

She opened his lantern, removed the empty votive cup and replaced it with a fresh candle from her pocket. "You'll need this tonight, old friend. It's the first of the month, and we both know what that means. My worthless nephew will be coming by, begging for money and trying to convince me to sell and move into the retirement home. Lord knows what it would cost me if he fell over one of these stones."

Grace stumped back up the path. Lush azaleas of red, pink, orange and white spread across the front of the porch. A thick carpet of marigolds clustered at their roots. Nestled within the blossoms were three smiling gnomes with an assortment of garden tools. Grace smiled and nodded at the gnomes. "They look especially fine today. Keep up the good work, boys."

She stopped at the bottom of the steps and brushed away a dry leaf from the open mouth of the stone lion that sat guard across from his mate. Slowly she mounted the steps and turned to survey her lawn, or more accurately her garden. There was no grass to be seen. There was a small dogwood tree on the right, a ring of purple and white violets encircling it. Beyond it a thick hedge of forsythia bordered the property on the right. On the left was a hedge of lilacs, planted so the color started white and gradually deepened from pale lavender to a royal purple as it reached the side of the ivy-covered cottage.

Across the front was a rambling hedge of soft pink roses. At the end of the path was a white iron arch and gate. The rose vines twisted over and around the ironwork until it was difficult to find the man-made structure beneath. To the left of the path was a rock garden filled with sweet william, black-eyed susans and multi-colored vinca. Three pink flamingos stood amongst the stones, poking their beaks into a patch of bleeding hearts. To the right was a circle of sunflowers standing more than twelve feet high. In their midst was a plump scarecrow with an old straw hat and flannel shirt.

Grace sighed and bowed her head. "Oh Lord, thank you for the beauty of your creation. And thank you for the joy it brings me." She straightened the bonnet on her stone goose, opened her screen door and then limped through the tidy living room and out into the kitchen. She fixed a cup of tea and watered the spider plant above the sink. She finished her tea, put the cup in the sink and then moved out the back door.

While the front of the house was well endowed with flowers, the back yard made it look like a desert in comparison. More than three acres in size, it sloped gently down to a brook that broadened into a pond. At the water's edge stood a massive weeping willow. The forsythia and lilac hedges from the front angled out and down, forming a living wall around Grace's garden.

She leaned down and lifted the cellar door open, reaching inside for her pruning shears and basket. She dangled the basket over her arm and hobbled down the long path to the willow tree, its branches so thick they obscured the trunk. Grace parted the hanging limbs and eased behind them. She sat down on a boulder and looked at the elderly masculine face carved on the trunk's surface. The natural runnels and whorls of the bark added to the effect, creating a full beard and long flowing hair. "Hello, Master Willow. But isn't it a glorious day?" The fronds stirred, carrying the sweet smell of honeysuckle on a light breeze.

"I knew you'd think so. I'm afraid I don't have much time today. Timothy will be coming so I have to bake some cookies. Still, I just wouldn't feel right if I didn't visit with you a spell." The breeze stirred again and Grace inhaled, deeply savoring the layers of fragrance first light and sweet then growing earthier until the rich tang of mulch hung all around.

Grace stood and reached out, stroking the carved cheek. "Don't you worry about me. I'll be back tomorrow and we'll have a nice long visit. I'll even bring a book. Now I've got to do a bit of pruning. Some of the roses are looking a bit spindly. I'm sure they won't mind if I take a few blooms inside. I do so love a bouquet by my bed."

Grace moved back out into the garden, passing by a reflecting pool and fountain. A trio of cement frogs watched her from their stony perch. At the edge of the water was a plastic boy. His pants were at his ankles and he looked embarrassed to be caught in the act of tinkling in the pool. Grace chuckled, thinking how her mother would have reacted to such a sight. She noticed a bird had left a calling card on the boy's hat. She spat on the corner of her apron and wiped the excrement away.

She continued along a winding path and reached a cluster of deep red rose bushes. There were tall trees, round shrubs and climbers trained up a white lattice fan. In the center of the roses a plastic Cupid hung from a shepherd's crook with a tiny arrow nocked in his miniature bow. He swayed in the breeze and turned as if to watch as Grace cut a basketful of blooms.

She started back the long walk to her kitchen. She passed a raised bed of red, white and blue gladioli. In the center of the bed stood a six-foot tall plywood Uncle Sam standing guard, his top hat in hand. She saluted as she limped past. The breeze rose again and set the nearby woodmen in motion, sawing back and forth on a log that never seemed to split. Grace paused to watch their fruitless effort. "I wish I had more talent. If I did, you wouldn't be merely black shadows."

In a nearby bed of ferns and lily-of-the-valley, another dozen gnomes peeked through the foliage. Each one wielded a tool; there were hammers, hoes, picks, shovels and pitchforks. "You must have been busy last night, boys. The garden looks perfect today." She bent down, leaning on her cane, and righted a sleeping gnome. "Guess you've been tossing in your sleep again, sleepyhead."

Beyond the flowerbed the garden became a meadow of wildflowers. The weathered remains of a split rail fence offered mute witness to the land's former boundary. Next to the fence stood an equally weathered farm wagon. Years ago, when Grace first bought the property, the field-stone foundation of a barn had been visible. She had used those stones to form the front walk, pulling them one at a time in a child's wagon.

She had planted an apple tree next to the wagon, imagining how the horses would have enjoyed waiting beneath it. Wrinkled, dry apples now dotted the bed of the old wagon shaded by the tree boughs. She brushed a wisp of hair away from her eyes. She chuckled as her fingers felt a cheek as dry and wrinkled as the apples. Grace didn't mind. She thought it was proof that she and the garden were a part of each other.

She shook off her memories and limped back to the kitchen. She mixed a batch of oatmeal raisin cookies and waited for Timothy. Just past ten she heard him arrive, the thumping music of his car stereo announcing his approach. Grace looked at her spider plant in the window. The tiny babies jumped in time to the music. She made soft comforting sounds to the plant, then moved toward the front door as the noise stopped.

She watched him fumble with the gate. "He's been drinking again, don't you know," she whispered, patting the goose's bonnet. The candle in her lawn jockey's lantern illuminated the path, but Tim tripped beside it. Grace winced and bit her knuckle as Tim kicked the statue. Her anger quickly turned to amusement as he hopped up and down on one foot, massaging the other and cursing. "Good for you, Amos," Grace whispered.

She opened the door as Tim stepped onto the porch. "Hello, nephew. What brings you all the way out here? Wouldn't you rather be in the city?" She hobbled back to the living room and sat down in a rocking chair.

Tim flopped down on the sofa. "Don't I visit enough, Aunt Grace? I thought you would like some company." His voice was petulant and slurred.

"Have you grown too old to hug me now, Timothy?" The rocker creaked, and the pendulum on the grandfather clock ticked as if waiting for an answer.

Tim grabbed three cookies and stuffed them in his mouth, dropping crumbs over the spotless upholstery. Grace continued rocking and waiting.

"I have a cold, and I wouldn't want to make you sick. You know, if you would sell this place and move into the home there would be someone around all the time. In case you needed anything and all. Why, how would I even know if something happened to you out here all by yourself?" He crossed his legs and lounged back.

"I'm not alone. I have my garden and all my friends. They're far more comfort to me than you or your mother ever were." She clenched her jaw, and pointed her finger at him. "I saw you kick Amos. And all he's ever done is light your path when you stumbled in drunk."

Tim jumped up. "For the love of God, woman! He's not real! He's just a statue, and a racially offensive one at that. After Mom and Dad died and I had to live here I begged you to get rid of it. But you never cared how many times I got the shit kicked out of me at school!"

"Sit down and mind your manners, boy. That was ten years ago. You were only here a bit less than two years. As soon as you turned eighteen you took the insurance money and squandered it all. You could have gone to college, made something of yourself. You are just as spoiled and selfish as your mother ever was!"

"How dare you! Grandpa left everything to you, and what did you do? You bought this dilapidated farm and turned it into a freak show! I couldn't wait to get out of here." Tim swayed over the coffee table, striking it with his knee.

"My father left me what he wanted, because your mother was married and had her own life. She was too busy to care for our parents when they needed looking after, but I was always there. Not that I owe you any explanations. If I embarrass you so, why are you here?"

Tim swayed again and fell down onto the couch. "You're all the family I have left, Aunt Grace. I suppose that should count for something. I'm sorry, let's just forget this conversation happened."

Grace leaned over and took her checkbook from her purse. "Let's not waste time pretending any longer, boy. You're out of money again and you need me to bail you out. You should have listened to me and invested the insurance money. Then you'd be collecting your own dividends instead of asking for mine." She filled out the check and tore it out, putting the book back into her purse.

Tim rubbed his hand across his mouth. "Don't be like that. I do appreciate you taking care of me when Mom and Dad's boat sank. A teenage boy isn't easy to put up with, I suppose. But you are right on some counts. I am like Mom in some ways. I'm not cut out to be a caregiver. I really wish you would consider selling this place and moving into town."

Grace handed him the check and stood. "This is my home, Timothy. I may be an old woman, but I'm not ready for the grave yet. I want to hear that you have a job when you come back next month." She moved to the door.

Tim followed, pausing to lean down and give her a stiff hug as he slid the check into his pocket. "Take care of yourself. I do worry about you." He clomped down the stairs and out to his car. The engine roared and the music throbbed, then faded in the distance.

Grace closed the door and went to the kitchen. She got a glass of water, and misted the spider plant with the sink sprayer attachment. "I know exactly how you think, Timmy. You plan to sell my home the minute I pass on. Imagine turning my garden into a shopping mall! I think you'll be quite surprised when my will is read." The wind blew, and the ivy scratched at the windowpanes.

* * *

The next morning, after breakfast, Grace put on her gardening hat and made her way down to the shade of the willow tree. A breeze parted the branches and she slipped inside to sit on the worn rock. "Good morning, dear friend. I am old, and I am tired. I wish I knew how old you are. I might never have found you under here if Amos hadn't told me to look. Has it really been almost forty years? We've shared many talks, you and I. And over the years we've added quite a few new friends. Still, you and Amos are my dearest and best." A warm breeze rustled the fronds and they brushed across her shoulders.

"I want you to know that I have taken measures to provide for all of you when I'm gone." The wind picked up and the leaves rustled like a melancholy sigh. "I know you don't want to talk about it, but we need to face the truth. I can't go on forever. However, you can."

Grace patted her apron pocket. "Last Sunday, after church, Mrs. Baker from the Garden Society and her attorney joined me for lunch. I signed my will, and have a copy right here." She pulled the paper out and held it up. "When I die, Timothy will get a token from my portfolio. The rest of my money and the farm will go to the Garden Society, provided the garden is maintained properly in perpetuity. They're going to turn the house into the Garden Society Teahouse. Won't that be nice?"

The fronds rustled again and a bright sunbeam filtered through. Grace leaned into the light, closed her eyes and sighed. "I have never been any happier than when I am here in my garden." She slid down onto the carpet of moss, turned on her side and rested her head on her arm. "I think I need a little nap. I know you will watch over me, won't you?" The will dropped from her fingers as her life slipped away.

The willow shuddered, the branches shaking as if in rage. The carved face twisted into a masque of grief, and sap leaked from its eyes. The carved lips pursed and whistled. There was a flash of green light and a tiny wood sprite appeared. "Go tell Amos the time has come. Grace is gone. Now it is our duty to care for her." The tree shook as the face sobbed.

With another flash, the sprite disappeared. In just a moment it returned. "Amos is on his way." The sprite's voice was musical, though the key was dark, minor and full of heartbreak. It hovered over Grace; its tears fell to her face. Everywhere a tear fell the years rolled away from her skin revealing a beautiful young woman.

It took the lawn jockey more than an hour to make his way to the willow. The sprite was flitting back and forth across Grace's withered leg. Gradually the stunted bone and muscle grew until in death Grace had the perfection she had been denied in life. Amos bent over and kissed her cheek. He looked up at the willow and spoke. "It will take time. The garden gnomes will dig a grave and the woodcutters will get the boards ready for the tinker gnomes to build a coffin. I think Sam would like to give the eulogy, though perhaps we all should speak."

The willow shuddered again, and sighed. "Since I am unable to move, I would ask that we bury her here beneath my branches."

Amos nodded. "It was her favorite spot. Can you cast a shield around her while we complete the necessary arrangements?"

The branches waved. "As long as Grace remains beneath my cover, she will remain as beautiful as she is now. Tell the others to take their time and do honor to her memory."

"Of course. There is not a one of us who would give anything less than the best for her." He bent down and picked up the will. "Did she tell you what she did for us?"

"Yes," replied the willow. "How did you know?"

"They signed the papers on the front porch over a pitcher of iced tea. I heard everything. The boy will be quite angry when he finds out." He tucked the will inside his coat, now silk instead of iron.

"It should be him that's dead, not Grace." A shower of tender leaves fell from the tree and formed a blanket over her.

"That is not our decision to make, my friend. I will go speak to all the others. Take good care of her." Amos turned to go. "We should be finished before he comes back again, I would think."

* * *

The moon was full and the sky was clear. Tim didn't notice that the lawn jockey was missing until he was almost to the porch. "Thank God," he muttered. "Maybe she's starting to come to her senses and got rid of that thing. Maybe she'll finally listen to me and sell this dump and let me manage her money."

He waited for her to open the door, and then looked at his watch. "Damn, it's later than I thought. I wonder if she's asleep? I don't want to drive all the way back out here tomorrow." He pounded on the door, knocking a wreath to the floor. An ivy vine fell from the jamb and wrapped around his arm. He jerked free and stepped backward, stumbling down the steps.

He reached out for the lions to break his fall, but they were gone. He looked around and noticed that all the lawn decorations were missing – no flamingoes, gnomes or scarecrows. "That's odd. I didn't think she'd ever get rid of any of that old junk. She probably put it in the back. Guess I'll take a look around before I go."

He wandered around the side of the house and into the back yard. There were thick clouds of fireflies hovering above the flowers. Along the path the blooms were twisted and mingled in a rainbow of color. "Bizarre," he mumbled. "Almost looks like funeral sprays. Wonder how she gets them to grow like that?"

He was so engrossed by the flowers that he tripped over the lawn jockey. He felt a sharp pain in his ankle, sat up and looked at the statue. "If I didn't know better, I'd swear you just kicked me."

"I did. Payback's a bitch, so they say." Amos kicked him again and walked away.

A young boy waddled over, his pants drooping around his knees. "We don't like you!" He peed on Tim's shoes and snickered as a goose hissed in the prostrate man's face.

"That will be enough. Grace wouldn't want us to act like that. Here now, let me give you a hand up instead of the hand-out you wanted." Tim stared up into the face of Uncle Sam, his hat now atop his head.

Tim jumped up and looked around. The back yard was filled with his aunt's decorations, but now they were moving about. Several gnomes marched past, pushing wheelbarrows full of flowers. The scarecrow took the blooms and fashioned them into wreaths and sprays. Two stone lions growled, rose to their feet and stood before the old willow tree.

Near the pond the artificial frogs began to croak and then started singing. Tim recognized the spiritual, "Amazing Grace," sung in a deep and somber bass. He balled his fists and rubbed his eyes. "This has to be one hell of a flashback, that's all. When I open my eyes it will all be gone." He mentally counted to ten and opened his eyes, only to find Uncle Sam shaking his head.

"I'm sorry, but the service was three days ago. If you came to pay your last respects, I'm afraid you're too late. Still, I suppose you'll be interested in this anyway." Sam held out the copy of the will. "Mind you, this is just a copy. The original is on file with her attorney."

The gnomes returned with another load of flowers, glaring at Tim as they passed. Uncle Sam stood between the gnomes and Tim, and then spoke. "It would probably be best if you left now, young man. Amos is not dealing with Grace's passing very well. I don't think he wants you here, and your presence upsets the others. I really need to tend to them."

Tim shook his head, looking like someone who had just awakened. "Service? You mean my aunt is dead? Then all of this is mine! I don't know what kind of trip I'm on, but once I sleep it off all of you abominations are out of here." Tim shoved Sam backward and stumbled toward the back door, mumbling to himself. "Break in, if I have to. Things will be clearer in the morning."

Uncle Sam strode up behind him, took him by the arm and stopped him at the door. "I told you to go. You simply aren't welcome here. The document will explain everything."

Tim yanked his arm free from Sam's grasp. "You're just a damned figment of my imagination. Leave me alone!" Tim grabbed the doorknob, but it was locked. He picked up a rock and shattered the window. Before he could reach through to unlock the door a commotion drew his attention to the cellar door in the ground.

A loud canine wail split the night, full of mournful sadness. The cellar door began to heave, and Tim could hear the clank of rattling chains. Heavy footsteps thumped up the basement steps and something hammered on the door until the wood began to split. The howl spiraled out again, accompanied by a high-pitched cackle and throaty moans.

"What the hell is that?" demanded Tim, trying to keep his voice from trembling.

"I tried to warn you, but since you refused to listen I think you are the one who is truly damned. You see, your aunt kept some of the seasonal decorations in the basement. Because of their nature they could not animate until the moon was full. I suppose they're a bit angry we couldn't wait for them, but Willow wanted to bury Grace at sunset. It seems they have awakened, and now they want to pay their last respects." Sam nodded toward the cellar door, as it broke open.

A werewolf leapt out and knocked Timothy to the ground, snarling at his throat. Tim struggled to get it off his chest, twisting his head away from the dripping fangs. Frankenstein filled the doorway and lumbered out, his arms extended in front. Tim began to moan, his eyes wide as he watched the living decorations stream out of the basement.

A witch raced out, jumped on her broom and circled overhead. Insane laughter assaulted Tim's ears, followed by the drone of an incantation. Green bolts of lightning leapt from her fingers and struck him in the legs; his pants began to smolder. He heard a soft rustle, and struggling beneath the wolf, he turned his head and saw a mummy shambling toward him.

A large bat flew across the garden and turned into a cloud of swirling mist. A vampire stood between Frankenstein's monster and the mummy. He spread his cape and stretched his arms around his companions. "Someone get hold of the wolf or there won't be anything left for us." One by one they fell on Tim, clawing, choking and biting.

Tim grew weaker and closed his eyes, praying for the flashback to end. Suddenly he smelled burning sulfur and opened his eyes, searching for the source. Satan stood nearby in a scorched circle, his tail twitching. "I heard your prayers, my boy. It will indeed end soon, and I will take you home."

Uncle Sam shook his head as Amos strode up beside him, chuckling. Sam looked down at the writhing mound on top of Grace's only legal heir, shook his head again and turned away. "I tried to warn him. I told him to leave. We all sensed the pain he caused Grace, but only the Halloween decorations heard every word he ever said to her, every threat and curse. All those years being locked in the basement gave them time to plan what they would do if they ever had the opportunity."

Amos picked up a floral wreath of lilies, roses and carnations tied with a bow of ivy. "You did the best you could. It isn't your fault that he wouldn't listen, but then I don't suppose he ever did take any sound advice. We can bury whatever's left of him tomorrow. I want to take this down to Grace. Why don't you come with me? We can tell Willow that Timothy received his inheritance tonight."

Anna Lowther's *short story "Miss Magnolia's Secret" is the lead story in the horror anthology Damned in Dixie, edited by Ron Shiflet. Her short voodoo tale "Gris Gris" is in the special Halloween 2007 issue of Sinister Tales magazine, and she has a pirate tale in the upcoming anthology Black Dragon, White Dragon edited by Rob Santa of Ricasso Press. It is due to be released by January 2008.*

WHATEVER HAPPENED TO BABY CHARLES?
by John Teehan

She was squat and wide. In the dim of late twilight she looked like an old tree stump and smelled of brackish swamp water. As for the other, he was tall and thin, bent nearly in half like a broken birch with rough ash-white skin peeling off him in curls. Respectively, they were called Bogsbottom and Kindlesticks.

"It is nearly time, my dear," said Bogsbottom, looking up at the darkening sky.

"I don't see how's a one could tell, my pretty thing," replied Kindlesticks, who twisted around and craned his neck to look. "One cannot see the moon."

"There is no moon tonight, my dear. But if there were, she would be rising high in the night, and therefore, it would be nearly time," said Bogsbottom, who knew these sorts of things. Bogsbottom spent a lot of time looking at the night sky.

"Wondrous," was all that Kindlesticks said for a while. Kindlesticks spent a lot of time looking at the ground.

The wind whipped about them. Kindlesticks creaked and swayed, making the dry, pale leaves about his head rustle. Bogsbottom remained still, but the evening's mad breeze carried her stale-water stink through the trees and beyond.

A small, piercing sound rose between them. Kindlesticks kicked the source of the sound and the keening turned into a wail. "Quiet that thing!" he hissed.

Bogsbottom reached down by her feet and unwrapped a blanket of dried moss, uncovering a babe that had lain hidden within. "Hush now, small thing," Bogsbottom said. She looked at Kindlesticks and clucked, "It is hungry. No need to kick the poor creature, my dear."

"It makes too much noise," Kindlesticks said. He turned away as Bogsbottom lifted the child into her stumpy, damp arms and rocked it. "The Shadow Procession is mad, I tell you," Kindlesticks said after a moment. "Gibbering, hound-howling mad."

Bogsbottom looked around cautiously, then nodded slowly and replied quietly, "They are all who remain, my pet. The old Fae are gone from these woods, but their spectrals linger still. Who are we to deny them their due? We could have left with the others had you not slept all that winter. Ages past."

Kindlesticks whirled and pointed a twig-thin finger at Bogsbottom. "Don't you blame this on me, love! We've been through this before. As I remember, you spent that same winter dozing under the ice!"

Bogsbottom continued to cradle the child until it ceased its noisery. "Only because I had given up trying to wake you, pet. And was I going to leave my dearest one all alone in these woods? Silly creature!"

Kindlesticks harrumphed and lowered his hand. "You should have gone, my love. You should have gone with the high ones and the rest of the old Fae and escaped this dying place."

They both remained silent for a while, then Bogsbottom whispered. "No."

For a while longer they stood, and Kindlesticks sighed, "And you were beautiful then, my treasure."

Bogsbottom smiled, "And you were most handsome. Ah, but how I wish the door hadn't closed. But we make do. We make do, my Kindlesticks."

The child began to cry again--small choking sobs of fitful discomfort. They listened to the small creature and watched it wave its little pink fists in the air. Finally, Kindlesticks snapped, "Still that thing, or smother it!

Someone will hear!"

"If the Shadow Procession does not hear, how will they know where to find their tribute?" asked Bogsbottom.

"I mean its humans--so excitable. They will find the babe, then what will happen to us?"

"What about us?" asked Bogsbottom. "They cannot see us here. We are under the protection of the Shadow Procession. That will only expire if we fail to make tribute this night."

"The humans will find the babe, then the Brigade will come and what will we have for them? Nothing!" Kindlesticks shivered and rattled like a bundle of loose sticks.

Bogsbottom looked up in the sky again, then looked down at the babe. "Poor little thing," she said.

"Hush!" Kindlesticks hissed. "Someone comes."

"The Procession?"

A dog barked. Far through the trees, beams of light swept through the wood. "No," said Kindlesticks, "cover that thing and keep it quiet!"

Bogsbottom wrapped the child again into its bundle, laid it down on the cold ground, and covered it with her body before it could cry out again. She sank halfway into the soft, marshy ground and became rock-still. Kindlesticks rooted himself into place, swaying only slightly in the stiff evening breeze. The sounds of human feet noisily tramping through the brush neared.

"I tell you," said a man's voice, "old Blue picked up the scent--and it leads right through here."

A small group of men approached the motionless Bogsbottom and the silent Kindlesticks.

"I dunno, Sam. I don't see how your dog could follow anything in this stink," said another voice.

"Blue's nose don't lie," said the first man, holding an old bloodhound by a leash. "Whoever took Anne and Charlie's baby came through these here woods." They stopped next to Bogsbottom and looked around. All of the men held flashlights. They scanned the trees and ground.

"Nothing but animal tracks here."

"Anything good?" asked a third voice, also male.

"Bird tracks, Jim, and keep your mind on our business. Whoever took baby Charles couldn't have gotten far. There's a highway over that there ridge, ain't there?"

"Over the ridge and on a spell, but yeah," said the man with the bloodhound. "Troopers supposed to have roadblocks up and down the whole county."

Blue sniffed around Bogsbottom and barked. The man holding his leash gave it a jerk. "Come on boy. We ain't got time for you to go rolling around in muck."

The dog barked again--this time at Kindlesticks, who stood behind a man carrying a large halogen light. Blue barked twice more.

"Stop that! I don't know what's gotten into this dog. Can track a fox through a hurricane most days."

"He's getting old, Sam," said the one called Jim.

"Nonsense. These woods smell like a sewer, and the babynapper probably knew that."

"Makes sense, I s'pose," said a fourth man with a deep, gravelly voice. "Sam's hound followed the scent into these woods at least. No surprise he's all turned about now. I betcha we pick up a new scent once we get over the hill."

The dog barked and strained at his leash.

"Blue, you stop that!" shouted Sam. He wrapped the dogs leash around his fist and aimed his flashlight off into the darkness. "Come on, fellas. Billy's got the right idea. Blue'll sniff out the trail again once we move on."

The men brushed past Kindlesticks, and around Bogsbottom and the hidden babe. They continued through the woods with Sam dragging the barking Blue behind him.

Bogsbottom and Kindlesticks remained still until the sounds of the men and their hound faded, then vanished, between the trees. After a while, Kindlesticks whispered, "Does it still breathe?"

Bogsbottom rose slowly from the muck and uncovered the child. It was sleeping, but its face was filthy with mud and dirty, green water. "It lives."

For a longer time, the two old creatures stood in the still of night. The men did not return.

"Maybe the Shadow Procession is not coming after all," Bogsbottom said. He looked at the sky and frowned. "If there were a moon, she would be at her highest now. Perhaps--"

"Hsssss!" went Kindlesticks. "I hear them approaching."

"I hear nothing, my pet," said Bogsbottom.

"Through the trees, love. Through the trees, the Procession comes. Look!"

Kindlesticks pointed at a cluster of old elm. In the black of a moonless night, the two creatures could barely make out the shifting of shadows. They were no longer alone. Through the trunks of the trees, darker creatures emerged and began to spread out along the edges. Black upon black, flickering shapes gradually took form until the two old folk of the woods realized that they were, indeed, in the presence of the Shadow Procession.

The spectral creatures crept through the trees and stood shoulder to shoulder amongst themselves, keeping a distance from Bogsbottom and Kindlesticks. Twelve there were in all. Tall. And blacker than a starless sky. They stood naked save for cloaks of tattered darkness which swayed in the wind. They made not a sound. The creatures of the Shadow Procession did not exude the grandeur of the old Fae as they had in ages past; they now wore mantles of dread and hunger. Their power was desperation. Power out of a fear of the dark. Kindlesticks shivered despite himself.

A small figure stepped out last from the trees and stood before the Procession. "Approach!" it croaked. Bogsbottom and Kindlesticks shuffled forward.

It was hard to determine if the speaker was a male or female of its kind, but the detail didn't seem particularly important. It wasn't like the others, but a low creature, a folk-of-the-wood as were Bogsbottom and Kindlesticks--mayhaps much malformed in these days of man. The creature (a male, assumed Bogsbottom) was short, though not as short as Bogsbottom, and thin, but not as thin as Kindlesticks. Its flaking skin was mottled with brown and yellow lichen. It (perhaps she, thought Kindlesticks) had a head like a lopsided mushroom, with hollow holes for eyes.

"Presenting myself as Mugbump, Speaker for the Shadow Procession," it said with a voice like a rusty door hinge.

Kindlesticks rustled forward and made an awkward, teetering bow. "Greetings to the Shadow Procession and to Mugbump. I am Kindlesticks, and with me stands Bogsbottom. Humble servants are we of the dark lords of the forest."

"You're having the tribute," Mugbump stated plainly.

Wordlessly, Bogsbottom stepped forward and held out the bundled babe. Mugbump reached out and took the bundle from Bogsbottom. He unwrapped the babe and looked at it. Behind Mugbump, the Procession stirred. Mugbump poked the child once in the stomach, eliciting a startled little cry. It turned toward the pack of shadows behind him and offered the child up.

The creatures snatched the child from Mugbump's hands, tore away the blankets, and hungrily surrounded the child. The babe, who had continued to fuss plaintively, let out a single piercing shriek that was suddenly cut off--leaving only the sounds of shadows rending flesh and bone--and feasting. Mugbump turned back to Bogsbottom and Kindlesticks.

"Accepting your tribute, my lords are. For seven winterings more having you their protection."

Kindlesticks bowed once more, his pointed chin scraping the ground. Bogsbottom followed with as much a bow as her short body would allow. "We give thanks and praise to the Procession for their generosity," Kindlesticks said.

Mugbump snorted. "Instructed to informing you, however, that this will be the last tribute accepting for this wood. Seven winterings after all, my lords removing their protection must."

Kindlesticks sucked in a wheezy breath. "What? That can not be!" he hissed.

Behind Mugbump, the twelve mockeries of old Fae continued to greedily consume the flesh of the tribute. "It means," said Mugbump, "that after seven winterings, the race of man will enter these woods, so it is seen. To drain. To raze. To build their machines and their houses of glass and steel." The speaker for the Shadow Procession gave a raspy sigh. "It is happenings all over, you see. In all the landings on this Earth, the remaining domains for Fae growings ever smaller. Even the Shadow Procession not being able to hold off the onslaughting of man and machines forever."

Bogsbottom let out a low grown. Kindlesticks just grumbled quietly, "You should have gone when you had the chance, my pet." He looked at Bogsbottom, then turned back to the speaker and to the ravening dark lords of the wood. "It's not like it was in the ages past."

"S'truthing," agreed Mugbump. "But that's the whying of the Shadow Procession."

"Just shadows," said Bogsbottom quietly. Then she looked up at the sky, "but perhaps in times to come?"

"We could follow the others from ages past? To the new home?" Kindlesticks finished hopefully.

The three misshapen folk-of-the-woods stood quietly amidst sounds of feasting. As the Shadow Procession finished consuming the sacrifice, they seemed to Kindlesticks a little more solid. Maybe a little more tangible--but they were a long way off from what they once were. A long time ago.

"Perhapsing," said Mugbump suddenly, who had apparently been contemplating times to come. "But for now, and for seven winterings, we existing as we have. No more, and perhaps a little lessening."

Privately, Kindlesticks thought them all lucky if they had even half that time before the Shadow Procession surrendered what little magic that lay stagnant in these woods to the machinery of mankind. For perhaps a winter or three, Kindlesticks and Bogsbottom could consider their little home safe and secure. But soon--too soon--it would be time to move on. Perhaps to colder lands in the north. Maybe to the dryer lands in the west. Maybe never to the lands beyond the Gate.

One by one, the creatures of the Shadow Procession melted back into the trees, as silent and as wordless as their arrival. Mugbump waited patiently, and with a nod of sad recognition to Kindlesticks and Bogsbottom, the speaker followed the Procession into the wood and on to their next tribute, leaving the two denizens of these particular woods alone in the night.

For a while, neither said anything. Bogsbottom waddled over to where the dark lords of the forest had stood. She poked a fat finger among the fresh white bones of what was once a human child.

"Poor little thing," Bogsbottom said to herself.

Kindlesticks tapped a dry, leafy hand atop Bogsbottom's head. "Don't be foolish. And look, my love. Is it nearly light?"

Bogsbottom looked up and nodded. "It will be light soon."

"It was a good night," said Kindlesticks, trying to reason whether spending the night giving tribute to the Shadow Procession was indeed as good as he wished it sounded. What had they really accomplished? Maybe it was more in what they learned that made the night not a total loss.

"I've had better," said Bogsbottom, who was more honest about such things.

For a time, they stood as silent and still as the woods around them. Then Bogsbottom slowly bent and picked up the bones of the human babe. Kindlesticks watched as she buried the remains under an old elm tree.

Winter would come. Then again once or twice more.

Then it would be time to move on.

John Teehan, *based in Providence, RI, has sold short fiction for anthologies by Mike Resnick, Sharon Lee & Steve Miller, a benefit anthology for Charles Grant, and most recently a story to the Bound for Evil anthology. He has also sold poetry and book reviews to Strange Horizons, poetry* to Star*Line, and have several nonfiction credits in various professional markets. He is the Production Manager/Art Director for the SFWA Bulletin, and is also a member.

© 2007 John Teehan

PAPA MORT

by William Blake Vogel III

The stars rise over a dying sun, and if their eternity were but a cosmic blink, it would last forever to that meager shining fated for the eternity of mankind. Papa Mort understood forever. Touching cold death as a lover embraces the one, he had known the limits of infinity. Still they feared him for this knowledge--the kind of fear that breeds an awed respect measured in solitary distance. He judged the ways and means of the souls of man. He had touched the Darkness and it had made a change in him.

Papa Mort had stared Death cold in the face and laughed. Like the raven he feared it not, and rode on the winds of what Destiny would will. He was alone, and he was cast adrift in forever.

Ryan's eyes were blurry when he first opened them. His arms straddled a long wooden beam, each hand being snugly tied down by leather cord. The cords had been bound and knotted so tightly that they were tearing his skin; his fingers tingled from deprivation of blood. These were the waking sensations that stirred him. As his senses expanded, sharpening from blunt awareness to heightened frenzy, he noticed more.

The room's ambient light came from the glow of three small fires. Against the skin of his arms, Ryan felt the dull gnawing of the roughly fashioned wooden plank into his taut, raw flesh. It was a blunt, aching pain that grated against his nerves. Moving his arms only made the sensation worse as the friction wore his skin raw. This was agony, and he suffered with no hope of deliverance from his nightmarish perdition.

"What Hell is this?" Ryan screamed. His voice echoed mockingly throughout the chamber's expanse. The Darkness heard his cries.

Then there came a voice from the darkness. Softly it said, "This is not Hell. Not yet." From the enveloping shadows stepped a man dressed entirely in white. His skin had been painted black, and then adorned in the semblance of a skeleton. The shadows dissolved around his demonic form until he seemed to glow dimly in the firelight. He was a menacing figure to behold.

Ryan's fear was almost overwhelming, and Papa Mort could sense it. He relished that bleak utterance wildly, as beast enjoys the fresh taste of blood after the savage kill. It pleased him.

Ryan's skin coldly crawled. Never before had he felt fear like this, and he prayed that he never would again. From words spoken in terror to prophetic revelation, his fate had already been cast. Kismet has an ironic cruelty.

Papa Mort grabbed Ryan by his hair, jerking his head back. The tears rolled down Ryan's face; his fear was expansive. But his crying eyes pleaded to a heart beyond mercy. Papa Mort had no softness for the craven. "Your actions have brought you to this point. You came to the crossroads, and the choice was clear. When a man sows his seeds to the wind he reaps the whirlwind. Now you're going to reap what you've sown."

Ryan cried out. The drool puddled behind his lower lip, mixed with curdled blood, and then spilled forth in a tumult. It dripped slowly to the floor, leaving a dangling trail behind.

Papa Mort smacked Ryan hard across the face. He clenched his jaw tightly in his hand, staring into Ryan's nearly closed eyes. "You sold drugs in my neighborhood. It poisoned their hearts; it tainted their visions. I watched my children die."

Papa dropped Ryan's head onto the crudely hewn board. "You asked before what Hell was this, boy? From your mouth to God's ear, or better rightly Satan's ear. Because you ain't knockin' on Heaven's door, that's for Hell sure." He laughed grimly as Ryan's eyes pooled with blood-stained tears.

The old man had a ghastly demeanor. Every aspect of his existence, even the pallor of his morbid soul, reeked of the charnel house,. "I can hear the saints beginning the dirge.

"My children think that I am a *Sandoma*, or a witch doctor as y'all would say in the English slang. But I don't need any Voodoo. The magic that runs in these veins is older than Palo, Santeria, and Voodoo all stirred together in a copper pot. Far, far older...

"It is as old as the mountains and as black as the night. We were all born to this destiny, and called each to his fate. And we shall see what the end of the road has in store for you——where your fate shall end the story."

The flames rose higher, and roared unnaturally in each of the scattered fires. Papa Mort stared back at Ryan and said, "So shall it be." Then his eyes closed slowly and opened again.

Mort held his hands out toward a fire. Ryan sobbed aloud. It had finally sunk in just how doomed he really was. The pain was the least of his worries, and the best of his troubles to come.

"Quit your cryin', boy. Maybe you'll find some mercy with God, but you sure as hell won't find any with me." His smile forebode the ill of what awaited.

Papa Mort went to the wall and retrieved a blackened human skull. From it he took a folded piece of cloth tightly shut with ribbon. "This neighborhood is mine. They are all my children here. Their magic is my magic... their power is my power... their pain is my pain."

He grabbed Ryan by the hair again and slammed his head down. "If God had wanted the world to be white, He would have covered it in snow." Papa Mort was very angry now, but he never raised his voice. He had no need to; Ryan was scared beyond his wits.

Mort lowered himself onto his knees. Unfolding his fingers, he revealed the small cloth envelope. He untied the ribbon and gently pulled back the folds of fabric. Within the center was a small mound of grey powder. Mort smiled cruelly.

"Between both worlds is where you'll be. Neither Heaven nor Hell, but for eternity"--blowing the dusty substance into Ryan's face.

Ryan gasped and choked, drawing it deeply inside. He strained for air as the dust violently burned inside of his lungs and throat. The onset of madness was instantaneous. "This is the Living Death. Aeons will pass, the stars will die, and you will suffer the more."

Ryan's body jerked violently. His vision blurred and gyrated liked an old, warped movie frame. Everything was jagged, and vibrated in a sickening hum.

Soon the bugs came crawling from out of the cracks in the floor. Masses of them scurried towards him, screaming and gnashing all the way like starving beggars. They crawled up his legs and arms, burrowing beneath his flesh as they marched ahead. The skin bulged in their torturous wake. These bulges rippled like waves towards his heart, flowing upstream to the very source. There was what they craved, the blood that is the life. The pain was excruciating. Ryan screamed.

Papa Mort laughed coldly. "The price of immortality is pain," he said. "Death will not have you, not for a while."

Ryan blacked out briefly as the magic made waste of him. Even then he had no peace. He had dreamed that this was all just a nightmare, but then the pain roused him once more.

His body had stiffened. There was no breath from his now cold lips. To the outside world he was dead. His soul was trapped in a corpse that had once been his own body. Now there was nothing left for him except pain and his growing madness in this wretched tomb of putrid flesh.

Such was justice in Papa Mort's world. It was a world where he was judge, jury, and executioner for those whose sins led them to his door. Seldom did they ever cross the threshold more than once alive, and never did they tell the tale of what took place there. Even the fool's tongue has its bounds.

Papa Mort slowly closed Ryan's eyelids. The last words that Ryan heard were those of Papa Mort. He said, "Darkness falls." His laugh echoed like a funeral dirge. Then all that was left was oblivion.

William Blake Vogel III *writes a unique brand of Classic Horror that bleeds with an old school grit. Influenced by the likes of Poe and Lovecraft, Vogel's style of Gothic/Horror reflects a deep love for the genre. He currently is working on his zombie opus, "The New Normal." W.B. Vogel has sold pieces to Grafika Magazine, Surreal Magazine, Champagne Shivers Magazine, Apex & Abyss, Night To Dawn Magazine, Black Satellite, Scavengers, Fantasque, Horror Carousel, T-Zero, Twilight Times, etc. He has also appeared in various anthologies including "Open Graves." More can be found at http://deepblackdream.tripod.com.*

RIDING THE OAK MILL BRIDGE

By Eric Christ

From his perch in the security room atop the Oakdale Mall, Lyle Osborne watched Rosie and her dwarf companion examine a rack of leather purses. When the dwarf turned and stared into the camera, his face shifted. His round head narrowed and widened, the eyes moved closer together until the eyebrows merged into an unbroken wall, his skin took on a greenish tint and leathery look, and his mouth broke into a grin.

A tiny row of ivory daggers was lodged into his gums.

Lyle jumped to his feet, hissing at the pain emanating from his knees and shooting up his legs.

He'd seen this creature before.

The dwarf's face shifted again, and he looked like a normal human being, with pale smooth skin and close-cropped blonde hair.

Lyle collapsed into his chair and stared at the monitor with a mounting sense of dread. The dwarf gazed into the camera with a knowing smirk. Wearing a dark blue suit with a white shirt and blue and red striped tie, he stood two feet shorter than Lyle's twelve-year-old grand-niece Rosie, whose blonde hair streaked down her back in pigtails, framing her yellow summer dress that was imprinted with blue and red flowers.

Lyle had seen Rosie only a few times since returning to Oakdale four months ago, but she once mentioned an adult friend shorter than she, who was very nice and often took her shopping at the local mall. Rosie had told Lyle the friend's name. It took him a second to remember it. "William," he said aloud. Rosie had called him Billy. "He's my own little Billy!" she'd exclaimed with a proud grin.

Rosie and the dwarf passed out of sight from the camera.

Lyle lunged to his feet, gripping the edge of the desk to support his aching knees. His hip sent out rhythmic waves of pain in tune with his pounding pulse.

He should call someone, but who? His boss? The police? They wouldn't believe him. Maybe Rosie's mother. But she lived 20 minutes away.

It was up to him.

"The kid's screwed," he muttered, but he grabbed his cane, left the security room, hobbled down the escalator, and rushed through the jewelry department to the mall entrance.

He spotted them four stores down, staring into the pet store. William turned his oval head and looked at him. Lyle's stomach lurched as they locked eyes. The tiny cretin grinned and beckoned with a pudgy hand.

Scaredy-cat. The voice sounded like Jim Hunter, his childhood best friend. Jim had called him that the night he disappeared. Lyle hadn't thought of him in decades. Why hear his voice now? He felt the answer lurking at the edge of his consciousness, but it stayed hidden in the shadows of his memory.

The monster tugged on Rosie's arm and they headed down the mall. Lyle started after them, trying to get closer as he fought through the crowd. They paused in front of a jewelry store, and then rounded a corner.

Lyle cursed his weakness. He'd worked construction since he was 18 years old, and all he had to show for it were two deteriorated knees and a left hip that needed to be replaced. Unable to work, he'd returned to Oakdale and moved in with his widowed sister. She charged him rent, which had forced him to take the security job.

As he hurried around the corner, he tried to remember where he'd seen William before. But all he could associate with the little monster was a paralyzing fear.

Lyle reached the glass doors and pushed outside into the oppressive heat of a Midwestern summer evening. Fading sunlight glinted off a battalion of parked vehicles.

Rosie and William were three-quarters of the way down a narrow aisle. "Rosie!" he shouted. With sweat popping out on his forehead and staining the back of his shirt, he set off in pursuit.

The two reached the edge of the parking lot, crossed the road that circled the mall, and disappeared into thick woods. Seven minutes later, Lyle arrived at the same spot, peering into the thickening gloom. A path snaked through the dense underbrush.

Since he'd moved fifty-some years ago, Oakdale had sprawled to the northwest, leaving this marshy forest undeveloped. The woods extended 30 miles to the next town, a wilderness with few roads and a handful of hiking trails.

Lyle glanced at the mall and its comforting veneer of civilization and safety. He was sorely tempted to give up his chase. But he tightened his grip on the cane and plunged into the forest.

The dense canopy and overgrown brush blocked out the sounds of the city, surrounding him in a bubble of surreal silence broken by the wind rustling tree branches and stirring fallen leaves and pine needles. Moss and lichen clung to tree trunks and ancient gray boulders, spreading their dank scent throughout the air. The sweat on his skin turned cool as he put his head down and hiked the trail. And tried to ignore the feeling that he'd left the known world behind and entered a twisted fairy tale.

Fifteen minutes later, his legs shaking and knees screaming for rest, he came across a rutted dirt road. Just around a curve lay the shuttered Oak Mill Bridge. Beside the entrance stood a vintage, bright red 1930s Mercury bicycle.

The bike stole his remaining breath, and he leaned against a tree. His murky memory cleared. The events of that night rushed into his head, with images of a bridge and a monster wearing Jim's blood....

Two boys pedaled their bikes down Mill Road through the deepening twilight. A full harvest moon bathed the road in gloomy light and cast the twitching shadows of skeletal tree branches onto the hard-packed dirt.

"We're here," Jim Hunter announced. They skidded to a stop before the final curve that led to the bridge. "You ready?"

Lyle gazed at the long wooden structure that stretched over the gurgling waters of Oak Mill Creek. With its rounded exterior walls, Lyle thought it looked like a giant serpent. Its white paint glowed eerily in the moonlight and its shadow-shrouded entrance gaped open like a gigantic mouth. "The floor is rotting out. That's why they're shutting it up this weekend."

Jim laughed. "That's just for cars. It's fine for two kids on bikes. I rode over it earlier today."

If it were daytime he'd race his friend across. But not at night. "I don't think it's a good idea."

"Don't be such a scaredy-cat."

Jim launched his Mercury forward and barreled around the curve. Lyle's hands tightened around the rubber grips as his friend approached the entrance and disappeared inside.

Dead leaves whispered their scratchy song as the wind skidded them across the road. A wispy cloud drifted across the moon, blunting its glow and casting the bridge beneath a thin curtain of darkness. The evening chill crept down Lyle's neck and squirmed beneath his coat.

He jumped when Jim cried his name. His voice sounded hollow. "Lyle! Get in here. You have to see this."

"You need to get out," Lyle shouted back. "It's not safe!"

"Sure it is. See?" Heavy thumps echoed from the bridge. "I'm jumping up and down. It's plenty strong."

Stop being a scaredy-cat, Lyle thought. The bridge was just a bridge, whether it was day or night. "Okay. I'm coming." He pushed off, rounded the curve, and was ten feet from the entrance when Jim said his final words. "There's someone in here with me."

Then he started screaming.

Lyle slammed back on the pedals, locking the brakes and slewing to an unsteady stop. "Jim!"

His friend's hoarse cries morphed into a moist wheezing. Lyle squeezed his eyes shut against a sudden onslaught of freezing tears. He should help Jim.

But his feet stayed rooted to the dirt.

The wheezing trailed off into a brief gargle. Then silence.

After several moments, Lyle opened his eyes. A tiny man stood in front of the bridge and spoke in a gravelly high-pitched voice. "You must be Lyle."

No taller than Lyle's seven-year-old kid sister, the man wore ragged flannel trousers with gaping holes in each knee, revealing knobby protrusions crusted with hair and dirt. A checkered flannel shirt draped his diminutive frame, with the sleeves stretching past his stubby fingers. The shirt was caked with dried mud and darker brown splotches that Lyle knew were blood.

But his face was the worst. Shaped like a squat egg lying on its side, his head was as wide as his shoulders, covered with reptilian oily skin, and topped by a ragged shock of ratty blonde hair. Squinty green eyes flashed beneath a wall of eyebrows that stretched ear to ear. Fresh blood coated his blunt nose, dripped from his narrow lips, and streaked across his craggy chin.

"Too bad you're such a scaredy-cat. I may not have attacked both of you." His mouth broke into a grin, revealing a line of sharp white teeth smeared red and flecked with bits of gristle. "Are you brave enough to save your own tasty skin?" The creature growled deep in his throat and charged.

"Leave me alone!" Lyle screeched, swerving his bike around. The back fender caught the monster in the knees, and he stumbled with an angry curse.

Lyle shoved off the ground and churned at the pedals. He leaned over the curved handlebars until his hands pressed against his armpits. His breath hitched in his throat and his cheeks stung from the icy wind as his feet pumped round and round. Hot sour bile shot into his throat but he swallowed it down.

He couldn't resist glancing behind him. Jim's killer sprinted twenty feet behind, laughing like a maniac and waving his arms above his head.

Lyle faced forward, rounded the first curve, and thudded through a deep rut. The front tire wobbled under the fender.

The monster's taunting laughter permeated Lyle's head. His lungs burned and his breath exploded out of his mouth in ragged gasps. Spittle, stark white in the moonlight, flew from his lips.

As he leaned into the second curve, he saw the monster's elongated shadow dancing beside him on the ground.

Then he struck another rock. The front tire fell off quivered inside the fender and snapped free of the frame. The bike nose-dived into the dirt. Lyle plunged over the handlebars and somersaulted onto his back, landing with a painful thud that blasted the remaining air out of his lungs. Unable to move, he stared at the night sky and waited for the inevitable.

His heartbeat pounded five times when humid breath caressed his ear. "I'll get you, Mr. Scaredy-Cat," the voice threatened in a rasping whisper. "I promise you that." Soft footsteps plopped against the ground and faded into silence.

After what seemed a lifetime, Lyle lifted his head and saw the twinkling lights of Oakdale.

Lyle opened his eyes and stared at the Mercury gleaming in the gentle starlight. Its red paint and silver chrome glowed in the milky incandescence. A black rubber grip rested against the bridge's termite-ravaged wood. He'd loved the bike once. Until that horrible night outside the Oak Mill Bridge. After that, it became a daily reminder of his cowardice, and he never rode it again. His father donated it to a local charity. Lyle hadn't thought of it since.

He approached the bike in a painful shuffle, drawn to it in a way he couldn't explain. He pulled out the mall's penlight and shone it on the edge of the rear fender.

The scratches were faded and nearly polished out, but legible. Lyle recognized them instantly. LO.

His initials. Right where he had carved them.

Lyle staggered backward and leaned against the tree, as if the bike were the monster.

But the Mercury was just metal and rubber. William was the real monster. The little fiend had somehow managed to find his old bike and leave it as a reminder of his childhood cowardice.

Jim's face popped into his head. His friend's dying scream echoed in his ears.

I may not have attacked both of you. William's voice mocked him from across the decades.

His best friend would still be alive today – if only Lyle had followed Jim onto the Oak Mill Bridge.

Now he had another chance. No doubt William thought he'd chicken out again. But Lyle couldn't do that.

"Time to ride the bridge," he muttered.

He slipped the penlight into his pocket and approached the bike, gently pulling it away from the bridge. He lifted a protesting leg over the crossbar and settled carefully onto the rock-hard seat. His back and hip sent out spasms of sharp pains. Laying his cane across the handlebars, Lyle grabbed the grips, wrapped his fingers around the cane so it wouldn't fall, and maneuvered the bike until it faced the bridge.

It was in bad shape. Leaning precariously to the left at a 30-degree angle, its faded paint was cracked and peeling away from the corroding wood. Shredded remnants of wide flat boards hung from the entrance's frame. The opening exhaled a slight stale draft that stunk of decaying corpses – animal or human, he couldn't tell – and solid waste. The floor had to be rotted out and crumbling under the unforgiving pressure of time and neglect. He may not make ten feet before crashing through the floor and plunging into Oak Mill Creek.

But he doubted it. He couldn't say what awaited him inside the bridge, but he was certain it wasn't that.

Lyle placed his left foot on the pedal, gritted his teeth against the expected agony, pushed off with his other foot, and then rolled through the entrance.

The inky darkness embraced him, wrapping him in a cloak of dank humidity. Fresh sweat streaked down his forehead and slithered down his back. The floorboards cracked and popped as the bike lumbered over mounds of debris and lurched through dips in the sagging wood. Even as the bike wobbled underneath him, Lyle felt a rush of exhilaration. He was finally riding the Oak Mill Bridge.

Someone called his name. "Uncle Lyle!"

He stopped by planting both feet on the floor and tried to listen over his ragged breathing. "Rosie! Is that you?"

"Help me!" The muffled voice echoed weakly against the walls.

"Where are you?"

"Under the bridge. Hurry!"

"Hold on!" Lyle leaned the bike on its side and cast the penlight's glow around the floor. Two feet away, a square piece of new wood lay in the middle of the floor, fastened to the faded and splintered floor with a pair of brass hinges. A small half-circle hole was gouged into the door opposite the hinges, and he inserted the handle of his cane and yanked the door open.

Lyle peered down into the opening. A steel ladder attached to the wall descended to the dirt floor ten feet below through a murky mix of flickering candlelight interspersed with pockets of darkness. The room extended to his left and out of view. "Rosie! Are you down there?"

"Uncle Lyle!" his grand-niece replied. "I'm here. Please help me!"

"Are you free? Can you climb out?"

"No, he tied me up. Please come get me!" Her plea broke off into hitching sobs.

"All right, I'm coming down. Yell if you see him, okay?"

Lyle knelt next to the door and reached out a foot, searching for the first ladder rung, grunting at the sharp daggers of pain that dug into his knee. His shoe hit something solid and he pressed down. The rung held.

Lyle slid over, wincing at the wood splinters gouging his hands and arms, and rested his other foot on the same rung. Trying to avoid additional stress on his knees, Lyle shifted his weight to his arms and took two steps down. Both knees throbbed; the left one felt like it was about to buckle.

With the cane in his right hand, he gripped the ladder with his left and descended two more rungs. Now just his head and shoulders were above the opening – the rest of him would be visible to anyone in the room.

He was about to take another step when a white-hot pain lanced across the back of his legs above both heels. He cried out and fell to the floor, his wounded legs collapsing beneath him and shooting out new jolts of agony. Muttering curses through clenched teeth, he scooted around on his rear end, holding the cane before him like a sword.

William and Rosie stood in front of a dark corridor lined with twinkling candles embedded high in the walls. William's tiny fingers were enveloped in Rosie's hand. They stared at him with gleeful eyes and fierce grins. William gripped a slender paring knife, its three-inch blade covered with blood.

"Rosie?" Lyle asked. "What's going on?" Blood continued to pour from his legs, soaking his pants and spreading out into a widening pool. The cane suddenly felt very heavy. He dropped it.

Then Rosie's face shifted.

The unblemished skin, sparkling blue eyes, perfect white teeth, and little-girl innocence were abruptly replaced by swarthy gray-green flesh pockmarked with dime-sized hair-sprouting warts and nickel-sized pus-oozing sores, squinting black eyes crisscrossed with thick red ragged lines, and jagged yellowing teeth rimmed with pale-pink bleeding gums.

Lyle's mouth gaped open in a vain attempt at speech.

"Did you think I was the only one of my kind?" William asked. "We all have our talents, some stronger than others. Eve can change her form to match any child, given time and practice. I can merely make myself more presentable." He stroked Eve's black greasy hair with loving tenderness. "She doesn't share my affinity for killing, though her appetite is just as ravenous." He turned back to Lyle. "She was swallowing your friend's heart as I chased you down the Mill Road."

"Where's Rosie?" Lyle asked.

"Tucked in her bed," William answered. He leaped forward and leaned his face so close to Lyle's that their noses touched. Lyle could smell the monster's fetid breath and tried to turn away, but the dwarf grabbed his hair and yanked his head around.

"I knew you'd come back here someday." William paused. "You

think you're a hero, but you've done nothing. I got you, just like I said I would."

"No," Lyle gasped. He stared into the monster's eyes and forced out a whisper. "I rode the bridge."

A moment of doubt flashed across William's eyes. Then it was gone. "Doesn't matter. I won. You lost." He danced back to Eve, grabbed her hand, and they turned and disappeared down the tunnel.

Lyle watched them go. His breathing grew shallow and labored. The murky light dimmed and blurred into an inky glob. His eyes closed as total darkness enveloped him.

Through it someone called his name. He opened his eyes and found himself standing in front of the bridge, straddling his Mercury with child-sized legs. The voice called again. "Jim!" he cried out, and rode across the Oak Mill Bridge.

Eric Christ *is a lifelong Phoenix-area resident who graduated from Ottawa University in 2000 with a Bachelor of Arts in English Composition. He currently works as a business analyst and technical writer, and in his spare time writes short stories, reads countless books, and sings along with his karaoke machine. His published works include "The Foster Parents" and "Pitchfork Man" in the upcoming charity e-anthology Black Box, "Rodeo Day" in Nocturnal Ooze – April/May 2006 issue, "The Jack-O-Lantern" in issue 8 of Shadowed Realms, "The Ghost" in the charity e-anthology Shadow Box, and "The Mirror" at BloodLustUK.com.*

GOOD DOG

R. Scott McCoy

Steve's lungs burned as he tried to make it to his house before the small pack of older kids caught him and beat the crap out of him. The welcoming committee had tried to pound him into the ground since he and his mother had moved into the neighborhood at the beginning of summer. Steve was small for a 9th grader, but so far his fear had given him the speed he needed. The gang of mostly older kids was getting smarter and more determined. He was sure that eventually he would fall, or be too slow bursting out of the school bus doors.

He had his key out and prayed they wouldn't come into the yard. No car in the driveway meant no mom for protection and his dog Terra was in the fenced backyard, unaware that he was even in trouble.

He took all three of the porch steps at one time and grabbed onto the door handle while shoving his key home in one move. He could see the kids out of the corner of his eye and forced himself to focus on the door. He turned the handle and was in and shutting the door as the head of the gang, a kid name Todd, reached the bottom stair.

"Get you next time... you little bastard!" Todd yelled.

Fists slammed against the door a few times for good measure, and then they left, probably to look for easier prey.

Steve sat down hard, tried to catch his breath and wished for hundredth time that his parents were still married and he still lived on the lake where his friends were. Transitioning from middle school to high school was hard enough, but moving in the same year was just too much.

Terra came in though the dog door and licked his face, taking away some of the pain. He sat there for a long time, looking into her golden eyes and petting her thick fur while she stretched out next to him. At least he had one friend. She'd always been there for him since he picked her out of the litter at his uncle's farm five years before.

Steve wished he could let her loose on his tormentors. He was sure she would hurt anyone that tried to hurt him. If she did though, she could get injured, and the authorities would definitely take her away if she bit one of the bullies. He couldn't stand the thought of losing her. She was such a good dog.

Steve nodded off while petting Terra, and she curled in next to him with her head in his lap.

* * *

David had always known he was above the rest of the herd, but now that he was a senior, it was even more evident. He roamed the school halls and watched people. He found their social behavior fascinating, although pathetic. There were so many possible victims that it was hard to choose. He needed someone small and easy to carry, but it was also important that whomever he chose had spirit. Not just attitude, most kids had that these days. He needed someone with what John Wayne had called "grit".

He leaned up against the wall so he could watch a small girl get books out of her locker. She was the right size, but something about her posture bothered him. Too timid. He was about to move on when someone ran into him and knocked the books out of his hand.

He looked down at the small boy who had run into him and smiled.

"Hey there. You all right?" David asked.

The small boy looked like a frightened rabbit as David reached his hand out to help the boy up.

"It's OK, I won't bite," Dave said.

The smaller boy took his hand and looked into his eyes. The boy's face drained of color and he looked away. David lifted him to his feet in one smooth, effortless motion.

"There you go, Sport. What's your name?"

"Steve. What's yours?"

"My name's David. Nice to run into you, Steve."

The boy named Steve forced a smile, but David was struck by the thought that Steve had somehow recognized him for what he really was. Not part of the herd, but a wolf in sheep's clothing. David smiled wider and Steve shrank back involuntarily.

"Well, Steve, I have to go now, but it was very nice to meet you."

He ruffled Steve's hair, picked up his books and walked away into the crowd.

* * *

Gym class usually sucked, but dodge ball was worse than most games. Steve could dodge well. He'd had a lot of practice, since he seemed to be the favorite target, but eventually he got too tired to avoid the hurtled projectiles. The gym teacher was an older version of the jerks that kept hitting him long after he had fallen, and did nothing to stop it.

As usual, he was last to get in the shower and last to leave the locker room. Todd and his gang were waiting for him when he got into the hall. Steve had made them look bad for the past couple of weeks by escaping their "justice," and it looked like it was payback time.

Todd's face was a mixture of joy and anger. His gang circled Steve, cutting off his retreat. Steve thought briefly that his strategy of running had been a mistake. After all, he knew they would catch him eventually, and he suspected it would go worse for him now than if he had just faced the beating on day one.

He opened his mouth to try to talk his way out of it when someone pushed him hard from behind. He stumbled forward into Todd's oncoming fist. It caught him hard in the right eye and spun him sideways. The pain was bad, but not as bad as Steve had feared for so long. Todd was taunting him, moving his mouth, and the other boys were egging him on, but he couldn't hear what they were saying. There was a roaring in his ears. Months of fear had been knocked out of him with that hit, and he balled his hands into fists.

Todd stepped forward for another punch, but it never landed. Steve swung a wild uppercut that caught Todd in the jaw, shutting him up and knocking him out. Todd's fan club fell silent. A teacher stuck his head out of a door and the pack scattered, leaving Steve standing over his unconscious tormentor.

* * *

David watched the show through a window from outside. He'd been about to leave and continue his search for another kid when he saw the look on Steve's face after he got hit. David expected him to start bawling like a baby, but he watched as Steve's face twisted with rage. David leaned toward the window and smiled when he saw that little fist connect with Todd's chin. The punch has lifted Todd a good inch off the ground before he crumpled into a heap.

Steve had grit. Steve was the definitely the one. Steve would be his first human victim. He would also be his last before he moved away to college. He'd be caught for sure if he started racking up a body count in such a small town.

Now that David had selected his victim, he needed to find out everything about him, starting with where he lived.

* * *

"Terra. Terra Bear," Steve called out again.

Terra had jumped the fence in the backyard before, but she never left the yard. She was a good dog and never missed breakfast.

"Terra!" Steve shouted.

"She'll come back, Sweetie," his mom said from the kitchen door. "Time for school. Try not to worry. She'll be back when you get home."

Steve looked into the dark woods behind their house for another few minutes and choked back tears. Somehow, he knew that she wouldn't.

* * *

"Time for bed, David," said Rachael as she went upstairs. "Shut down the computer."

"Just fifteen more minutes?" David pleaded. "I'm almost done with this paper for history."

He was such a good boy. No video games for her David; he wanted to finish his homework. He was so smart, one of the few high school seniors working online towards his Bachelor's degree. David had finished all his requirements for graduation halfway though his junior year, but he said he wanted to graduate with his friends.

"All right," she said, "but just fifteen more minutes, then it's lights out. You need your rest."

Rachael couldn't help but smile at him. He was so earnest and handsome, such a good boy. She kissed him on the forehead and ruffled his reddish brown hair. David had the hair and the deep blue eyes of his father. If only he could see David now, how proud he would be. She kissed him one last time for good measure. David rolled his eyes in mock exasperation and then kissed her back.

"Good night, Mom. I love you."

"I love you too, Sweetie. Don't let the bedbugs bite, and if they do..."

"...bite them back," David finished with a smile, then looked back to his screen.

Rachael went back down the stairs, past pictures of her family. She lingered at a photo of her husband, holding little Davie in his big La-Z-Boy chair, a huge goofy smile on his face. Two months after the photo, a drunk driver had taken him away. Her vision blurred as she entered the living room. She brushed her eyes clear as she sat down on the coach in her cozy spot and opened her book to where the hero was just about to dispense some serious justice.

An hour later, Rachael turned off the lights and checked the doors before going upstairs. On the way to her room, she went in to check on Davie, as she had done every night of his life. She crept in and leaned over him. She smelled his hair as she kissed his forehead lightly. "I love you," she said in a whisper. Then she crept back out and shut his door.

David's eyes popped open exactly thirty minutes after his mom kissed him goodnight. He pulled back the sheets and climbed out of bed. He removed his pajamas and slid open the bottom drawer of his bureau. He took out a black two-piece cold-weather running suit and a pair of black dress socks. He put them on and reached under his bed for his old sneakers. They fit a bit snugly; his mom had tried to throw them out because they were "so worn there was barely any tread left on them!" Perfect.

He eased his window open and pulled himself out using the branch of a large oak tree. From the branch, he slid his window shut. He was confident that the two Tylenol PM's his mother took every night would keep her from noticing his absence.

The late fall night was cool, but no breath yet showed in the dim light coming from the garage across the alley. He climbed down the tree into the darkness of his back yard, which was blocked off from the rest of the world by an eight-foot wood privacy fence. He had removed the leaves earlier in the week, and the grass made no noise as he passed.

He also kept the gate well oiled. It opened and shut without a sound as David entered the alley. He walked slowly but steadily, staying in the shadows as he crossed several yards on an unmarked path known only to him.

The woods loomed ahead, dense, dark, and welcoming. This stretch of forest skirted the entire western edge of his typical small Wisconsin town. The population was 6,562, according to the sign on the main road that ran through on its way north. The woods were a mix of pine, birch, maple, oak and poplar. The ground was covered with years of leaves and needles that gave off a pleasant scent of decay. The soil was loose, black, and easy to dig. It was ripe for planting.

David took in the familiar smells as he went deeper into the woods. After ten minutes, a small clearing opened in front him. A decrepit wood shack, black with rot, loomed at the far end of the clearing. It leaned forward eagerly. Its door hung open like a mouth, set in a permanent leer. It called to him.

As he approached his hideaway, he remembered his delight at finding this forgotten place three summers ago. He looked down at the ground, sensing the bones just below the surface. David was a precise young man and could recall the intimate details of each kill and burial. Several squirrels were underfoot. His first cat kill was three feet to the left and two feet down. There were more cats up ahead. He loved cats, but was sure there weren't more than a dozen ways to actually skin one. Dogs were harder to take. They were more likely to be missed and so much louder. They were also more difficult to carry, but an important step in his development.

David smiled at the thought of tonight's work. It would be his first human kill, and he had no intention of getting caught. He must be sure of every detail. He went through the checklist. First the tools: wheelbarrow, stolen 1 year ago; common rope found at any hardware store; duct tape, very common; surgical gloves from the school nurse's office; coveralls from a feed lot; homemade chloroform from a recipe found online and thoroughly tested on large mammals; a stolen towel to soak in the chloroform; a gallon sized Ziploc bag to hold the towel; and most importantly, his knives.

He had stolen many knives over the years. His first was an old steak knife from home. Some were from stores where and when he could safely take them. Most were from people's houses when he practiced entering and exploring, undetected. Practice makes perfect. He had learned a lot. They were his first trophies, but not his fondest. They were only tools, important, but just tools.

He took off his belt and then slid it back on, adding his two favorite, sheathed knives: one on each hip, where he could reach them quickly with either hand.

The bones were his real prizes: a bone from each of the animals. Numbering more than fifty in all, they were different shapes and sizes. He kept them in an old metal lunch box under the floorboards. They were buried just six inches from the surface, and he longed to touch them. No. He never took them out before a kill. There were rules, and the rules must be followed.

Another twenty minutes at most and the town would be asleep. He used the time to go over the details of his plan. With the tool check completed, he could stop thinking about it and move on to the route. The trail was clear enough for the wheelbarrow and ended within fifty feet of Steve's house. It was a rambler with the bedrooms in the back facing the woods. A four-foot high wire mesh fence surrounded the backyard. A large dog door panel was installed in sliding glass door. No dog now. No barking. David had made sure of that the night before.

She had been a big mixed breed. Golden retriever and probably lab that had barked at the slightest noise. Poison had been out. David didn't want the dog dead before he got to it. He would need to do more research on non-lethal ingested poisons. He needed something that would knock something out but not kill, and wear off in a short period of time. Until then, he had his Internet chloroform recipe. A fluffy animal squeaky toy soaked in the stuff had worked nicely on the bitch.

It'd been good practice and a good time. It'd taken the dog thirty minutes to die. There had been so much blood in the big animal. He had known this of course, researched it and planned for it as with everything, but the amount had still surprised him. She had been a good dog. Her eyes had pleaded, her gagged mouth whined, and her body had squirmed. Yes. She'd been a very good dog.

Steve wasn't any bigger than his dog and probably wouldn't last nearly as long, which was a shame. However, people felt fear more than any animal could. He was sure of that. He would see the pleading in the Steve's eyes, along with the fear and the agony.

Stop it, he told himself. Work the plan.

He had to stay focused or he would make a mistake. Tool check done. Route good. Now his action plan: 1. Gloves on. 2. Take the wheelbarrow down the trail to the edge of the woods. 3. Open the fence gate and leave it open. 4. Enter the house through the dog door and open the sliding glass door. 5. Go to Steve's room and take the chloroform rag out of the Ziploc bag. 6. Place the towel over his face and lay on top of him. 7. Put towel back in Ziploc bag. 8. Take a sock from his room. 9. Carry him out the door and close the door. 10. Bring him to the edge of the woods and put him in the wheelbarrow. 11. Gag him with his own sock and cover his mouth with duct tape. 12. Hog tie him with rope and push the wheelbarrow back to his true home. Where David should have a whole hour to play with and bury him before he had to go to bed. Tomorrow was a school day, after all, and a growing boy needed his rest.

Scritch scratch.

He turned toward the sound, curious but not alarmed. Nothing much moved out here at night, or in the day anymore, for that matter. There might still be a few raccoons around.

Scritch scratch.

It was closer this time. It sounded like small claws on a tree. He pulled a wrist rocket and a couple of small round stones out from under the floorboards and eased over to the edge of the door. He still had about fifteen minutes before it was safe to approach the house. Plenty of time to add to his collection and a good diversion to keep his mind occupied while he waited.

He moved to the wall just to the left of the entrance, then eased to his right and peered carefully out the door with only his right eye.

Scritch scratch.

David couldn't see anything. He had excellent night vision, and there was some light coming through the clear November sky from the waning moon. Even so, there was no hint of movement.

Scritch scratch.

This time the noise came from behind the shack, he was sure of it. He would be able to ease out of the doorway and get around to the right, using the building to screen his movement. Slow and silent from years of practice, he eased out the door. His excitement grew as he moved, reveling in his skill as a hunter.

Scritch scratch.

Louder this time and higher up on the old twisted oak that grew behind the shack. He froze, not wanting to startle the animal. He lifted his eyes slowly up to the place in the tree he had heard the noise and shifted his weight so he would be able to spin and shoot in one fluid motion. He frowned. There was nothing on the branch where the sound had come from. He had not seen or sensed any movement.

Scritch scratch.

Then he saw it, something small and white. He could see tentative movement as the thing skittered down the branch toward him. It was small, about the size of a small red squirrel, but it wasn't red. It was white.

Albino? Cool.

He had seen pictures but never had the pleasure of taking one. He raised his arm, aimed, and then released the stone in one lightning-fast well-practiced motion. He knew as he let go that it would be a good hit.

Scritch scratch went the squirrel, unaffected by the stone that should have turned the side of its head to jelly. Instead it moved closer down the branch. Its little whiskers twitched at him.

A large twig snapped. The sound was loud in the still woods. It had come from about thirty feet behind him.

Now he was annoyed. He didn't miss. Not at this range. And now there was another animal behind him.

This is my retreat, not Grand Goddamned Central Station for the animal kingdom. I rule here!

He turned around while he reloaded the wrist rocket and drew the pouch back to his ear.

There in the middle of his personal graveyard was a white cat. Not snowball white, but pale white. It almost glowed in the thin moonlight. He released straight for the head, and the stone lashed out. He heard it hit the ground behind the cat and stared incredulously at the beast.

No way had he missed a target on the ground at thirty feet. No fucking way!

He sensed more than saw motion to his right. He spun and reached for another stone. Coming from the edge of the woods were a dozen animals. Pale white cats, squirrels, raccoons and a few dogs. A poodle with an over-sized collar growled at him. It took a step forward and growled again. It looked like his first dog kill, the little yapper that had lived at a house on his path to the woods. That couldn't be, he had killed it over a year ago after almost getting caught on one of his late night excursions because it had barked at him. He had made the damned thing suffer for that. He had taken a big risk and kept it alive for three days as punishment. No way this was the same dog. It had been black. This one was white, like the cat, like the squirrel....

He dropped his wrist rocket and pulled out his knives. The one in his right hand was a Vietnam-era KA-Bar Marine knife with a 7-inch razor sharp blade, and a 1-inch sharpened back blade that met in a wicked point. The other was a short fat blade with a gut hook on the back. It had a half moon curved design and was made for skinning.

He crouched low and started for the poodle. More animals appeared all around him, and in the center next to the poodle a large pale dog sat on its haunches.

What the hell was going on?

He turned back to his sanctuary and saw he was surrounded.

A low rumbling growl drew his attention back to the big dog, and he prepared to lunge in for the kill when he stopped. The dog wasn't white. It wasn't anything at all. He could see the ground through it. The animals all seemed to grow pale, then solid again, like ripples across a pond, as they tightened the circle around him.

He lashed out at the bitch with the big knife and cut through nothing but air. He slashed to his right at a raccoon that leaped at him. He watched the blade pass clean through. He felt the creature's impact and its claws as it grabbed on to his arm.

Impossible! If he couldn't touch them, they couldn't touch him. This had to be a dream. He had to be asleep. He needed to wake up. He had to escape this nightmare.

More animals leaped on him. He shook frantically, trying to break free. He started to run and felt sharp teeth sink into the back of his left ankle. He tried to scream, but nothing came out. He took another step and felt another bite, deep in his right calf. He fell down, rolled onto his back, and tried again to break free. Small teeth pierced him in a dozen places. The leader of the bizarre pack loomed over him. He looked into its eyes, which seemed to become more solid the longer he stared.

"You're dead!" David croaked. "I killed you. Killed you all. You belong to me. To meeeee."

The dog returned the flat dead stare for a long moment, and then it lunged forward so fast David felt the teeth on his throat before he registered her movement. He heard a wet ripping sound and his neck jerked up, forcing his head back. He smelled the hot blood as it spurted across the dead leaves. His head lolled forward and he saw his flesh disappear into the dog's mouth. The bitch became more solid. He tried to speak but nothing came out.

Stupid dog. He would be dead in two or three minutes and he barely felt any pain. Where was the fun in that?

He watched as the animals moved back to the center of the clearing and surrounded the bitch. They seemed to get larger, wispy, and then they dissolved and joined together into a thick mist that got smaller and smaller until only the bitch remained. No longer white, her golden fur glowed in thin moonlight.

Bad dog, David thought as his vision faded. Bad. Bad dog.

* * *

The dog took one last look at the bad, dead thing in the clearing, then turned and headed down the path. Her breath puffed out in little clouds of steam. Brittle leaves crunched under her paws. The woods opened to reveal a fenced-in back yard and a house beyond. The back gate was shut, so she broke into a trot, then sprang forward. She cleared the fence and jogged toward the sliding glass door. She went through the dog door in one fluid motion. The flap swung back and forth twice before the magnets held it in place as her nails clicked across the kitchen floor. She went left down the hall and into the boy's room.

She watched him sleep for several minutes, then leaped up onto the bed. The boy stirred in his dreams, letting out a quiet sigh as he rolled on his side. The dog moved forward and stared at him. She slowly lowered her head toward the boy's face.

"Terra. Terra Bear. Good dog," he said, still dreaming.

Terra Bear. Yes, that was her name and she was a good, good dog.

She licked him once on the cheek, then turned around in a circle several times. She clawed at the comforter to get it just right, and then lay down at the boy's feet and closed her eyes.

R. Scott McCoy *was born in the wilds of Alaska and raised in Minnesota, where he currently lives with his wife, two daughters and three dogs. His work has been appeared in Blazing Adventures Magazine, Anathema, Bewildering Stories, Shroud Magazine, and in the Help Anthology for Preditors & Editors. Scott is the Publisher of Necrotic Tissue, a horror ezine and is an Affiliate Member of the HWA.*

© 2007 R. Scott McCoy

144 ABOMINATIONS

STARVELITO
by Lon Prater

I. No More Fat

Gene strained, clawing at his shoelaces like a drowning man. His face was red from exertion and the meager strings of soft muscle buried in his flabby neck had begun to cramp. Finally, he got the second shoe tied; a small victory perhaps, but enough to celebrate. Besides, after today he wouldn't be able to eat like he was used to anymore.

Gene flopped back into the easy chair, wiping dampness from his face with an embossed fast food napkin. He looked around, his eyes alighting on last night's box of shrimp fried rice. No good, it was empty. He grabbed a pizza box from the garbage piled on coffee table and shook it. Bonanza!

Gene pulled out not one, but two cold stale slices and began chewing them with effort. Only when he was finished did he think to look for something to drink. Lucky for him a two-liter bottle of Pepsi was just within reach. He upended it, letting the warm fizz pour down his throat. To think, he'd never be a slave to his hungers again. After the procedure, he'd be on the fast track to weight loss. By the end of the first year, he'd be as skinny as the day he met Rachel.

He set the bottle down heavily at the thought of her. The liquid sloshed and foamed, a bottled black sea. The surgery wouldn't bring her back. She had remarried, divorced, remarried again--this time to a minister. She finally got the kids she always wanted: two boys and another one on the way.

After Rachel left, the numbers on Gene's scale had just kept climbing. One day the needle stopped at twenty pounds past zero and he tucked it away in the back of a closet. He had no idea how heavy he was now, but he knew that he had to have continued gaining.

But all that was going to change, had to change. A trip across the border to Dr. Cansada's private treatment center for obesity, and he'd be on the road to health and wellness. No more palpitations, spots in his vision, chafing thighs, or enormous clothes. No more stares and whispers. No more pretending not to hear fat jokes.

No more fat, period.

Well, not immediately. The procedure was a new one, not approved in the States, or anywhere for that matter. It wasn't the gastric bypass, the one where the surgeon basically cut your stomach in half and then reattached your small intestine to the reduced organ. And it wasn't the new banding procedure, where they wrapped a tube around your stomach and filled it with saline until the organ was squeezed into a full-feeling hourglass shape.

Dr. Cansada's procedure was secret and unique, or so his website claimed. From the limited information available, the procedure was similar to, but much more successful than, the newest concept of inserting a balloon through the esophagus and filling it while in the stomach. From the hints on the doctor's website, it did involve putting something down the throat, but what exactly wasn't specified.

Apparently, the doctor was pretty serious about protecting his trade secrets. From all indications the weight came off faster than with the other techniques, and stayed off. Another huge benefit was the lack of extended hospital stays or recovery times. An hour under the gas, then you were free to go home and eat whatever you felt like; presumably the device inserted acted as some kind of appetite inhibitor.

This was the part that appealed to Gene, made it worth the trip to Mexico and paying the good doctor out-of-pocket. No cuts, no blood, no down time, and no hunger. And it was just hours away.

Gene huffed to his feet and shuffled toward the overnight bag staged in the little foyer. He took one last look around, then edged sideways through the door whistling a burger joint jingle as he closed it softly behind him.

II. Don't Drink the Water

The doctor's office was as clean and modern as any back home: the furniture new, the walls papered and adorned with tasteful framed art. A red-lipped beauty in glasses was perched behind the front desk. Gene felt the ends of his grin press into the heavy flaps of his cheeks. Maybe even better than home.

"May I help you?" she asked. Her voice was deep and rich, melodic with the rhythms of her native tongue and a touch of something almost European.

Gene let the grin bloom into a full-fledged smile. "I'm Gene Hankins, here for the procedure." The way his voice turned up at the end almost made it sound like a question. Pretty girls always made him a bit nervous.

She nodded in recognition and handed him a clipboard full of paperwork to fill out. He enfolded it in one meaty hand and maneuvered himself into a chair. Nice touch, he thought, settling into one of the comfortable padded chairs. These were big enough to seat even the plumpest of patients.

After the paperwork and credit check gods were appeased, the woman ushered him through a frosted glass door into a brightly lit hallway lined with dark wooden doors. The air was cold; Gene's breath trailed out behind him in ragged frosty puffs. She led him to a room at the end, checked his vitals, and told him the doctor would be with him shortly.

Gene hopped up on the bed and waited. And waited. He was just about to go back to the front desk and ask if the doctor had forgotten about him when a fragile skeleton of a man entered the room. Gene checked his watch. Shortly meant about twenty-two minutes here in Mexico, apparently.

Dr. Cansada was a study in emaciation. Veins showed through the thin skin of his face in a way that made it look like watermarked vellum. A fabric belt was knotted at the narrow waist of his white coat. He'd wrapped the ends around himself several times, but they must have come loose; one dangled in a limp bow while the other belt tip was crumpled into a pocket. Wire-like fingers toyed with a stethoscope that seemed about to fall from the twig that was masquerading as the doctor's neck.

"You're wondering if I tested the procedure on myself, yes?"

Gene jerked his gaze over to an empty patch of wall. "Well, did you?"

The doctor did not answer. A bony hand dipped into the pocket of his lab coat, returning with a photograph. He handed it to Gene. "That was me, two years ago."

"No way." The picture showed an immense man reclining on a red couch that sagged wearily in the middle. Gene squinted at the image, then at the doctor. The plaintive eyes were definitely the same--if a bit less vibrant--as those on the real life doctor in front of him. "This is you?"

Dr. Cansada nodded.

"Any long term effects, second thoughts?"

The little man's eyes flashed as something unreadable passed across his face. "What effects could there be? I eat when I hunger, and stop when I've had enough. That's how I lost over a hundred and sixty pounds in the last two years. I'm healthier now than ever before."

Gene stared at the famished-looking man. Now is the time to back out, if you're going to. "And you're never hungry?"

"I swear to you"--the doctor stressed each word--"I'm almost never hungry."

"There's no restrictions on what I eat? I can have whatever I want?"

The doctor gave a skeleton grin. "Well if I were you, I wouldn't drink the water while you're here. Otherwise, drink plenty of it. Listen to your appetite, it won't steer you wrong."

"Then I'm in," Gene said. "Where do you want me?"

Dr. Cansada waved a hand at him. "Just lean back, and I will administer the anesthetic. You will be unconscious for about an hour while I perform the procedure. When you leave, just listen to your appetite like I said, and eat whatever you get hungry for, whenever you're hungry for it. The weight will come off all on its own."

Gene leaned back in the hospital bed. He stared hard at the picture one last time. The heavier Dr. Cansada looked back at him with reassuring eyes. Gene gave the photo back to the doctor, and closed his eyes. Hasta la vista, Fat Ass Gene. He felt the needle poke into his arm just moments before the darkness slithered over him.

III. Svelte in No Time

It was hard to keep from smiling. Gene felt lighter already. He barely remembered the grogginess of waking from his procedure, or taking the cab back to the hotel. He'd fallen woozily into bed and slept through till morning. After a truly hellacious piss, he rushed off to the airport for the flight back home.

He hadn't been hungry even once in the three days since, and he'd never felt better. And he was losing so fast. He grinned at himself in the bathroom mirror.

"It's working, you handsome devil. You'll be svelte in no time."

Not being hungry, he simply didn't eat. Using all the money he saved by not buying food, he bought smaller clothes three different times that month. He considered shopping the thrift stores until his weight stabilized, but decided against it. Why waste an opportunity to make that smug bastard Kevin from the plus size store jealous as hell?

Kevin wanted to know what his secret was, how he could lose so much weight so quickly. "Isn't not eating supposed to slow down your metabolism? And how is it you don't feel hungry at all?"

But Gene could give him nothing more than a non-committal shrug. He had wondered about the superior results himself, even tried to call Dr. Cansada's office, just to make sure this was what should be happening. The number was no longer in service. Emails were undeliverable. The website was 404.

They hadn't overcharged his credit card and he was getting outstanding results. So Gene wasn't too worried about the good doctor. He just kept drinking water and listening to his appetite. Just what the doctor ordered.

The only down side was the constant need to urinate. All day, all night, he was letting go like a fire hose. The fat was melting off of him like butter. Every three or four hours he was pissing the greasy mess out of his system.

At the end of the first month, he had dug the scale out of his closet. Five pounds past zero. Incredible. He whooped with joy. This called for a celebration.

But Gene had no appetite for a victory meal, which faintly disappointed him; the thought of eating anything made him nauseous. Nowadays, he went for long walks instead of taking his meals, feasting his eyes on the people on the streets and sidewalks instead. When am I going to be hungry? he wondered--but it was a whisper even in his mind, for fear the weight loss would stop sooner than desired.

One night that next week (a milestone day, as he had dipped below three hundred to 297 that morning), the squirming in his stomach began. It seemed insignificant at first, easily mistaken for gas. He still wasn't the least bit hungry. Worry began taking little fishlike nibbles at him; nothing he couldn't swat away with a trip to the scale, or a look in the mirror.

His body had rebelled at the very idea of food for forty-odd consecutive days. Thinking about it put a little flutter of fear into his stomach. Or was that fluttering the thing the doctor had put inside him; maybe come loose or something?

What exactly had the doctor put in him, anyway? Gene decided then and there to go see an American doctor and find out what it was--once he got below two hundred.

IV. Confidential Agreements

Gene stared down at the scale. Two hundred and seventy-eight pounds. The last time he had been in the two-seventies was the day he'd signed the divorce papers, almost eight years ago. Rachel had looked especially prim and gorgeous that day; she wore a white dress with little red rose buttons that reminded him of their wedding day.

At least she had had the courtesy to show up without her new boyfriend. Justin or Jared or something like that: an accountant with thinning hair and a pointy beard who looked like he'd be more comfortable doing Kerouac readings than figuring depreciation.

The business with the lawyers was quick, but not quick enough to avoid the need to make uncomfortable small talk. She didn't mention the extra weight he was carrying; he didn't bring up the engagement ring already on her finger. Kerouac hadn't lasted for her either. Maybe she had a knack for picking sterile men. Gene hadn't been with a woman since. But maybe now that his weight was getting under control, that would change.

Maybe he would ask Sasha from the office out to dinner. Probably lunch would be a better first date. Take it slow.

Gene laughed at himself for having the thought. Why take a woman to dinner when you can't even smell food without getting nauseous?

His head swam a little as he stepped off the scale. Even thinking about thinking about food set The Thing In His Stomach to churning. Gene laughed again; a seasick sound to match the green-tinged face in his mirror.

The Thing In His Stomach. Whatever the Mexican doctor had put there seemed to have taken on a life of its own. Or maybe it had taken over a bit of Gene's life. With Pavlovian regularity, it squelched every inkling of hunger. At the same time, it had apparently sent his body's furnace into overdrive; he was burning fat faster than anyone he had ever heard of--so fast that he was beginning to get little flaps of loose skin under his arms and around his knees.

Now he knew why no one posted their experience on the web. It wasn't the confidentiality agreement; it was that the results were too incredible. He'd be hooted out of any chat room or forum faster than he could type in his "hundred-plus pounds in six weeks" success story.

But maybe there was something wrong. Dr. Cansada's technique was experimental, after all. What if the thing in Gene's stomach had given him cancer? Didn't people with cancer lose a lot of weight all of a sudden?

Cancer reminded him of Rachel again, and her minister husband. Didn't he donate time at a hospice? Disgusted with himself, Gene concentrated on hurrying through his morning rituals, and getting in to work on time.

He was still getting a kick out of seeing the reactions of the people in his building: "How ya doin' it, Gene?", or "Looking good, Gene," they'd say, and Gene would just beam back at them; smiling the smile of a man with one less chin than last week. The Thing In His Stomach was giving him back his body; it was still up to Gene to take back his life.

Which brought him to Sasha's cubicle around lunchtime. She was busy simultaneously taking an order over the phone and playing Free Cell when she saw him. She flashed Gene a chipper smile, clicking out of the game and entering the customer's information with a practiced clatter of the keyboard.

When she finished, Sasha swiveled toward him. "What's up, Gene?"

"I was wondering if you'd like to go to lunch with me today? My treat." Just saying the word "lunch" earned him a knot of gurgling discomfort. He was never going to get a date if The Thing In His Stomach kept this up. Look, I won't eat anything, he thought at it, and amazingly, the queasiness subsided. Surprised, he pressed on: "I don't bite, promise."

Sasha's eyes twinkled. "The way I hear it, you don't eat at all."

Well, I can't deny there's a little less of me these days." Gene gave her what Rachel used to call his puppy dog eyes, and silently cursed his subconscious for sabotaging him with thoughts of her. "What do you say?"

"I can't today, Gene. Some of us have to go to the gym to lose weight. And it's Friday. If I don't go today, it will probably be Monday before I make it there again." Hazel eyes looked up at the acoustic tiling for a second as she thought. After a moment, she graced him with another smile. "How about you come with me? It'll be fun, and you can tell me how it is you're losing so much weight."

Gene batted his puppy dog eyes at her. "You don't have an ounce of fat on you, Sasha. Besides, I don't have any workout clothes. Why don't we skip the gym and I'll tell you all my secrets over"--a whisper of nausea here—"salad... at Fitzi's?"

Sasha blushed a delicate pink at the compliment, then shook her head. She didn't seem to notice the way he had struggled over the word "salad."

"You're sweet, but I can't skip the gym today. Maybe Monday we can do lunch?"

"Monday it is, then," Gene said. "And I might even go look for gym clothes over the weekend. You can teach me which way to run on the treadmill or something."

She stood up, grinning at him coyly. "Maybe I will."

* * *

Gene made it back to his cubicle before he broke into a sweat. He had goosebumps on his arms. A lunch date with Sasha! He patted his diminishing belly. Things are looking up, amigo.

Normally, even "good" stress like this would send him running for a fast food drive-through window; today he went to the Big and Tall store instead, and bought the smallest sweats on the shelf from Kevin, who was perhaps not so happy for Gene as he should have been. "I'll be losing my best customer, you keep this up."

That night Gene dreamed he was a suave and savvy executive, closing a high-stakes contract with a talking bottle of mezcal. "You can eat all you want," he told the bottle, "but just don't drink the water."

V. Every Friend Needs a Name

That weekend, it seemed like everything Gene did was somehow in preparation for the date, or with Sasha in mind. He thought about Sasha's yellow-gold locks while his stylist jabbered how this new cut would look better on him, now that his face was getting to be a bit less round.

He thought of Sasha's slim, precise fingers as he clipped his nails Sunday night in front of a Sopranos DVD. He wondered what it would be like to take Sasha on a boat. They'd never even have to leave the marina.

He even agonized over which shirt and tie to wear, finally settling on the chambray shirt with a Brooks Brothers tie. His mother had given it to him before she died; it was the only tie he owned that didn't remind him of Rachel.

After marveling anew at his bladder's amazing capacity, he stepped on the scale. He had lost another five pounds since Friday. He got an old belt from the back of his closet, wrapping it around him. He had grown out of it a few months after Rachel moved out. The belt was just a bit on the snug side now; he'd probably be loosening it a notch by Wednesday.

* * *

Fitzi's used to be a nice place, and maybe it still was. Gene couldn't concentrate on much. The sights and smells of food were nearly unbearable. When Sasha ordered a chicken salad, Gene felt his gorge rise. He managed to order the same, with water, but only after promising The Thing In His Stomach that he wouldn't eat it. When the plates arrived at the table, wave after wave of nausea rolled over him.

He could hardly carry on a conversation. He dared not touch the fork. Despite all that, he must have been at least a little charming; Sasha had asked him again about coming to the gym with her the next day. He agreed, somehow, and before his seasick mind could register it, they were in her car again, on their way back to work.

Gene escorted her to her desk, then went straight to the restroom; he was glad no one else was in there. He locked the door to keep it that way.

Gene leaned in front of the urinal, pressing his sweaty forehead against the cool tiles on the wall. As another record-breaking urine stream began, Gene let out a long sigh of relief. The nausea was finally, completely gone.

Why was he worried about it in the first place? There was nothing in his stomach to vomit. Thinking rationally didn't help, though. Gene knew he'd feel that horrible lurching in his innards again, soon as he got too close to food.

As the stream finally began sputtering down to an oily yellow trickle, he thought that maybe his internal amigo wasn't turning out to be such a good friend after all. But when he tightened his belt all the way to the last notch, Gene's pants still felt like they were loose enough to fall off, and that made every missed meal, every nauseous moment worth it.

"You sure are hungry for my fat, little buddy," Gene said aloud to the Mexican weight loss device. He patted his midsection. "Every friend needs a name... I'm going to call you Starvelito." He chuckled. "You already know who I am."

Something stirred slightly in Gene's stomach, in the slow, comfortable way a sleeping dog might shift to welcome a belly rub. Gene turned the metal latch, unlocking the bathroom door.

"Starvelito, my friend, you keep doing what you're doing. We're going to get along famously. Famously."

* * *

By the end of the month, Gene couldn't recognize himself--or his life. He had bid Kevin at the Big and Tall Shop "Adios" two weeks ago. His weight was just on the heavier side of two hundred. And Sasha... Whoa, Sasha! Their relationship had progressed from that awkward lunch date to today's event: looking for an apartment to share.

And she was a tiger in the sack, too; full of ideas. The one involving the whipped cream had (quite literally) nearly killed him. His old buddy Starvelito had no interest in taking any food onboard--even under such delicate circumstances. It made that fact known with a violent retching session. Talk about ruining the mood.

Sasha was walking across the empty apartment toward him, her heels making soft echoes on the bare floor. "What do you think, Gene?" she asked him.

Gene had already learned to read that expectant twinkle in her eyes. "It's nice and big. Available now. The price is right. You love that breakfast bar. Why not?"

Sasha squealed and jumped on him, straddling him in a bear hug. "Do you really think so? I do like that bar."

Gene smiled. "Unless you want to keep looking..." He gave her a peck on the cheek. "I thought you liked the view here best of all. And it's so close to work."

She kissed him full on the mouth. "God I love you, skinny man."

He squeezed her a moment then set her back on her feet.

She beamed at him. "I know you can't eat, but I want to celebrate. Let's go to that new restaurant on Durante."

Starvelito began writhing hysterically. Gene imagined that if he pulled his shirt up he would see the flesh of his stomach pressing out with every pulse and twitch. He clenched his jaws shut, fighting off waves of nausea. It was getting harder and harder to negotiate with the little bastard.

"I got a better idea," Gene managed to gasp out. "I'll pay the deposit and you can order in for yourself while I start moving us?"

Sasha pouted but relented in the end. "You know, Gene, you really should see a doctor."

But Gene didn't go see a doctor. He couldn't even think of it, not now that he was approaching 160. Sasha worried nightly over how fast he was losing, but always told him how proud she was of his willpower. He couldn't tell her that he'd had an experimental procedure performed in Mexico. That would only make her worry more. The story he had given her was that he was getting a series of shots of vitamins and appetite suppressant that the FDA was testing before final release; he had hoped that would explain everything.

Then one night as she lay next to him, her fingers tracing the spiderweb of unnaturally slender stretchmarks around his waist, Sasha had asked why his skin wasn't hanging off of him like one of his old suit jackets, since he had lost so much so fast. Gene had told her that was an unexpected side effect of the shots.

Sometimes he wondered if the relationship wasn't going as fast as his weight loss; if both of them weren't going too fast. But never for long: in both cases, the end results were too satisfying to meddle with.

VI. Familiar Cravings

On Gene's thirty-eighth birthday, he weighed a ridiculous 110. He looked as much a skeleton as Dr. Cansada had that day in Mexico; more so, given the eight inches in height he had on the doctor. Sasha was too sentimental to let the occasion go by without a cake, even if he couldn't eat it.

"At least you can blow out all these candles," she said before disappearing into the kitchen. She never called him "skinny man" anymore. A bit later he heard her singing to the accompaniment of an electric mixer.

Gene had developed an uneasy alliance with Starvelito. He was able to be around food, to smell it, to even have it on a plate in front of him—so long as he made absolutely no move to eat.

He still took greasy leaks in the mornings, but nowadays they were more of a squirt than an unending geyser. Starvelito still allowed him water, and lately Gene had been getting more and more thirsty. His stomach poked out roundly beneath the wireframe cage of his ribs. Sasha made nervous jokes about him being pregnant.

While Sasha was cooking, Gene tried to watch a bit of the ballgame, but it wasn't holding his interest. He felt like Starvelito was in there strumming a small guitar. Every so often he felt a small riff of vibration echo through his stomach and down to his balls. As he sat there analyzing the sensation, it began getting more and more intense.

His mouth began to feel like it was coated with coppery dust on the inside.

"Come on, birthday boy. It's time to blow out your candles and make a wish."

He tried to shake off the weird vibrating sensation, for the most part unsuccessfully. His balls felt oddly swollen as he walked. Can take care of that tonight, he thought, giving Sasha a lecherous grin.

"I wish I was as rich as I am thin," Gene said. Sasha laughed that earthy guffaw of hers, and Gene laughed with her.

She smiled at him. "It won't come true if you tell," Sasha teased.

"Well, maybe my real wish is to be twice as rich--oh, can't tell you that either, huh?"

She swatted at him with a dish towel and he pretended to dodge.

"That cake looks delicious," Gene said. "Chocolate used to be my favorite, you know."

"You mentioned that." Sasha wrung the towel in her hands. Gene could tell from the look on her face that if this had been any day but his birthday, she would have launched in to begging him to see a doctor again. He kissed her, then took his seat in front of the well-illuminated cake.

"You sure you didn't put too many candles on here?" he asked. "It seems a little hotter than I expected, and all that heat is making the chocolate icing smell sooo good."

"You've earned every one of those candles, Gene. Now, make your wish and blow them out, before Mr. Hankin's cake becomes as famous as Mrs. O'Leary's cow."

Gene made a sour face at her, then let it fade into a smile. "All right, can't have the new apartment burning down, I guess." He took a deep breath and felt another aching strum, this one radiating from his testicles, and much stronger than before. He let the breath out slowly.

Concern wrinkled Sasha's forehead. "Something wrong?"

"Nope. Nothing." Gene felt a tickling in the back of his throat. "Just needed a deeper breath for all these candles, is all. Here goes."

He took another deep breath, felt another strum. This time he didn't let it stop him. Starvelito wasn't going to ruin this for him. He had no intention of eating the damn cake; all he wanted to do was blow out the candles, make his wish, and take a happy woman to bed that night. A deal was a deal, after all. Even the ones you made with Mexican weight control implants.

Even as he began to blow, he felt his mouth flooding with saliva. He splattered the entire cake with it. Sasha's face fell, then recovered into a pleasant mask, the sort a person might wear when visiting a nursing home resident at changing time.

Gene's mind reeled. His cheeks felt cold and slack. They both stared at the fat globs of spittle running down the candles, sheening the chocolate icing. He had put them all out, Yes he had. Not much chance of getting his wish, though.

He reached tentatively across the table and pulled out a candle. Sasha, pale and trembling just a bit, looked on. The candle was a simple white pillar, barely two inches tall. A thick string of saliva hung between the candle and the cake for a long moment, then snapped.

At the same moment, something in Gene snapped as well. He put the spit and icing covered bottom of the candle in his mouth, wiping obliviously at the slobber coating his chin at the same time. Food. The sugary chocolate sat there on his tongue for just long enough to taste it, then on impulse, Gene swallowed it.

Sasha's eyes widened. The nursing home look had completely evaporated. Now she watched him like an expert cook might watch a meringue beginning to solidify.

Gene sat there feeling the chocolate slide down his throat, thinking: I broke the deal. I should be running for the toilet to puke up my colon. His stomach—and the thing in it—had grown suddenly still. Expectant. The saliva was running freely down his face and throat now. He looked up at Sasha. She put the towel on the table beside him and stepped back, wary.

Gene's words came out in a kind of astonished gurgle. "Gonna eat now."

Sasha nodded slowly, and took a careful backward step. "I'll get you a fork," she said, her voice tight and high.

Gene paid her no mind. He was plucking candles from the spit-soaked cake as rapidly as he could. Before Sasha had backed up far enough to reach the silverware, he was scooping great handfuls of it into his mouth, making animal noises as he pushed the food in.

Gene had never felt such hunger in his life. It had stolen upon him like a sudden rage. The part of him that could think at all focused on making sure he could breathe in between mouthfuls, and that he didn't chew a finger or bite the inside of his mouth on accident. That part of him tried to ignore the odd tickling coming up the back of his throat, the way every swallow was followed by a strum in his sack.

As he crammed in yet another chunk of the unrecognizable birthday cake, Gene pictured Starvelito as a smiling Tequila worm in a sombrero, surreptitiously slipping tapeworm tentacles up his esophagus to greet the brown mess and hurry it along.

When the cake was gone, Gene picked up the towel, shook the crumbs off of it, and wiped his face gingerly. Sasha was a statue in the kitchen. Wisps of blond had come crazily loose from the bun. Gene flashed a gritty coffee-ground smile at her.

"That was really good, Sash," he said, "Could you make me something else?"

Gene's appetite returned for all of two hours. Two glorious hours. He ate Ho-Ho's and ice cream, deli meat and scrambled eggs, and so many frozen burritos that he thought he was going to learn the language if he ate another bite. Sasha kept giving him worried looks, but Gene was beyond caring. After so long with nothing to eat, just having food in his mouth felt so good. The full feeling in his stomach was painfully pleasurable.

After what started out to be incredible birthday sex--which was cut short by such an explosion of pain at the end of the first round that he had passed out--Gene dreamed of worm forests. Hundreds of televisions tangled in a web of glistening, undulating branches. There's nothing to fear, a large black set hummed into his head. He threw handfuls of cake and fire at that screen, then at all of the others, enraged.

A DEAL IS A DEAL! he shouted. The more he threw, the wetter the cake became, until it felt like he was throwing warm lumps of ground meat at the shuddering worm trees. All of the screens flashed white at that, then flickered to blackness in unison. The worm trees twittered at him. Time for spin-off, Gene.

VII. To Dream of Being Pregnant

Gene woke up late the next morning to the sound of Sasha puking. Poor thing was in the bathroom making the most godawful noises. Gene rolled over and looked out the window. The sun was half-hiding behind some fluffy clouds, but other than that, the sky was electric blue and empty.

The phone on the bedside table began to ring, and Gene picked it up grudgingly just as Sasha turned on the water in the bathroom sink. He heard her begin to brush her teeth, as he spoke into the receiver. "Hello?"

Silence for way too long, then: "Gene?" A woman's voice.

A thrill of excitement went through him. "Rachel?"

A controlled voice answered. "It's me."

Sasha's teethbrushing hadn't lasted long. She was already back over the toilet, vomiting again. At least the splattering sounded like she'd made it to the toilet.

Gene had forgotten how much he missed Rachel. "Where are you?" he asked, using one finger to blot out the noise of Sasha's gut emptying. "Everything all right?"

"I'm fine, Gene." More silence. "How've you been?"

Gene could still hear Sasha retching and gasping like someone who had nearly drowned. "I've been good. Lost a lot of weight. Down to 110."

The shock was apparent in her voice. "You're kidding. And what is that noise in the background?"

"My girlfriend's sick," Gene said, kicking himself soon as the words were out of his mouth.

Rachel didn't repeat the word out loud, but Gene knew she was repeating it in her head. Girlfriend.

"I'm in town doing a fundraiser. Thought maybe you'd like to join me for lunch...."

Sasha was spitting viciously now behind the closed door of the bathroom. Gene rolled his eyes up to the ceiling for a second then said, "I'd like that."

"You don't think your girlfriend would mind, do you? You can bring her if you want."

"No, she's a bit under the weather, but she wouldn't mind anyway."

"Good," Rachel said, then gave him the name of the restaurant. "About an hour from now?"

"That sounds fine," Gene said, wondering what he was doing even as he said it.

When he hung up the phone, Gene realized that Sasha hadn't made even a peep in the last few minutes. He pulled on some boxers and knocked softly at the bathroom door. "Sash? You okay, sweetheart?"

She answered him in a weak, whispering croak. "I'm sick, Gene."

He gave a commiserating chuckle. "Sounds like it. You want me to get you anything? I have to run out and pick up something anyway."

"Pick me up some Pepto, w—" The words were cut off by the sound of her agonized retching.

"Will do, sweetheart. Back in a flash."

* * *

Gene met Rachel at a classy little cafe by the water. Salt smells and harbor bells greeted them at the door.

"I ended up with a box of your old pictures, Gene," she said, setting the box down in the empty spot where his plate would have been. "You're looking fit."

Her eyes said he was looking sickly as one of the cancer patients at her husband's hospice, Gene thought. "I suppose so," he said.

They made uncomfortable small talk—her eating broiled fish, he nursing an ice water—then Gene thanked her for bringing the pictures. He kissed her upturned cheek as they parted, immediately wishing he had just shaken her hand instead. Or not even come. It hit him then just what a jerk he was being. Sasha was sick and where was he? Running out to catch up with an old flame.

"Gene?" she called, about to duck into her cab. "Take care of yourself. And do tell your girlfriend I hope she gets better."

"I will," he said, then checked his watch. He cursed. Where had two hours gone? Sasha was going to kill him. He picked up her medicine at the pharmacy, flowers from a street vendor, and hurried back to the apartment.

Inside, it was dark and cool. Gene stepped quietly through the living room and into the bedroom. He could hear Sasha's regular breathing from under the rumpled covers. At least she was able to rest. He went out to the kitchen and returned with a spoon.

"Sash," he whispered. "I got your medicine, if you want to take it now."

She stirred, moaning a little in her sleep.

He shook her gently. She rolled over to look at him with glassy eyes that didn't appear to recognize him at first. She was so out of it she didn't even seem aware of how long he had been gone.

"Gene?" she said.

"I'm right here," Gene said, suddenly feeling every bit the putz. The damn pictures hadn't been worth the trip. Neither had seeing Rachel. Not with Sasha so sick. He cursed himself again for being a hopelessly obsessed fool. The lady here in front of him meant the world to Gene, world-record stomach flu and all. What a fucking ass I am, Gene thought, stroking a clump of damp golden hair out of her face.

"Are you ready for some medicine, or do you want to see if you can keep anything down?"

"Oh God, no." She shook her head weakly. "I can't even stand the thought of putting anything in my mouth at this point. I tried to eat a banana when I first got up, but my stomach is empty now, and it's happy that way. I'll just let it be for right now." She kissed his fingers when they touched her cheek.

"I dreamed I was pregnant," she said.

Gene's hands went cold. "You're not, are you? We've been using protection. Except for last night—" He blushed, then continued, "Not that you could be pregnant so quick, but I don't think we got far enough last night—"

She cut him off. "I'm not pregnant, skinny man. It was just a really weird dream." She graced him with a tired smile. "But don't expect me to swallow ever again. I don't know what you ate that made it taste so bad, but it was awful."

Gene shrugged, the ends of his mouth curling up apologetically as he did. He pulled the covers up to her delicate neck. "Why don't you get some rest? You could use it."

Her eyes were already closed, but she smiled at him anyway. She was purring the soft snore of the exhausted before Gene had the bedroom door shut behind him.

VIII. A Make-up Strategy

The next morning Sasha was up and around before Gene. She bounced on the bed beside him, kissing his nose until he opened one cranky eye.

"Someone's feeling better," Gene said.

Sasha smiled. "Now I know the attraction of bulimia. I lost ten pounds yesterday."

Gene bolted upright. "You did?"

"Yep. Looks like you aren't the only one that can lose weight fast around here."

Gene felt Starvelito begin jiggling in his stomach. Almost like the little fucker was laughing. Gene looked Sasha's narrow frame up and down.

She gave him a wicked smile. "Not this morning, mister."

"You have to see a doctor, Sash." Gene's strangled tone robbed her of her smile, but only for a minute.

"Yeah, right. I'm fine now, Gene." She giggled, then seemed to remember something. "Where did those pictures on the kitchen table come from?"

Gene cursed. How could he have left those damn things out? "Someone brought them to me," he stammered.

Sasha's temper flared in an instant. "While I was so sick yesterday, you were out getting pictures? Who is that woman in all of them?" she demanded.

Gene sighed. "Rachel. My ex. I told you about her. She was in town on business and brought them for me."

It went badly from there, with Gene apologizing profusely and insisting that nothing had happened and Sasha alternately grilling him with pointed questions and calling him names.

She wouldn't speak to him the rest of that weekend, wouldn't even stay in the same room with him. Gene had to admit, he probably deserved it.

At work the next day, when Gene went to Sasha's desk to offer lunch and another round of apologies, the brunette in the next cubicle told him that Sasha had punched out early.

She's probably leaving me, Gene thought. Packing her bags right now.

After giving it a moment's thought, Gene left work, hoping to have a make-up strategy ready before he got to the apartment.

IX. Skin and Bones

The fridge door was open, and it was empty. The same was true of the pantry. From his angle by the door, Gene could see a litter pile of upturned food boxes, opened cans, and empty leftover containers spilling out past the edge of the breakfast bar.

Gene jangled his keys to break the uneasy silence, then hung them on the hook by the door. He took a slow step into the apartment, looking all around, and listening to the silence grow colder.

"Sasha?" he called. There was no answer. Her convertible had been parked below; it had been a little sideways, actually, like she had been in a hurry when she parked it.

"Are you here, sweetheart?" God, if she was here, calling her sweetheart under these circumstances would likely bring her out spitting venom. There was an odd smell in the apartment, one that Gene could not quite recognize; it was sweet and pungent, like vinegar and honey, but there was something faintly rancid to it as well.

As Gene entered the bedroom, the smell became much stronger. It seemed to be coming from the open bathroom door. The exhaust fan was clattering away in there, even with the lights out. He glanced across the room at the dressing mirror. The outfit Sasha had been wearing this morning was heaped on the floor in front of it.

His stomach growled. Not the everyday sort of hungry rumble, but a gurgling animal growl that made itself heard even over the noise of the fan. A coldness swept across Gene's body as he lurched into the master bathroom.

His feet splashed on the tile floor, and Gene looked down. "What have you done to her?" he screamed down at his own stomach, at Starvelito. "What the fuck have you done?"

The tiles had a geometrical cornflower pattern, now darkened and submerged beneath a viscous golden pool. Sasha's panties lay crumpled and soaking by the base of the pedestal sink. There was no sign that she had begun to pack her things, not in here, and not in the bedroom. She'd come in here to pee; judging by the urine-covered floor, she hadn't made it.

Gene reached down and picked up the panties. They were cold and wet and smelled so strongly that he wanted to throw up. The little bastard in his stomach made that odd gurgle-growl again and Gene flung the soggy bit of cloth into the trash.

"You shut the fuck up!" Gene shouted, not caring who heard. He repeated it, pounding a fist beneath the protruding cage of his ribs. He felt Starvelito flopping about inside his belly, and the feeling made him choke back the tickle of empty vomit he felt rising up in his throat.

Gene left the bathroom fan running and pulled the door shut behind him. "Where is she?" he asked the thing in his stomach. But Starvelito didn't so much as move.

Gene pounded his stomach again, and made for the kitchen. His urine-wet shoes made a scrunching sound on the hardwood as he crossed the combined living/dining room. He rounded the breakfast bar and jerked to a stop.

A jumble of geriatrically narrow bones and thin flesh lay curled in a ball on the kitchen floor, facing away from him. The frail body was surrounded by a mountain of upturned cracker boxes, stacks of empty cans, open jars on their side leaking juice, and all the rest of the food that had until today been tidily arranged on the pantry shelves and in the fridge.

Gene gasped. He stared at the back of a tiny blond head, trying to say her name. It kept catching in his throat. Starvelito gurgled again; Gene didn't respond to the sound.

His mouth kept working soundlessly as he took in everything. Sasha hadn't been heavy to start with. The sudden uncontrollable need to urinate, all that vomiting when she tried to eat a banana the other day, her rag and bone body on the floor before him, the littered aftermath of an enormous hunger....

Gene leaned down to touch her shoulder, his whole body trembling. With a gentle tug, he pulled the emaciated body over.

He jumped back. "What the—" was all he managed to get out before he began dry heaving and Starvelito started up a loud and angry chorus in his gut. Between the retching and Starvelito's frenzied flopping, Gene's midsection felt like a washcloth being wrung out, and at the same time like a grocery bag full of rattlesnakes.

He looked again when he was able. Sasha's mouth was wide open; her bloody tongue hung to one side by a few well-chewed strips of muscle. Her eyes were wide open and glassy. But it wasn't Sasha that had made Gene lose control; it was the oily black slug thing that had slipped from her mouth as he rolled her over.

One of its many feelers continued poking the plastic wrapper from a Ritz crackers package. Another feeler, this one translucent, siphoned orange crumbs into a tiny toothless maw. Yet another turned toward Gene, stalklike, and began bobbing at him merrily.

Starvelito began making a keening gargle noise, loud and fast. The slug on the floor twitched a bit, then belched a cloud of swampy smelling gas. A slender grey-green appendage telescoped from inside the creature's mouth and began making the same noises as the thing in Gene's stomach was. All the while, little crumbs of Ritz cracker kept churning up the little siphon tube and into its mouth.

This was too much for Gene: too much to picture her standing naked at the mirror staring at her diminishing body; too much to smell her last piss marinating her panties on the bathroom floor; too much to see her withered remains on the kitchen floor, shuffed off by that fat-craving creature like a jacket that no longer fit.

He lifted his foot; it left a faint yellow track on the vinyl. Inside him, Starvelito howled. On the floor before him, the slug beast turned two more of its grease-caked appendages Gene's way. It looked comical for a second, this hundred-legged slug, cocking its headstalks as if someone had asked it a particularly hard science question.

I'll take Fucked-up Biology for a thousand, Alex, Gene thought, then commenced stomping and stomping the thing on the floor. It squealed pitifully, and Starvelito--God, he had one of those in him?--began inching its way up out of his stomach.

The one on the floor was leaving little smears all over, and chunks of something foul and black clung to the sole of Gene's shoe. Some of his kicks were so violent and out of control that they struck Sasha's face; he severed the rest of her tongue with his heel by accident. It lolled there on the white floor beside the sharp metal lid from a can of green beans.

When the slug fell silent and unmoving, Gene collapsed to the dirty floor beside Sasha. Tears stained his face and sobs wracked his body. He held his swallowing muscles tight, and Starvelito, tired of butting against the narrowed passage, apparently gave up and slithered back down into Gene's gullet. Starvelito's gurgling noises had turned into a grating whistle, barely muffled by Gene's thin curtain of skin.

It could have been crying too, for all Gene knew. He used the plastic wrapper from the Ritz crackers to put Sasha's tongue gently back into her mouth.

Anyway you cut it, it's going to look like I killed her.

X. An End to the Problem of Hunger

Sasha's starved body had shriveled quickly, to the point that it would now fit easily into a big duffle bag. The bag was still open, and leaning up against the wall. A tuft of blond poked over the edge, mocking Gene as he scooped up the food garbage with a dustpan. The dweller in his stomach had gone curiously silent.

Gene was doing his best to avoid looking at the scattered remains of the slug thing, Starvelito's obscene spin-off. His thoughts went back to that day in Mexico. The skeletal Dr. Cansada promising that Gene would never go hungry, then putting him under and--what? Vomiting a slug into his sleeping mouth?

But how had Sasha gotten the thing inside her?

Gene finished sweeping up the last of the food garbage and jumped up to sit on the breakfast bar, forcing himself to face the pulpy mess of multilimbed slug on the floor. Sasha had been feeling ill the morning after his birthday, and damn if he hadn't surprised them both with his appetite that night. Not just at the table, but in bed, as well. At least at first. And that sickening strum in his balls . . .

"Oh God." Gene moaned. "No. No. No. No."

She'd swallowed him that night; he had come so suddenly, so painfully that it had knocked him out, ending the fun early.

Gene wiped cold sweat from his forehead then spat on the thing he'd given Sasha on his birthday.

He pounded his fist into the breakfast bar over and over. If that was how it got into Sasha, how had it gotten into him? He pictured Dr. Cansada jerking off a baby slug into his anesthetized sleeping face, and gagged, rocking his head from side to side in an unbelieving disgusted arc.

He spat again on Baby Starvelito, then retrieved the pictures he had gotten from Rachel the day poor Sasha had been puking up her newly infested guts. There hadn't been enough fat on Sasha to last more than a few days. The disaster in the kitchen had been the result of her last frantic efforts to feed the hungry worm thing inside her.

He brought the pictures back and tossed them into the same bag as all the trash without looking at them.

He knotted the garbage bag at the top and shook a new one open, catching a hint of pine as he did so. He blew a hard puff of air out through his nostrils. Still no sign of life from the boarder in his belly. How in the hell was he going to get it out of him? Now that he was thin, he could stay this way on his own, couldn't he?. Would a doctor believe his story long enough to take a look? And what would they do with Starvelito when they got him out?

Probably find a way to get rich off breeding the nasty things and selling them to people as heavy and desperate as he used to be. Gene held his breath while he scraped all the little parts of the creature into the newly opened bag, doubting it still smelled of pine.

Now that the trash had been removed, Gene could see all the places where the floor was stained with sticky black pulp. He tried mopping it up with hot water and a disinfectant floor cleaner; the residue was made of more tenacious stuff than even the folks at Lysol had planned on, apparently.

After trying every other chemical under the sink, even scouring the floor with an abrasive powder, Gene got an idea.

He whistled as he pulled the jug of bleach from the laundry room shelf. He felt Starvelito twist a bit inside him as the clear liquid began pouring from the jug's angled mouth.

The oily smudges came right up, bubbling like an Alka-Seltzer under the chlorine deluge. Gene smiled his relief; in short order, the floor was clean and evidence free. It took only a few minutes more to get the bathroom floor into the same condition.

Just for fun, he doused the slug body with a capful of bleach. The grey-green headstalks disappeared first, followed rapidly by the rest of the slug thing. It was gone like it had never existed. Starvelito let out a little whistling sound and made a tentative move to scuttle up Gene's esophagus.

Gene clenched the swallowing muscles, hard. "You're not getting out of me, you little hungry fuck. You hear me?"

It must have understood, because it seemed to coil itself back up again.

Gene wondered what he was going to do. He was at an impasse. As soon as he went to sleep, Starvelito would be creepy-crawling his way through Gene's body, or sending out more little slug babies to cure the world of fat people.

This has to end today, Gene thought. He took the garbage out in three loads, then lugged the duffle bag with Sasha's body in it down and left her in his trunk.

He took Sasha's sporty little car down to the worst part of town and waited by a bus stop. When the bus pulled up, Gene wiped the steering wheel and her keys down with a napkin, then boarded the bus, leaving the engine running. A trio of tough guys were already leaning against it when the bus pulled away from the curb.

Next he brought down all of her possessions, even the urine-soaked panties from the bathroom. He drove to a hardware store, bought a shovel with cash, and then went as far out of town and into the woods as he could manage without getting lost.

By the time he had buried Sasha and her things, paid his tearful respects, and hiked back to his car, the sun was low and red in the distance. But worse: he was starting to get hungry.

The drive back to the apartment was something from a nightmare. He was starving, aching: utterly empty inside. It took all he had to make it home without stopping to eat--without stopping to feed the slug in his stomach.

Back in the apartment, Gene made sure the door was unlocked, and took one last look around. "You're hungry, aren't you?" he asked the undulating thing behind his belly button.

He pulled out a pen and a pad from the junk drawer. Sasha had started a grocery list on it: Bananas, Yogurt, Cheerios.

Gene scribbled through her list, and wrote a message of his own.

SHE LEFT ME, he wrote. IT'S NOT WORTH IT ANYMORE.

Gene set the pad on the breakfast bar where it could be seen easily from the door, then grabbed a tall glass from the cupboard. It felt cold in his hand. Starvelito began to squirm.

"Don't worry, little buddy," Gene said aloud. "I just want a nice cold drink, then I'll eat whatever my stomach tells me to, forever after."

The squirming subsided, but Gene could feel the creature in there quivering like a hairless Chihuahua that expected a treat.

"Oh, you'll get your treat all right," Gene said, filling the glass from a tall white container. He put the cap back on the jug and reached for the phone.

He stabbed his finger into the nine, then the one, then the one again, and laid the phone down on the bar.

"Here's to good health," Gene said, then poured the contents of the glass down his throat.

He could feel the bleach bubbling violently inside him, and suddenly his face was full of clean white floor. His body began to spasm, and he could feel the burning liquid vomit in an arc from his nose and mouth.

As the white floor faded to black, his brain began to lose traction on reality. If he survived this, he would eat himself sick: swallow, swallow, swallow. Take it all in, every dripping, every crumb. Fill up that empty place inside over and over until it stayed filled forever.

Gene thought he could hear Sasha, back from the gym, back from the grave, pounding and yelling at his front door. He heard a rush of music, a mariachi serenade of splintering wood, someone shouting in his ear.

Then nothing.

Among many other things, **Lon Prater** *is the lucky father of two great girls, the even luckier husband of a truly amazing woman, a servicemember, stunt kite flyer, youth soccer coach, former editor of Neverary , and a* *writer of odd little tales.*

THE WATER GOD OF CLARKE STREET

by Kevin Lucia

It was a cold day, and Carolyn O'Hara was pissed off at her imaginary friend, Bob the Water Sprite.

"I hate you, Bob," Carolyn whispered fiercely, trudging through cutting winter wind, kicking snow piles with frozen feet, "I hate you, hate you, hate you! Adam Stillman thinks I'm a stupid freak, and it's your fault!"

"I hate you."

As she walked, Carolyn self-consciously whispered swears she'd heard other girls use in the school locker rooms before gym class. Each whispery curse sent frosty white plumes into the winter air, which crystallized on the pink scarf wrapped around her neck and mouth.

I'm never talking to you ever again.

Ever.

She scuffed home from school, her feet demolishing loose snowdrifts piled along Main Street. Having forsaken pigtails long ago because they were for kids and she was now a sophisticated sixth grader, her solitary ponytail swished back and forth in time with her angry steps, cooling her neck even more.

Of course, her toasty old jester cap with tinkling bells would've been a welcome accessory today, but she'd also left that behind years ago, exchanging it for a pair of grown-up pink ear muffs – though in truth, the jester hat had been much warmer.

Carolyn's sour thoughts weren't on her cold neck or her accessories; instead they dwelt on what happened today in sixth period study hall. It had been the most devastating day in her life, and she had Bob the Water Sprite to thank for it.

Adam Stillman was the most popular boy in her grade; athletic and graceful, shaggy brown hair mused in a skater cut, under which lurked dreamy blue eyes that dug deep into all the secret, gushy places inside when he looked at her. He was WAY above her, though – she, the frumpy, mildly chubby smart girl who read books, wore clashing plaid skirts with glasses that sported black "Ugly Betty" frames. She was his math tutor and spent every sixth period study hall with him, which was the best she could possibly hope for.

Of course, she probably wouldn't even have that anymore – if the look of horror she'd seen in his eyes today was any indication – thanks to Bob the Water Sprite and his frightful prank this afternoon.

"Stupid," she huffed, "I was so stupid to cast that spell last night. Why'd I ever let Bob talk me into doing it?"

She aimed on the fly and kicked a small chunk of ice, skittering it off the sidewalk and into the iced-over road, where it rolled with a resounding tinkle. Bob had grown increasingly unreliable as of late, and this afternoon's disaster was only the most recent fiasco. For the past several months he'd been out of sorts, showing up when she hadn't conjured him, or when she did conjure him, he'd play coy and not show up for hours, maybe not at all.

When he came to her last night, proposing a way to trick Adam into kissing her, why had she expected it to be anything different than another chance for Bob to embarrass her?

The O'Haras' modest ranch on Spear Street was only two blocks away from Clifton Heights Schools, so paying the town fee for her to ride the school bus was "superfluous," a big word Dad used a lot that Carolyn knew meant "silly." Because it was silly for Dad not to want to spend the extra money, even though he got lots of it being a lawyer; she hadn't ridden the school bus since the end of first grade.

Her family – like most today – was very busy; she usually walked home alone. Though her sometimes-nice older brother Bryan was willing to drive her to school in the morning, he couldn't take her home because he always played afterschool sports. Dad often worked late, hardly ever making it to dinner (or her dance recitals for that matter); and lately Mom had been too busy to pick her up because of all the grown-up parties she threw at other families' houses: gala events with odd names like Lia Sophia, Pampered Chef, and Domestic Delights.

The wind chilled her, and she shivered while hunching deeper into her jacket. "Dammit," she whispered, thrilled at using the "big swear" she'd heard Dad mutter once when he'd hit his thumb nailing the bottom step of her tree house ladder back into place... when he'd still had time for that sort of thing.

For a minute, her cursing felt deliciously rebellious, but another stiff gust blew the hot feeling away, leaving her tired, cold, and still mad. Somewhere deep inside, she knew she shouldn't always walk home alone. Someone in her family should care enough to come get her.

"Right," she clacked, "just like someone should get home in time to make supper so we don't have to eat microwaved crap every night; like someone should do the dishes so I don't have to always do them."

There were a lot of somethings that shouldn't be, which Carolyn unfortunately knew well. Girls her age shouldn't walk home alone, and Dads shouldn't frequently work late with pretty secretaries Mom called "slutty little tramps" when she thought Carolyn wasn't listening. Moms shouldn't leave eleven-year old girls to experience their blooming womanhood by themselves, and Carolyn should've learned about her period from Mom, not by herself – like the day she'd almost passed out at the sight of the white, pristine porcelain toilet bowl filled with thick, scarlet blood at school.

Girls her age also shouldn't have imaginary friends like Bob the Water Sprite; however, after this afternoon, she finally had to admit to herself that Bob was anything but imaginary.

She sighed as she stopped at the corner of Main and Allen, glancing across the street at old man Chin's pizza place. The front window of Chin's Pizza & Wings, framed by deep, fire-engine-red brick, throbbed with a welcoming glow, and though Mr. Chin would probably let her sit there and warm up, she had no money. Soaking up the warm, oily odor of crust, sauce, and garlic without eating a slice would be torture.

She looked closer at the pizza joint, saw the battered red Chevy truck parked alongside the curb, and grimaced. "Oh, great," she muttered, "Scum-bag alert, big time."

It was probably better she didn't have any money, because inside Chin's at a table close to the front window sat the infamous, legendary, downright scummy Jesse Kretch. Standing very tall, large, and wide, Jesse Kretch had gone to school with Dad, who often called him the "jester of Clifton Heights Senior High." Carolyn had a hard time imagining him in a clown outfit and a jingly-hat, but she figured that really meant he'd been picked on a lot in school.

That her father been one of those doing the "picking on" wasn't a surprise.

According to the stories, Jesse had lived in Clifton Heights all his life, never graduated high school or attended college, and didn't have a steady job. During the winter he worked at the lumber mill; in the summer he bailed hay for local farmers or collected scrap metal with Cletus Smithers. He was dirty, smelly, and sweaty; none of her peers went near him, for fear they might catch an infection that would make their toes rot off.

Her classmates swore a mass of buzzing flies held court around Jesse's head, and though she hadn't believed it, an unnerving encounter with him on the sidewalk this past summer proved the story true. She still shivered at the memory, because although she was only eleven and didn't know much about anything, there was something instinctual she sensed about Jesse Kretch that made her very afraid of him, indeed.

It had been a normal day last summer as she walked down Main Street, so intent on signing out some new books from the town library that she hadn't noticed Kretch sitting at the lone picnic bench in front of Dooley's Snack Shack, enjoying a bowl of vanilla ice cream smothered in Cool Whip, topped by a lone, slightly wilted cherry.

Walking while mixing songs on her iPod, she'd distantly heard someone say, Hey…wait up, and without thinking halted, turning to face Jesse Kretch. There he'd stood over her, bowl of cherry-topped ice cream in one hand, eating it slowly, spoon by spoon, as he looked down at her with dull, pale eyes.

Thin lips smiling on his narrow face, he'd mumbled, "Hey… lissen, kid? You want the rest of my ice cream? I'm full; gotta get back to work." He'd paused and gestured to the prunish cheery leaning sideways on top of the melting mound, "Look; it's gotta cherry on it and everything."

Smelling vaguely like rotten peppermint and the cigarettes Dad had recently tried to quit, he'd extended his bowl of melted, tepid ice cream – small crowd of black flies indeed buzzing - smiling in a way that made her feel squirmy inside. His long greasy hair fell to his shoulders; he stood hunched, and though Carolyn wasn't sure, she thought he was missing at least three teeth

She'd gaped at him, caught between her parents' contradicting commands to always be polite but never talk to Jesse Kretch, the sounds of Britney Spears' "I'm All Grown Up" blaring in her iPod's ear buds.

After what seemed like forever, she'd jerked head, rasping, "No thanks," and scurried away from the looming Kretch, no doubt leaving him staring after her. There had been a sense of wrongness in him, a vague threat she couldn't identify.

She'd kept the incident secreted away inside her heart-shaped lockbox, never telling anyone, least of all her father. She felt a little bad about that, though she didn't know why; maybe because she instinctively knew Dad would be pissed at her encounter with Kretch, and it felt naughty not telling him.

Though she'd always been "Daddy's girl," keeping something secret, holding it close and not telling anyone, felt good. The secret was hers, no one else's, just like Bob the Water Sprite.

She sighed again, glanced down Allen to make sure no one was coming, and crossed the street, leaving the pizza joint and the awful Jesse Kretch behind. All the while, she thought about Bob and how Adam Stillman would never talk to her again. She knew Adam wouldn't tell anyone about what happened, (unless he changed the story, lied, and told everyone she kissed him), but his predicted silence wasn't the least bit comforting, because of course that meant he didn't want anyone to know he'd kissed someone like Carolyn O'Hara.

"Bob, I swear," she muttered as her feet hit the curb on the opposite side of Allen Street and she continued out of town, "if I ever do conjure you into the real world, first thing I'm going to do is kick your furry little blue ass."

She tittered at her use of ass. She'd started experimenting with swear words lately, and out of all her new sayings, anything involving "kicking ass" was her favorite. It made her feel tough, hard, stolid and mean.

All of which she wasn't, of course, but it was nice to pretend.

Of course, a wispy voice muttered in her ear, if you'd just take up Bob on his offer, you could be all of those things... and more.

She pushed the thought away, and kept walking.

She wasn't retarded; she knew most girls her age shopped, downloaded songs to their iPods, had sleepovers, and whispered in heated, hormonal tones about "making out" with "hot eighth grade boys" and wondering about their "things." Her peers would call her a freak if they knew about Bob, but she didn't care. She was different, always had been, always would be, and she never intended on changing.

Instead of "hanging out" at the mall, she loved to read, hidden in quiet places like the "Wooded Den," a small copse of trees behind her house whose lowest branches hung several feet above her head, intertwined like a thatched roof; the floor a soft, quilted rug of browned pine needles. There she read everything from *The Brothers Grimm* to classic *Nancy Drew Mysteries*, even *Harry Potter*; she claimed Claudia Gabel's "chick books" as guilty pleasures. She soaked up adventures, love stories, mysteries, and chilling tales as if they were tonic for her soul.

She'd even read stuff written by two guys named Whitman and Thoreau, checked out from their modest town library. Though she didn't totally understand what they wrote, phrases like "I went for a walk in the woods" and "sucking out the marrow of life" burned her inside, imparting a truth that made everything else seem childish in comparison.

Unfortunately, loving books so obsessively had caused her troubles with Bob in the first place. If she hadn't loved reading so much, maybe she wouldn't have peeked into a big book entitled Incantations, the Spirit World, and the Necromani left lying around last year by her visiting cousin Heather from nearby Inlet, who called herself a goth or wicca or trance, she couldn't remember which because it changed monthly.

Then, she never would've snuck into the guest room and perused the tome, glancing over her shoulder, flipping through its parchment-like pages while Heather was out "getting stoned," as her brother said she was always doing. Carolyn only had the vaguest ideas of what that meant – it was something like smoking, only worse – but she really didn't care. As long as Heather was too busy "smoking a bowl," (another of Bryan's euphemisms; which didn't make sense because Carolyn had no idea how someone actually stuck a bowl in their mouth and smoked it), she was free to snoop through the fascinating book as much as she wanted.

It had been an odd book, which figured because Heather was odd. Heather, who'd attended and dropped out of a "king's ransom in colleges," dressed in black clothes and claimed she had her own personal ghost that followed her everywhere. Very pale, even in the summer, she always mumbled, walking around with a far-away look in her eyes. Brian said she smelled like weed, and though a bittersweet aroma did linger around Heather, Carolyn had never smelled weeds like that, so she figured Brian was lying.

In any case, perhaps if she'd never flipped to the page labeled Dagon, Water God and whispered the weird-sounding chant underneath the majestic picture of a half-man, half-seahorse, Bob never would've shown up in her full bathroom sink two days later, and today she wouldn't have been so mortally embarrassed in front of the guy she had a crush on.

"Sometimes," she whispered as she spied Black Creek Bridge and Clarke Street, a road running parallel to the creek down to the lumber mill, "I wish I'd never met you, Bob."

Are you sure about that? that same voice mocked with certainty. If Bob hadn't come along, you would've spent the last year alone, like always. Is that what you want – to be alone all the time?

Carolyn shoved the thought deep inside the dark lock-box of her heart and stalked forward.

She'd certainly had lots of fun with Bob over the past year. It had been wonderful having someone to talk to, even if he was imaginary - though the spell she cast and today's disaster had finally led to speculation that Bob wasn't imaginary at all.

She wasn't sure how she felt about that.

Her mistrust of Bob had crept in slowly. At first she'd been enthralled by her secret – talking and sharing her troubles with someone no one else could see. Initially, Bob had been witty, lightly sarcastic, a "bellyful of fun," as her Uncle Wayne would've said.

Unfortunately, things had changed. Even though he still told her stories she mostly liked, some of them had been frightening, darker than usual. Also, he'd been mean lately, playing awful tricks on her, like waiting until she got near a body of water and then popping out, yelling, "BOO! I'm gonna gobble ya right up!"

This always scared her, but he seemed to think it was funny; and sometimes, Carolyn wondered if his threat to "gobble" her up was only a joke, or perhaps something more - which she always dismissed, of course, because it was stupid.

Still, something was different about him, and she never knew what he was going to do next.

"It's like playing with Mrs. Snowballs," she whispered as she neared the bridge, "every time I pet her, I wonder if she's gonna go nuts and claw me."

Mrs. Snowballs, her Aunt Sylvia's cat, was old and starting to lose its mind, and could never decide anymore whether it was a friendly lap cat, playful kitten, or bitter old feline marm who'd soon as take someone's eye out than let anyone touch her. Lately, Bob was the same way; she never knew what was he was going to do. He still made her laugh often enough and listened to her secrets – she'd told him about Jesse Kretch – but a couple times he'd been rude enough to almost make her cry.

That, and she couldn't dodge the sense that he lied most of the time.
It was very hard to know for sure, because his fantastic storytelling was the most entrancing thing about him. It was as if he knew what she craved most: stories, wildly entertaining and imaginative stories. He'd thrilled her with heroic tales of bravery in battles between dragons and ogres, and amazed her with the courage he'd displayed facing them all. She drank the stories in, never once questioning their truth.

Now, however, she wondered how much of a valiant hero Bob had actually been.

Up ahead, right before the bridge in a ditch on the left side of the road, she saw a wide patch of ice, gleaming in the sun. The sight diffused some of her anger and released the little girl within, and she broke into a jog, forgetting about embarrassments in front of boys she liked, strange, stinky men, and unreliable imaginary friends.

As she ran towards the ice patch, she spread her arms into steadying wings. At its edge she hopped – just a tiny bit, because hopping too high would throw her off-balance and onto her ass – and touched down on the ice, feet completely flat, legs flexed as she crouched for balance, arms spread like rudders.

She closed her eyes and she slid across the ice, brisk winter air burning her face and eyelashes, cheeks and forehead. For a moment she forgot her troubles and they faded while she slid forward in a solitary dance. Things were good – at this moment, they were good.

"Hey, Baby Cakes!" came the cheerful, gritty-gravel voice she knew so well, "What's shakin,' ma belle?"

Carolyn's anger returned, and she frowned. Clenching her hands into fists without opening her eyes, she tensed her thighs – good thing Mom had made her take skating lessons every year since kindergarten – lifted and jammed her right foot perpendicular to her left, and in a flurry of frosty snow and ice shards, came to a sliding stop.

She opened her eyes, hugged herself, and glared at the ice, under which Bob the Water Sprite floated, wide, toothy smile greeting her. His long, furry serpentine body stretched out for what seemed like miles under an ice patch that was only two or three feet deep, his outstretched hands sporting four slender fingers which pressed up under the ice. A patch of wavy tendrils on his head - looking like exotic undersea vegetation – rippled slowly back and forth in currents Carolyn knew couldn't be there, while silvery, almond-shaped eyes twinkled.

Bob looked something like a fuzzy seahorse crossed with those wannabe Muppets on the Cartoon Network called "Fraggles." He sported catfish-like whiskers on either side of a long, narrow face, and even sported a tuft of small, soft tendrils as a short beard. He didn't have any ears or legs; his body ended in a tapered, triangular point. Along his back was a spinal ridge that looked a lot like the ridges on the iguanas in her science textbook at school, which sparkled with an ever-shifting kaleidoscope of colors.

Bob grinned, flashing rows of perfectly square teeth. "Lookin' good on that ice there, Carolyn. You could kick Michelle Kwan's ass any day."
Even though the sprite used her new favorite swear, she didn't laugh or smile. Carolyn scowled and said, "I don't wanna talk, Bob; I'm pissed at you. Go away."

Bob spread his hands, smile stretching his narrow, rubbery face into an amused leer. "Aw, come on, Baby Cakes – don't be mad. The spell worked perfectly, didn't it? Ya got just what ya wanted – a big ole' wet one, right on the lips!" He leaned closer to the ice, cupping his mouth as if he was a kid hiding in the rear of a classroom, and whispered, "Didja get any tongue?"

"Bob!" Carolyn squealed, kicking the ice with her boot. "That's gross!"

The Water Sprite threw back his head and guffawed, furry hands on shaking belly, mouth opened so wide Carolyn could almost see down his gullet, and her stomach twitched as she wondered what hid down there in the darkness.

"Stop it!" she squeaked again, wishing her voice was stronger, less girlish. "Stop laughing!"

Betrayal twisted her belly, making her sick. She clenched her hands tightly, biting her lip, using the flash of pain and slight coppery taste of blood to keep the tears away, but it was hard not to cry. She never knew anymore when the razor-sharp point of Bob's merriment would turn upon her, and even though he always acted like it was all in good fun, she sensed a darker face that he hid from her.

"It's not funny, Bob," she grated, remembering Adam's shocked, almost disgusted expression when he realized what he was doing, "Adam's probably never gonna talk to me ever again, and it's all your fault."

Bob's laugh trickled off into a chuckle, and he wiped merry tears from his eyes as he gasped, "Oh Carolyn… my dear, innocent lil' Carolyn. Yer so precious when ya get mad; I swear I could just eat ya right up."

Carolyn fidgeted. Her stomach always gurgled when Bob said things like that, because of a hungry twinkle in his eyes. Pushing her nausea down, she murmured, "It wasn't supposed to be like that, Bob. You said the spell would make him kiss me on the cheek, not on the mouth. That was so gross."

Gross, yes, but in reflection – though she wasn't about to tell Bob this – Adam had tried to push his tongue into her mouth for a second, and she still didn't know what to do with the sensations that aroused. It had made her sick to her stomach and excited to think about his tongue touching hers, but the feelings were so intense, she pushed the memory back into her heart-shaped lock box.

Bob shrugged his furry shoulders. "Ah, what can you say, kiddo? Boys 'r boys, after all; walking balls and hormones, and not much else, 'm afraid. Besides"--he glanced at her with the same look she'd seen some of her male classmates give other girls(the pretty, popular ones, never her, of course)--"it wasn't all that bad… was it? Admit it… ya liked it when his tongue tried to get in yer mouth, didntcha?"

Carolyn stood rock still, her face cold, something icy swirling in her stomach. She supposed it was dumb to think Bob wouldn't know about that, seeing as how he'd made Adam do it in the first place. That's what the spell had done; after all - let him inside Adam, even if only for a second or two.

There were other spells, of course, chants and incantations she'd copied off that fateful page of Heather's book, including one that would free Bob. She didn't know how that worked, exactly, but she guessed it was probably something like what happened with Adam… only for longer.

She stared at Bob, eyes wide, and opened her mouth to speak, but found she couldn't. She was suddenly afraid of Bob the Water Sprite.

Bob, meanwhile, had straightened. His furry little shoulders were thrown back; his arms crossed over his chest. His face softened, his air now of concerned parent, rather than lascivious pervert. "You know, Carolyn, in some ways I'm gettin' a little worried about ya."

His concerned tone caught her off guard and she blinked, confused. "Whaddya mean, worried? About what?"

Bob sighed and floated back and forth, pacing like Dad usually did when either addressing her dropping grades, or explaining why she was still too young for pierced ears, lipstick, eye shadow, or any of the other grown-up things all her peers did. "I'm worried, kiddo, 'cause you ain't got nobody else but me, y'know? It breaks my heart, 'cause I'm worried ya'll be alone forever. That's why I put some extra mojo into the whole Adam-spell-thingie; I just don't wantcha to be alone."

He stopped his ethereal pacing, casting an apologetic glance. "I'm sorry if the tongue-thing weirded ya out, kiddo. I was just hopin' maybe the kid would take a shine to ya is all."

She supposed Bob was trying to make her feel better in his odd, twisted little way, but his words hammered her the way the anvils from Looney Tunes always crushed poor, misguided Wile E. Coyote into oblivion. It was one thing to know she was alone –smell, taste, really know in her bone's marrow – but quite another to hear it so calmly announced, as if it were a detached commentary on her multiplication skills.

She looked at Bob and realized it wasn't a far trip to hating him.

"Bob...." She swallowed. It was hard, because she loved him too, in a way. In a small town where most girls aspired to be like their pop culture idols, it was lonely for an imaginative girl like her. Bob had been great company, and some of the stories he'd told her about fighting off evil wizards and battling trolls while single-handedly defeating underwater monsters had filled her lonely days with color, wonder, and amazement.

Still, today's disaster was too much. She wasn't sure why; perhaps something about his apology rang false, maybe she sensed he was lying and had always meant for Adam's forceful tongue to probe her mouth as another mean prank. Maybe she sensed he really wasn't worried about her, nor did he care about her loneliness.

Suddenly, in a moment of revelation, she sensed the pitch before the wind-up, and suddenly knew with a hot flush of resentment that all his feigned concern was nothing more than prepping for his ultimate agenda – coming into the world.

"Hey, c'mon, Baby Cakes," Bob quipped, clearly eager to commiserate, "turn that frown upside down, willya? I've got the answer to all yer problems; you've known that for awhile now. All ya gotta do is take the plunge, and I can make you the most popular kid in town."

He grinned, showing lots of teeth that looked much sharper than moments ago, and leaned closer, pressing his palms against the frosty underside of the frozen puddle's surface. "You know the words, Carolyn. You've said them to yourself lots, practicing late at night, alone in the dark when you thought no one watched. You know 'em by heart now, I'd even guess." He paused, his grin fading, silvery eyes swelling. "You've no idea what wonderful things I can show you, Carolyn," he croaked, "such wonderful, delightful things. The whole world could be your stage; you'd never be lonely again."

She licked her lips, looked away, the faint, peppermint taste of Adam's breath – he used the same freshener she did – still lingering. Even though Adam's disgust hurt, even though he probably deserved what Bob had done to him because of it, what Bob wanted was wrong. Coming into the world had been Bob's desire from the day she'd conjured him, and it was clear the only reason he'd befriended her was because he wanted a way into the real world.

He was using her.

She sucked in an icy, burning breath. "No," she managed, hands clenched at her sides. "I can't."

Bob leaned forward, hungry hands caressing the ice. "C'mon, sweetie... it ain't so bad, honest. When you finally let me outta here, we'll be pals forever. We'll have such fun. I promise." He clapped his fuzzy hands together, rubbing them gleefully. "Carolyn, ya can't even imagine what it'll be like."

Carolyn shook her head, face pale and cold against the wind.

Bob rushed on. "Like I've toldja lots of times before, it'll be great. You'll see and hear things like never before, you'll know stuff no kids your age know – ace school for the rest of your life, howdya like that? – and you'll be stronger, faster, quicker."

He leaned closer to the ice again, piercing her with a penetrating gaze. "And that's not the best part, is it, sweetie? You'll be able to do whatever you want, Carolyn," he murmured, "and you can have anyone you want, for the rest of your life. No more being alone. When I'm inside you, everyone will want a piece of your action, savvy?"

The last two sentences snagged like fishhooks in her heart; tugging, twisting. She had the barest ideas of what "being inside" meant; all she could imagine was a strange image of Bob playing with a "Carolyn marionette," but the thought of having lots of friends and not being alone...
The thought of tasting Adam's sweet peppermint lips whenever she wanted...

She swallowed, looked at the blue Water Sprite, who at this moment appeared tender, almost forlorn. "I'm lonely too," Bob whispered, "I know what it's like, kiddo, to be surrounded by folks and still be alone. Your parents don't give a rat's ass for ya, and you know it. Dad's too busy messin' around with the secretaries at work; Mom's too busy throwin' parties for every bored mother hen in town, and Bryan?" Bob paused, rolling his eyes and sighing. "Sheesh. He thinks Cousin Heather smokes too much weed? That's like the cannabis calling Mary Jane green, kiddo."

She didn't understand who Mary Jane was, but he waved the euphemism off, saying with a gentle air of finality, "You conjure me up, Carolyn, and you'll never be alone, ever again."

She wanted to say yes.

More importantly: she needed to.

Want.

Need.

There was truth in Bob's words; that was the horrible thing. She knew her parents' love was merely dutiful, and Bryan was, well, an older brother. The fact was, her family would probably never notice the difference.

"You're the one, kiddo," Bob revered, "the best. I've spent a lot time searching, choosing, looking for the best, and out of all the others... you're the one I want."

A light in the darkness sparked, sputtered, and flickered on.

An instant replay of his words – "out of all the others" – carved something cold in her stomach.

"What do you mean?" she breathed, eyes narrowing as she regarded Bob with renewed suspicion. "What others?"

Silence, as Bob floated in the fathomless puddle, staring back, until he finally muttered sotto voice, "Oh, damn."

"What others, Bob?" Carolyn repeated, comforted that the weather was so cold, hopefully no one would be out to see her shouting at a frozen puddle of water, "what others?"

The charade cracked. Bob gave up and smiled, but this was an ugly, perverse grin, showing his predator's teeth. "What, ya think yer the only one?" he sneered. "You think yer the only kid to summon me and beg for someone to listen to your dirty little secrets? I got a whole laundry list of kids like you, a freakin' little black book of whiney losers with no friends, who ain't got nuthin'."

Carolyn jerked; Bob's words were an open-handed slap. The urge to flee clanged against her frozen legs, locking her into place. She swallowed, throat tight, and wheezed, "No... that's not true. You said I was your only friend, the only one in the whole world."

Bob's nasty grin widened, showing more teeth than she thought imaginable – rows and rows of sharp, razor-like teeth – and he pressed himself against the ice. "Kid, I've got tons of friends, and they're just like you – weak, pathetic, and alone."

Sudden tears trembled on her eyelashes, and then froze in the cold as she bit her lower lip, shaking her head quickly back and forth in short, jerky sweeps. "No," she sniffed, her anger doused by heavy loneliness, "s-stop staying that."

The blue, fuzzy little monster – as she now thought of him – pushed back from the ice, folding his arms. "Oh come on, it's true. Sorry princess, ya gotta grow up sometime. First of all, there's little Timmy Johnson, living right at the end of South Street? He's a pain; all he does is complain that daddy beats him when he's drunk, 'cause poor little Timmy likes poetry, which makes daddy worried he's gay, so he tries to beat the gay out of him every now and then."

"S-stop it, stop it…"

"….there's also Jenny Tillman, you know – the one who wears the purple eye shadow and short little skirts the boys all like? She pretends she's really dumb, 'cause when she shows her smarts, her trailer-trash mommy beats her 'cause she's worried her little girl is smarter than she is. Then there's Billy Hopkins." Bob counted each child's name off on an extended blue, worm-like finger. "The fat kid with the black hair and all the pimples?" He sighed. "Well, all I can say is that kid watches way too much Internet porn for his own good."

Fresh tears flooded her eyes, and she wrapped her arms around herself, shivering in the suddenly suffocating cold. She reeled with the torrent of names; Bob was lying, had to be.

Bob smiled again, gently. "It's not like I'm cheatin' on ya, sweetie – I'm not even the same guy when I'm with them. One kid I talk to through the TV; another over his short-wave radio; another plays PS2 with me all the time – and to good old Billy, I'm 'Buxom Babe in Biloxi Who Likes to Drink and Party' on his freakin' Myspace page." Bob smirked, twirling a furry finger next to his ear, "That kid's one sick puppy, Carolyn. Make sure you don't bend over to pick up nuthin' around him, 'cause his eyes'll head straight for your bumpy little ti…."

"SHUT UP!" Carolyn screamed, eyes closed, tears washing her cold cheeks, fingernails cutting angry white crescents into her palms.

Silence. Perhaps even Bob sensed he'd almost gone too far, as he fell quiet for several seconds before offering, "Yer the only one I ever told stories to, Carolyn. I promise. Only you."

Carolyn inhaled, her lungs burning, and she wiped her face with the back of her hand, which of course didn't help much because of her frosted mittens. Grunting, she ripped one off, turned it inside out, and wiped her face as best she could. Muffled by knit wool, she rasped, "Why? Howcum so many kids? Why?"

When no answer came right away, she stomped the ice, her voice shrill. "Why?"

Bob shrugged. "I had ta find the best, strongest, most imaginative kid, right?" He waved a blue hand, adding, "I know I played ya, but I don't want to bond with a loser; I wanna bond with a sure thing, and I'm tellin' ya, that sure thing is you."

She sniffed, wiped her eyes again with the ineffectual rag of a mitten, and coughed.

Out of all the others.

Carolyn clasped her hands to her chest, feelings of betrayal blooming anew. "You're lying," she croaked, her throat sore from the wind and the cold, "you're not lonely at all – not with all those other kids, and you don't need me or want me...."

Bob smiled again, but this time nervously, perhaps sensing he was losing ground. "Listen, Carolyn, all those other kids don't mean nothin', 'cause I'm pickin' you, get it? Yer the one I wanna bond with!"

"No, Bob, you don't want me at all; you just wanna use me to get out...."

"Aw, c'mon," Bob snapped, "don't be a freakin' little sissy, Caroly...."

Carolyn glared at the Water Sprite floating just beneath the ice. His form was no longer oddly attractive or strange, but repugnant and disgusting. Perhaps knowing he'd overplayed his hand, Bob backpedaled again, stuttering, waving his arms, "No, no, wait kid.... I didn't mean that...."

Carolyn stomped her foot again with renewed fortitude. "No," she spat, "I'm not letting you out, Bob. I want you to go away and never come back. Ever."

Silence. Bob stared, hands flexing, whiskers and furry tuft of hair waving back and forth, but completely still otherwise. Something glittered in his fathomless, black eyes, and for the first time in her life, Carolyn O'Hara knew she looked death deep in the face.

Exploding, the Water Sprite attacked the ice, pounding and flailing with all his might, howling and thundering away. Carolyn screamed, scrambled, slipped and fell to the hard, icy ground. Fear flowed through her as she saw the ice's surface tremble and shake and even in some places crack, as an unearthly green glow fired to life beneath, spreading into the gray winter evening.

"Stupid, stupid, stupid little bitch!" Bob yowled as he pounded, each blow harder than the last, shaking the ice. "Say the goddamn chant and lemme outta here; lemme outta here now! I get outta here, I'm gonna tear you to shreds, you worthless piece of....!"

With an ear-splitting howl, Bob swung a mighty blow, which struck the ice hard enough to bow it outward. Cursing, Bob spat, "You damn, damn, miserable little kid!" A portion of his rage spent, Bob placed his hands on serpentine hips and hissed, "There's a bit of the bedtime story I forgot to tell ya, sweetie. Guess what happens to all the other kids when I finally get free? After me and the lucky one bond, we get to have some fun – and I mean some serious gut-munching fun. The first thing we'll do is settle with all the folks that've pissed us both off. Know what I mean?"

Somehow Carolyn scrambled to her feet on shaking legs, and despite her brave refusal to free Bob, cold terror shook her. She stood, trembling, teeth clattering.

Bob leaned in, dark eyes glittering. "Oooh, that's right, sister… if one of those other kids lets me out, and not you… I'm comin' to your door first, and then I'm eating your and mommy's and daddy's and Bryan's guts for dinner."

She was scared. Maybe Bob was lying and maybe he wasn't, but some-where, deep inside where dark things screamed and crawled and cried, she knew Bob would someday get out and come looking for her, to do the bad things he promised. If he looked and sounded and even smelled like someone else, how would she ever know?

"Let me out," Bob cooed, "and we can have all the fun you want, do whatever you want. I mean, I may ask for a few small favors"--he shrugged, looking like an innocent blue Fraggle again--"but what's some people-meat compared to all the power and friends in the world, right?"

To her childish horror, a small part of her wondered just how bad it re-ally would be.

With a great sob, Carolyn choked back her tears.

"You've really got no choice, do you?" Bob whispered, almost omni-scient in reading her despair. "You've only got me, babe – and that's it."

A memory; a spark – a light fearfully lit.

Choice.

Her choice.

She brought Bob into the world… not Bob. She read the chant from the book… not him.

He couldn't do anything.

"But I can," she whispered. "I brought him here, so I can...." She stopped, afraid Bob would hear, afraid she was wrong and the blooming magic inside would be destroyed by speaking it aloud.

...I can make him go away.

Everything stopped; the wind stilled, and Bob's voice faded away. There was nothing but her and the realization she could make Bob go away.

"Well babe, what's it gonna be? Are you an' me gonna party, or am I gonna hafta find some other kid to hook up with, and then come back here and eat yer guts?" Bob chuckled, raising his furry, blue-caterpillar eyebrows as he did so, looking impish. "I gotta be honest; I'm of two minds. Yer the best kid out of the whole lot, buuut..." He leaned forward, pressing hands and face against the ice. "I bet you're also the tastiest, too. Either way – I'm gonna have a bellyful of kid-meat by tomorrow morning, that's for sure."

Balling her fists, she stepped up to the ice's edge and looked down at Bob the Water Sprite, her former friend – and now monster.

She breathed, swallowed, rocked back and forth on her toes, and squeaked, "No. Go away."

Surprise registered on Bob's face, and Carolyn saw something else there, too.

Fear.

"Carolyn," he reasoned as he folded his hands, "it don't quite work like that." He smiled, exposing his teeth. "You can't just make me go away."

Somehow, she knew he was lying. "No," she said, emboldened by this knowledge, "that's not true. I can do whatever I want; I can make you go away, because I don't want you here anymore."

His smile hardened; anger simmered in his eyes. "If that's what you want, sweetie, so I can come eat your eyes out later..."

She stomped her foot, and to her surprise, Bob flinched. "No! No more lies, Bob, no more, you can't hurt me, because I said no. You can't touch me!"

With a roar that shook the ice, Bob the Water Sprite ballooned, swelled and grew into a rippling mass of nightmarish muscle. No longer a little sprite, but now something a cross between a man, lizard, and snake, Bob became something ancient, primal, and evil.

Carolyn went deathly cold at the sight of him.

"Listen girlie," he screamed in a deep, hollowed out voice, "I AM DA-GON! I get what I want, ALWAYS, and I AIN'T about to be stopped by the likes of you!

"LET! ME! OUT!" Each bellow was accompanied by a horrible blow to the ice, which shook and heaved with great splashes of spectral green light.

Carolyn closed her eyes, plugged her ears….and screamed back.

"GO AWAY!"

She screamed for the days and nights of loneliness, wondering where her family was, why they left her alone all the time. She screamed from the hole in her heart where "Daddy" and "Mommy" were supposed to be: black, aching holes that hurt all over. She screamed and screamed and screamed for the best friends she didn't have, the sleepovers she never went on, and the parties she never went to.

She screamed for the stories that were her life, she screamed for herself.

The instant the words left her lips, a concussive blast exploded from the frozen puddle. Ice and water and snow and frost flew everywhere, shards of coldness biting into her skin. Everything was bathed in a sickly green glow, and the air was rent by a horrible, inhuman scream born of darkness, of dark things crawling and crying.

The blast's force threw her backward and she fell, arms and legs akimbo, hands and feet flailing for purchase and finding none as she wheeled into the street. She slipped and turned, her feet sliding to a stop at last, a droning truck horn filling her ears.

She looked up just in time to see the battered, red form of metal she'd last seen parked in front of Chin's Pizza barreling down upon her. She froze, unable to move – her mind locked into place by this final, curious, horrible twist – as she saw twin blazing eyes rush towards her; the paint-chipped, battered metal grille filled her vision…

With a sickening crunch and screeching brakes, Jesse Kretch's swerving red truck punched Carolyn May O'Hara fifteen feet, and while she flew through the air she had the dimmest sense of deja vu, as if she were skating on the frozen puddle again….

…she slid gracefully across the ice…

…bones crunched, blood burst….

…brisk winter air burned her face and eyelashes, cheeks and forehead….

….gravity snatched her, flinging her toward frozen snow banks…

…she forgot her troubles as they faded away…

She plummeted; fell down, down, down – forever down.

...she slid forward in a solitary dance, and things were good...
...her body landed, bones snapped, spine ripped...
...they were good...
....and finally, she fell.

* * *

Jesse Kretch lurched out of his truck's cab, a gash above his right eye pouring blood down over his confused face. Bone-weary from pulling extra shifts at the lumber mill, mind clouded by too little sleep and too many Pabst Blue Ribbons, Jesse stared at the fluffy pink mound crumpled atop the embankment alongside Black Creek Bridge.

Drunken wheels spun and whirred in his head as disjointed puzzle pieces from the last ten minutes fell into place. Normally, after having a few beers at Chin's, he dragged himself to his truck and slumbered at the wheel while he sobered up, the windows down just enough to avoid choking to death on the exhaust.

He squinted as he stumbled towards the pile of pink fur – please be a deer please be a deer oh God be a deer please – bright sun glaring off winter hills, working in tandem with the blood from his wounded forehead to distort his vision. Today, for some reason, he'd gotten into his truck and driven away, despite knowing he'd had a few more beers than normal. As he slogged through wet snow, he remembered nothing but a gray streak of swirling colors, shifting, sliding tires and loud, harsh noises.

And there was the mound of pink, fluffy fur – ringed with something like white cotton, he saw – lying huddled in a heap on the snow bank.
A burst of harsh wind, and a small pink mitten puffed away from the pink and white mound, upward, over, and the down the embankment towards Black Creek below.

A pink mitten....just like the ones he'd gotten for his niece from the Family Dollar in Boonville last Christmas, because he'd no idea what to buy a kid he barely knew.

Bright pink mitten, flying away forever to the ice fields of winter; and there – a tuft of wind puffing up the ends of what looked like a long, pink scarf.

Jesse's world splintered, cracked, crumbled.
"Oh shit," he mumbled, scrambling forward, a mindless machine of desperation, "oh shit, oh shit, oh shit!"

* * *

Carolyn blinked, slowly. She tried to breathe, but her throat – packed tight with rent flesh, ruined cartilage – only twitched. She licked her lips and tasted the saltiness of blood, but couldn't swallow because of the wrecked throat. She felt nothing below her neck.

She felt no pain, anger, or sadness, which she thought strange. Most kids don't think much about dying, and Carolyn hadn't been any different in this regard, but she'd thought about it a little – would it hurt, would she be sad? – the basics, of course.

There was none of that. She was just tired and wanted to sleep, and that was fine by her.

Carolyn.

Her name came from so far away, it sounded like the wind, and as her last few neurons sparked and fizzled and died out, it didn't matter much, because it was a whisper lost among fading recollections and dying memories.

Carolyn. Hey...Carolyn!

One last neuron in her head flared, allowing her to hear as the rest of her blood-soaked brain shut down. Even though she lay facing away from Bob's puddle and her neck was shattered, she imagined turning her head towards the puddle, imagined the blue face of one she had called friend peering over broken shards of ice.

"B-o-b." Her lips never moved, neither did her tongue, yet somehow the sound cracked between her bloodied, torn lips and crushed trachea.

Yeah, it's me - holy shit! Lookit you! Damn, I never meant this to happen, Carolyn, honest I....

"N-o," she somehow wheezed past broken bones and clotting blood, "m-o-r-e."

Huh?

She tried to breathe, and her whole body convulsed. When she finally stilled, she continued. "N-o. M-o-r-e. L-i-e-s."

Bob sighed. *Yeah, I get it kid. No more lies. Sorry I had to play dirty like that, but I always win, kid; I always win.*

She imagined him shrugging. *Well, the endgame's come, kiddo. You in or out?*

Time hung. She wasn't afraid of dying; didn't care she was leaving her family behind, and for some reason she didn't fear what she'd face on the Other Side. She wasn't angry or in pain; and oddly enough, Adam Stillman and all the boys in the world no longer meant anything to her.

In fact, there was only one thing she feared losing, above all others. Stories.

Her stories; everyone's stories. Stories she'd read; stories she'd make. Hell, even though he was a bastard, she feared losing Bob's stories most of all.

She closed her eyes, and felt something small and subtle slide loose inside and hang over the abyss. She licked her lips and rasped...

"I-n."

* * *

Jesse Kretch sank to his knees next to the little girl – the poor, awful, dead little girl – sobbing openly, great tears running down his face and into his mouth, snot bubbling from his nose, leftover blood from his forehead wound trickling in and mixing, almost like strawberry sauce. His head still pounded – from the drink or the accident, he had no idea – and he blubbered, shaking his head, not knowing what to do, realizing with dimwitted horror that now he'd probably get sent to a real jail after all these years; maybe a big one where huge black guys would make him their bitch, all because he'd drunk too much and hit a little girl with his damn truck..

The girl lurched once, and he cried out. She coughed, hacked up clotted blood onto the snow next to her, rolled her crooked neck straight with several audible clicks and snaps, looked at him, and smiled.

"Sweet," she tittered, "fuckin' awesome!"

Mouth hanging open, gagging, Jesse Kretch promptly pissed his pants.

It happened much faster than any sober human eyes could follow, so Jesse was no match in his drunken stupor. The little girl whipped her body around in a mighty jerk to the clacking and snapping of bones re-knitting, then leapt to her haunches, lingering there for just a moment as something predatory flickered in eyes that shone a bright, sterling silver.

"Huh," she said with interest, "this will be different."

She jumped and he flung up his arms, but she batted them aside as she drove him back onto the cold ground. Jesse's head cracked against the winter-hardened asphalt, filling his head with a great pressure that made him sleepy as everything spun around. Blackness rushed in, and the last thing he saw was the skin of the little girl's face melting away to reveal something horrible and scaly and slimy and dark and blue underneath, serpentine tongue flicking, teeth snapping.

He shuddered as the girl's head shot for his throat, and Jesse Kretch knew no more.

* * *

Brisk winter air burned her face and eyelashes, cheeks and forehead as she stood very still, arms outstretched for balance, standing on one foot, though in perfect control. For a moment her troubles faded as the winter air crystallized her breath, and things were good – for a moment, they were good.

WHAT THE HELL? Bob screamed. WHAT THE BLOODY HELL? Carolyn May O'Hara stood on Black Creek Bridge's guardrail, balancing on one foot, arms stretched out, feeling the wind blow through her hair. She no longer felt cold or hurt or angry or sad; she felt nothing, she merely felt there, and that was good enough. She knew things now: deep, ancient, primal things, and her insides crackled with centuries-old power.

All was quiet; Jesse Kretch's pickup still sat stalled, Jesse himself passed out on the ground several feet in front of the truck, unmolested, none the worse for wear.

She was at peace.

Bob the Water Sprite – Dagon, Water God – was anything but as he railed within. I can't fuckin' believe it! All this time stuck inside the fuckin' water, no people-meat for AGES, and you won't let me tear into the guy who ran you down in the road like a dog! What the hell?

Carolyn smiled a picture of a world-weary traveler who'd seen more than she ever wanted to. Allowing Bob inside her so freely had produced an unexpected, yet delightful result.

"My body, Bob," she whispered as she fluidly hopped to her other foot on the slippery, icy guardrail with nary a tremble or slip, "my rules."

No fuckin' way! It's never been that way, and it's never going to be that way, EVER! She imagined furry little Bob pounding away on a bright pink door within, to no avail. *I'm hungry, no one's going to miss that beer sloshed asswipe... so let's dig in!*

"Bob," she mused as she gazed at the iced-over creek below, "Ever have anyone who actually liked having you inside them?"

Again came the mental image of Bob, this time leaning against the pink door, arms folded, petulant. Yeah, one time – a guy named Edgar, back in the 1800's. He was a trip; a writer, and half nuts. Didn't last long; he liked his opium.

Carolyn nodded, still smiling, a knowing look in her eyes. "What was it like being inside someone who wanted you there?"

Her image of Bob grew thoughtful, his expression softening and slivery eyes twinkling. *A lot of fun, actually – like workin' as partners, instead 'a buttin' heads all the time.*

"I bet you compromised a lot."

Bob's imaginary face smiled. *Yeah, we did, kiddo; we did at that.*

"Are you hungry, Bob?" she asked.

Bob straightened, a hopeful look dawning on his furry blue, whiskered, Fraggle-features. *Could eat a goddamn horse.*

"Well then," she remarked as she turned, hopped off the guardrail, and headed across the bridge (hat, mittens and scarf forgotten because the cold no longer bothered her), "I know the perfect place. You game?"

Bob grinned, teeth glinting as he leaned against the pink door in her mind. *Lead on, sister.*

A small glow of contentment filled Carolyn as she skipped out of town, Jesse Kretch left sprawled in the snow to wake up later with a headache, hangover, and unanswerable questions. She hummed a bright little tune any literary scholar would recognize as The Bells, and wondered if Adam Stillman was busy this evening, and if he'd like to have company for dinner.

Kevin Lucia *is a full-time English teacher and part-time graduate student at Binghamton University, enrolled in their Masters of Arts in Creative Writing program. His nonfiction has appeared in Title Trakk, Infuze, Nappaland Literary, and he writes a weekly column for his city newspaper, The Press & Sun Bulletin. His fiction has appeared in Liquid Mind Dreams, Starlines Science Fiction/Comic Book Magazine, Millennium Science Fiction Magazine, Coach's Midnight Diner, Le Belles Lettres, Twisted Ink, and Infuze. A recent piece of flash fiction entitled "City Smells" is forthcoming in an anthology published by Edit Red, his short story "Monsters" was recently accepted by The Ghost Story Society's All Hallows magazine, while another story entitled "The Sliding" will appear in the December/January edition of Darkened Horizons.*

THE AMBROSIA SUPPER CLUB

by David Dunwoody

The original owner of the Ambrosia Supper Club wanted the building to look like "a drop of nectar cascading down the side of the mountain", the mountain in question being part of the Klamath range in northwest California. The owner's brother covered the joint's walls with chalk-white stucco and placed spotlights on the ground around the building, so that the club would be visible from the mountain's base – and it did indeed resemble a glowing teardrop sliding over the mountainside, flanked by dark rock.

The club's original clientele consisted both of local folk and tourists lured north to catch a glimpse of the building, described far and wide in near-mythical terms by its owner – "Just a bit of the nectar of Olympus, fallen to Earth." The interior was simply decorated, with a modest-sized dining area and an open kitchen where customers could watch the staff prepare their gourmet meals. A spiral staircase in the corner of the room led to the offices upstairs.

The Ambrosia Supper Club's financial take eventually tapered to a sustainable but unimpressive point, though the legend of the place never died at all. Still, it was enough that the owner was ready to hang it up and head south in hopes of creating a new sensation. The club shut its doors for a brief period, and was then purchased and reopened, with little fanfare and little changes to the design or the menu. The new owner, a man named Mister Chith, never came down from his office over the dining floor and never the displayed the showman's attitude of his predecessor. The club still survived on its reputation, never again the tourist boon it had once been but a survivor nonetheless.

The present-day clientele were mostly older locals. Younger people made up the staff, including one Vetta Lewis, chief hostess, an ebony-skinned beauty with a shining smile. On the last night of the Ambrosia Supper Club's operation – an unplanned event, mind you – Vetta descended the spiral staircase from Mister Chith's office at six o'clock p.m., the restaurant's peak hour, and made her way to the podium at the entrance to greet those who'd made their reservations. "Well, if you don't look ten years younger!" she exclaimed as Mrs. Donahue was escorted in on her husband's arm.

"You're too kind," came the reply. "It must just be the occasion – fifty years for Edward and me."

"Congratulations! Let's bring you right over to your usual table." As Vetta led them into the dining area, she unpinned from her lapel a note Mister Chith had just given her. Sure enough, in his strange left-leaning scrawl, he'd written Donahue silver anniversary – on the house – serve raspberry cheesecake for dessert.

Chith was an odd, quiet man but neither his kindness nor memory ever ceased to amaze Vetta. The oddness of his character wasn't just due to his name – awkward to say, like the sound one made biting off her own tongue – it was his appearance too. The man had no face. There was only a yawning snarl of scar tissue where his eyes and nose should have been, and beneath that, a toothless gaping mouth that no longer produced sound. He communicated only with notes penned in that unusual scrawl, the same scrawl he used to keep the books. How did the sightless Chith manage to write at all, let alone handle the club's receipts on his own? Just another of the many mysteries surrounding him.

Vetta was long-used to his look, though it had never really bothered her. He emanated such a gentle calm that it was difficult to do anything but wonder at the man. And the cats – he had several felines that wandered the offices upstairs, all of whom adored him. It seemed like every day there was another cat that Vetta had never seen before, as if ferals simply came in and out of the club as they pleased, or at Chith's pleasure.

After seating the Donahues, Vetta rushed to answer the phone at the podium. A man was trying to make a last-minute reservation. "I might be able to get you in at eight-thirty..." she began.

"Party of ten," the man rasped.

"Oh, there's no way we can manage that. You should have called much sooner." Vetta frowned into the receiver. "I'm sorry."

"Party of ten at eight-thirty." The man didn't sound old or infirm; maybe just stubborn.

"I'm sorry," Vetta repeated, "there's no way I can fit you in tonight. Not at all."

"We'll be eating steak, all of us – steak tartare, no sides. And we want one table. All of us at one table."

"Sir, again I'm sorry, but we can't fit you in at all. Good night." Vetta hung up and turned to receive a young couple.

The phone rang. It almost seemed to have an insistent, nagging tone, and she knew immediately who it was. "Ambrosia Supper Club, this is Vetta, how may I help you."

"Party of ten. For eight-thirty. The name is Lugal."

"Sir, I can't help you. Goodbye."

She hung up. The phone jumped in its cradle with a shrill ring.

"Ambrosia—"

"I want a table tonight, you hear me? We'll be coming one way or another and we want a table to sit at! A table for ten!"

She slammed the phone down, giving the couple before her an apologetic look. "Right this way." She ignored the next ring.

The pager on her waist vibrated. Mister Chith wanted her upstairs. She seated the young couple and motioned for another hostess to take over, then headed for the spiral staircase.

Chith was sitting behind his desk with an orange tabby sprawled across his lap. It purred loudly as he ran his fingertips through the hair on its tummy. His other hand was composing a note.

Who's calling?

"Someone wanted to make a reservation for ten at the last minute. Ten people, not ten o'clock. I told him it was impossible. He keeps calling back."

Name? Chith wrote.

"Lugal."

Chith set the fountain pen down and placed both hands on the cat's sleek body, running them up and down its throbbing length as the purrs increased in volume. His featureless countenance seemed to darken. Vetta waited, and he tore away the top paper on his notepad and wrote again.

Transfer the next call upstairs.

"To your phone?" She had no idea why there was even a phone in the room. He could listen, but not speak; she didn't even know the line's extension.

But Chith nodded. She checked the phone to see the extension. "All right. If Lugal calls again, I'll just put him through."

She went back downstairs and heard the phone screaming from the entrance. "Let me get it," she called, trying not to disturb the patrons around her as she rushed through the tables. The head chef, Grant, looked up from the kitchen and met her eyes. She shook her head: it's nothing. The bald man nodded and went back to the grill.

Vetta grabbed the phone. "Ambrosia Supper Club."

"I want a fucking table for ten. And I want it at eight, not eight-thirty."

"I'll transfer you to our manager." Vetta said through clenched teeth. Before Lugal could reply, she placed the receiver down and sent the call upstairs.

"Who was that?" asked the other hostess, a young blonde named April.

"Some asshole keeps calling," Vetta replied, keeping her voice at a whisper. "Mister Chith is taking it now. I have no idea why."

"He's taking the – how?"

"No idea about that either."

Vetta looked toward the staircase. The orange tabby was sitting on the top step. It stared at her with glittering green eyes. Then it hopped out of view.

She felt something brush against her legs. A brown-and-white tabby made a figure eight around her ankles, then headed into the dining area. She stooped to catch it, but it bolted; a second later she saw it going upstairs.

"Where'd that little guy come from?" she wondered aloud. "April, you stay here for a while. I'll see how it's going with that call."

Vetta crossed the dining area, stopping by the Donahues' table. "How's everything so far?"

"Oh, Mister— Mister—"

"Chith."

"Yes, he sent down this lovely bottle of wine. Thank him, will you?"

"Of course. And by the way, you'll be having raspberry cheesecake for dessert."

Mrs. Donahue beamed. "How did you know? I haven't had that in years! My mother made the most wonderful cheesecake, it simply melted in your mouth. But I don't know if my stomach can handle all this food."

"We'll send it home in a box." Vetta smiled at Mr. Donahue, who patted her hand. Then she went upstairs.

Mister Chith was sitting with the phone at his ear. Several crumpled pieces of paper lay on his desk. Vetta could hear Lugal's obscene yelling. She waited to see how her boss would reply.

He turned his faceless face toward her and motioned for her to leave. "Just checking," she whispered, and backed out. She pulled the door almost all the way shut. Leaving just a sliver of space between the door and the jamb, she peeked into the office.

Chith clutched his notepad in his fist. A gray cat raced across the table as he searched for his pen, then wrote, the phone still cradled next to his ear. He stabbed furiously at the paper. Then, the toothless void of his mouth moved, trying to shape a word; a small, high-pitched sound came from his throat. It sounded like a mewled "no".

Lugal roared. Chith dropped the phone and threw the pen across the room. The orange tabby leapt into his lap, and the gray feline returned to the desktop. Vetta saw other tails flying about below desk level: black, brown, and calico. When Chith's head lifted up, she stumbled back, hustling down the stairs.

Had he been trying to speak to this Lugal character? What had he been writing on all those pieces of paper? Anxiety knotted in Vetta's stomach. She leaned against the service counter looking into the kitchen. Grant walked over. "Hey, you sick?"

"No, just worried. Chith's having it out with someone. I saw him on the phone."

"On the phone, huh?" Grant didn't seem to know how to react. He pushed a plate of noodles into a server's hand. "You look sick, Vetta. Doesn't look good on you."

"Gee, thanks." She hated how direct Grant was sometimes, and with that nasal East Coast bite in his voice.

"Hey, I'm just saying. You're the hostess, you gotta look tip-top. As for me, I'll be covered in sweat and grease by the end of the night."

"Don't let any of the customers hear that."

Grant chuckled. "I'm not trying to be hard on ya. But if Chith's having a bad night, you've gotta be on it, little girl."

"You're right." She couldn't be preoccupied with whatever was going on upstairs. She had to run the restaurant.

After pecking Grant's cheek, Vetta crossed the dining area to the entry-way and excused April from the podium. The phone rang. "Oh shit," she breathed, then answered. "Ambrosia Supper Club."

"What time do you open tomorrow?" A young man's voice. Thank God.

"We open for lunch at eleven." Vetta hung up and glanced at the reservation book. It was nearing seven, and the Gordon party for six-thirty was a no-show. She could move up the Watterson party, if they were here. She looked up to search the waiting area.

A large man with a face full of thick, bristly black hair filled her view. The smell of rot hit her nostrils, and she grabbed a handkerchief, clutching it to her mouth. "H-hello, welcome, name please?"

"Lugal."

His eyes bored into her, blotted and bloodshot. Jesus, he was the size of the front door and he smelled like a corpse. He was wearing a ratty gray suit with stray hairs from his beard stuck to it. His eyebrows – eyebrow, really – looked filthy, greasy, as did the mop of hair on his head.

And his skin was a sickly pale.

"It's only seven," was all Vetta could manage to say.

"I know." Lugal rasped. "I'm here to speak with the manager. Did I talk to you on the phone?"

"Yes, yes you did." She spoke through the silk handkerchief. Was he a mound of spoiled meat beneath that awful ugly suit? She felt like she was going to throw up. Lugal leaned into the podium. "You couldn't get me a table for ten at any time this evening?"

"I – God – I—"

"Is there a problem?" Grant tossed a towel fresh with goat's blood over his shoulder and crossed his arms. "Hi there." He smiled broadly at Lugal. "Anything I can help you with?"

"I've come to see the manager," Lugal growled. Really growled. His huge meaty hands curled into fists. Grant spread his feet apart and blocked the dining area. "You got an appointment?"

"Grant, I can just call up—" Vetta began.

"No you can't, and you know it." He turned back to Lugal. "I said, appointment? Hell, you even got a name, buddy?" He looked over the man's suit. "You can't come in here like that."

"What's wrong with my clothes?" Lugal snapped.

"Ain't your clothes, though they're second-rate," Grant shot back. "It's the smell of death comin' off ya. Haven't you taken a shower this year? Listen up. I run the back of this restaurant and Vetta runs the front. Neither of us likes you and neither of us thinks you have an appointment with our man Mister Chith. So why don't you turn around with your greasy hair and your second-rate suit and walk the hell on out of here before I break something?"

Grant was all smiles the whole time, but he was deadly serious. He'd come up on the streets of Queens and the only thing that made him happier than crafting a perfect meal was kicking the shit out of someone.

Lugal stared down at the chef, fists at his sides, his chest swollen with rage. Vetta still had the handkerchief pressed to her face as she cowered behind the podium. The diners didn't seem to have noticed any trouble yet; April moved from table to table with her megawatt smile and kept everyone's attention on their plates.

"Well?" Grant said.

"When do you close?" Lugal asked quietly.

"Ten o'clock, sir."

"I'll be back at ten. Party of ten."

Lugal turned, casting a wave of decay over the whole entryway, and walked out of the club.

"Who the fuck was that?" Grant muttered under his breath.

"I can't believe you threatened him." Vetta gasped. "Grant, that man could kill you with his bare hands."

"Maybe. But if he did, he'd have half the kitchen staff ramming cutlery down his throat. Fuckin' guy was like a walking stiff, wasn't he? All that hair growin' on him like moss on a burial vault. Fuck him. If he comes back at ten with his pals, me and my crew will take care of them outside. Okay? And you'll still be here, so I'll have you waiting upstairs with your staff and Mister Chith."

"We should tell Mister Chith about this."

"Nah, don't bother. Poor guy can't really do anything about it, much as he'd like to. That's why I'm here, Vetta." Grant patted her shoulder. "You know you're actually looking a little better. Get that napkin outta your face."

He walked back to the kitchen. Vetta sagged against the podium. April was beside her in half a second. "Tell me everything."

"There's nothing to tell. Asshole couldn't get a table, Grant thinks he's going to come back and have an old-school rumble in the parking lot with the cooks. I really think Chith ought to know about this. I'm going upstairs, okay?"

She left April and headed for the spiral staircase. Grant waved at her with a don't-you-dare expression on his face. She steeled herself and marched upstairs.

"Mister Chith?" She opened the office door. "I—"

That was it. All the breath in her lungs and all the words in her brain fell to the floor of her body like broken glass. She just stood and stared.

Beneath an open window, a gentle breeze rustling papers, Chith had been torn apart. Most of him was still in his chair, though the desk was covered in blood. There wasn't a cat in sight, not even a scrap of hair – they must have left, or he sent them away, before—

Vetta fell to her knees. A severed arm with three fingers lay in front of the desk. He used to work those fingers behind cats' ears like a masseuse, putting them into a coma. He'd given Vetta a shoulder massage once and, she was ashamed to recall, she nearly had an orgasm as he kneaded her nerves. Mister Chith, who loved cats and spoke with little notes and was somehow truly magic, was now just dead meat scattered about a room.

There was a bent fork on the floor. Chith had amused the wait staff bending forks and spoons with his mind, or so he implied (Vetta was sure there was a logical explanation but she sure didn't know what it was). This looked like one of the forks he had bent, except on the curled tines there was a bit of his muscle. Vetta threw up on the carpet.

She rose and, making sure there wasn't any blood or vomit on her clothing, went downstairs. She went straight to the podium. "April, what time is it?"

"Barely seven-thirty."

"Go home. Send all the wait staff home."

"What?"

"Please. Please please please just do this. Now. I'll handle it. I need to go see Grant."

She walked on trembling rubber-stick legs into the kitchen, where Grant was filleting a bass. He turned and set the knife down, replacing it with a cleaver. "You're white as a sheet."

"I've sent all my people home." Vetta said. "I'm going to tell any patrons who come through the door that we've had an emergency and have cancelled all future reservations. I'll send them home with a coupon for a free entrée. Everyone who's here, let's just hurry them out and comp their meals if they're unhappy. Mister Chith is dead. He's been ripped to pieces upstairs."

"Jesus Mary." Grant took her hand with his, the one that wasn't holding the cleaver. He stared into her eyes. "You mean it. Every word."

"Yes. Grant, I'm so scared right now. We have to get out of here. We have to call the police."

"No." His voice, trembling as it was, sounded defiant; in the blink of an eye, his shock had turned to anger, and Vetta knew that his stubborn pride would never allow him to flee the restaurant, nor leave the matter to the police. All the other men in the Ambrosia family were the same way. When they heard of Chith's death it would only harden their resolve and seal their fate inside the club... whatever that turned out to be.

The halved bass stared up at Grant from the cutting board. He plucked its eye out and swallowed it. "I'll tell my boys. I'll send the ladies out the back though. We'll double as wait staff for the time being, until we get everyone out of here. Most of the orders are done or getting there already. Vetta, you need to go too."

"No, I can't leave. If I leave... Grant, I've seen him. I saw Chith dead and if I leave now, whatever is supposed to happen at ten is going to happen now."

"Okay. I think you're right. Sit tight right here." Grant walked through a cloud of steam, back into the kitchen.

Vetta stood stock-still beside the dead one-eyed bass and listened to the clinking of silverware and glassware as customers enjoyed their meals. She turned her head slightly to see April ushering her people out the front. Good. They'll be alive tomorrow.

April looked at her. Vetta mouthed: Go.

Grant walked past Vetta and out to the Donahues' table. "Looks like you're about full. You want that cheesecake in a box?"

"You know what, I think we can handle a slice as long as we're here." Edward Donahue said, smiling. Grant clasped his hands and smiled back. "It's no problem at all to get you that box. Meal's on the house, you two."

"But we'll have some cake—"

"I'm just gonna get the box." Grant almost said something he'd regret. Instead, he sent the words upstairs, and his eyes teared. Edward Donahue frowned a little, then nodded. "Why don't we box the whole thing up, dear.

I'm a little tired."

Other customers were leaving as well, and April was pulling her coat on as she turned a party away, the phone next to her ear. Vetta smiled admiringly from the kitchen.

The Ambrosia Supper Club was cleared out at seven forty-five.

Grant's men gathered in the kitchen, each staring at Vetta. "What's the story?" asked Vincent, the sous chef. Grant stepped in behind Vetta. "Okay. Listen up. Mister Chith—"

"Hey, look." Vincent pointed out of the kitchen, toward the stairs.

The cats were coming down. One at a time, they trotted down the spiral staircase and filtered into the dining area. Some leapt onto tablecloths, and others lay beneath chairs. Vetta thought she heard them all purring, and remembered that sometimes cats purr when they're anxious, or in pain.

"Chith's dead." Grant said. He raised the cleaver. "Fucker butchered him upstairs. He's outside with — how many of them are there, Vetta?"

"Party of ten," she whispered.

"There's ten of us. We're gonna take care of them, tonight, right now, no police. We're gonna settle this and that's it."

Vincent nodded at Grant. He plucked a butcher knife from a bowl of dishwater. "How'd they get Mister Chith?"

"I think they got in through the second-story window," Vetta answered. "I don't know how. But the cats... he sent the cats away."

Grant shook his head. "I don't know nothin' about the cats. Fucker's outside. C'mon." He led his boys through the dining area, each in their spotless white uniforms with their names embroidered on the breast.

Outside it was dark. The city below was quiet, and a cold wind made its way around the mountain. The Ambrosia Supper Club, a frozen drop of nectar illuminated by spotlights, was silent as the grave.

The only cars in the parking lot belonged to the employees. Lugal and his party stood on the asphalt.

Lugal's face was covered in blood. So was his jacket. "Doesn't matter," he coughed. "Second-rate shit."

His brothers all looked like him, filthy and hairy, with a pallor of death. They all began taking off their suit jackets.

Grant brandished the cleaver and stepped forward. "You should never have come here. Mister Chith was a good, gentle man and you killed him out of fucking spite. You're gonna die for nothin'."

"Child," Lugal said in his guttural tone, "I've only come to eat."

They changed.

The bristly black hair tore from every pore of their flesh, and the men fell forward, shoulder blades rotating underneath the skin with a loud CLACK-CLACK-CLACK!! Lugal's men screamed in agony, kicking off their pants, some of them too late; those pants tore and fell away in ribbons. Bones arranged in human form unlocked and rolled about under the skin, and Lugal's men screamed and screamed and Grant's boys could only watch in utter horror as the wolves came to life.

Lugal's mouth opened, bled, extended – his jaw dislocated and shifted to allow a bridge of bone from his throat to come out through his nose, catching a sleeve of skin, becoming a horrible snout. His knuckles folded back and rolled on the asphalt, along with the rest of his joints; and the hair settled and the transformation was complete.

The wolves leapt onto the men.

Grant went down first, Lugal smashing him into the ground, dashing his skull to pieces to that his head became a bag of bones sloshing around in brain matter. Lugal tore open Grant's chest and began the feast.

Vincent landed a perfect blow with the butcher knife, driving it beneath a wolf's chin, but the animal batted his hands away and ignored the steel in its throat. It reared up over him. Vincent fell on his ass, crying. The animal tried to howl, and blood sputtered from its mouth. It tore his face off in a rage.

Vetta was in the club, watching through the front door as the wolves each selected a chef and took him down. It was a lightning-quick massacre and suddenly all the fanfare was over and there was just the sound of contented munching.

Munch munch munch in the dead of night.

Vetta screamed.

The Lugal-wolf looked up from Grant; it had prepared his chest cavity like a soup bowl, and its snout was drenched in crimson. Its eyes locked with Vetta's.

Like Chith, it tried to form words with its alien mouth, groaning:

"I eat you nooooooooooow."

Lugal loped toward the club's entrance. Vetta staggered back into the podium, knocking it over. She rolled over and ran through the dining area – the cats were gone again! "GODDAMN YOU!" she screamed at them, stumbling up the spiral staircase.

The hall had three doors. The one at the end was Chith's office, and it was still open. All the cats were there.

The orange tabby stood in the open window beyond Chith's desk. It stared at her, as if calling: this way.

She ran into the office, slipping in blood, vaulting over the desk and running into the windowsill. Downstairs, glass and tables crashed; the wolves howled.

The window was a two-story drop into some bushes. She could just jump out and scurry down the mountainside. But what about the cats, all these cats...? She turned to look at them.

All the crumpled notes that Chith had written while on the phone were being batted into a pile on the desk. She took one of them from a Persian and opened it.

for burning

That was all it said. She opened another, and another; the same.

She yanked the top desk drawer open and found the Zippo. Tears streaming down her face, she ignited the pile of paper. It went up with a whoosh and the cats jumped back.

Lugal reached the top of the stairs. He saw her, behind the burning desk. His jaw CLACK-CLACKED as he forced words through his snout. "STUPID! BITCH!"

Vetta turned to jump out the window. She felt the hem of her skirt catch on the windowframe, on some errant splinter; and she heard Lugal stalking down the corridor, seconds away from sinking his claws into her flesh. In spite of herself, she glanced over her shoulder at the wolf.

The ceiling in the corridor groaned and sagged downward. The entire hallway seemed to warp, and she knew it couldn't be the result of the fire; the raging beasts were bringing the club down around themselves.

Lugal leapt back from the doorway, cringing as the hall shook. Vetta, jostling about in the window, stared into his hate-filled eyes.

Lugal let out a miserable howl. It was answered by others from downstairs. The pack was in retreat. He began backing down the staircase, his gaze never leaving Vetta.

Then the ceiling came down.

Vetta tore her skirt free and jumped.

The night sky and the ground below were the same shade of midnight black, and then everything was black, sound sight taste smell touch, she was unconscious.

Vetta woke up at the bottom of a slope, nestled in leaves. It was dawn. The smell of smoke was thick in her nostrils. She sat up and realized she was still on the mountainside. The little winding mountain road was just a few yards away, and it would take her up to the Ambrosia Supper Club if she dared go.

She stood up and brushed herself off. She didn't look too bad, but she smelled like she'd slept by a campfire. The foliage around her was green as ever, though, wasn't it?

As she headed up the road, it wasn't so.

It turned gray, then black, then it was all a charred smoking mess. A fire truck perched precariously on the shoulder rained water down on the ruined woods. A stout fireman jumped down and ran to Vetta. "Hey! Don't you work at – up there?"

She nodded. He took her by the hand. "Are you all right? Have you been out here all night? Jesus, did you breathe in any smoke? Are you hurt? Let me look at you. Where were you?" Other firemen surrounded her like she was some kind of wonder, and Vetta just nodded in response to their questions.

She walked with them up the road. The fire, they said, had started at the club (which had closed early, God bless) and made its way down the mountain just a bit before the fire department hit it, and they'd spent all night containing the blaze, raining water down on the beast from all sides. It seemed to be dead now. They were, for the first time, venturing into its heart – and they hoped Vetta could tell them about the fire's origin.

"I don't remember much," she said. "I fell out an upstairs window. Or I jumped..."

"You must have jumped." The stout fireman put a blanket over her shoulders. "It's all right. It's common for the trauma to take your memory away, at least for a time. We're just glad you're okay."

"Did you find anyone else?"

"Well, we just barely put out the club fire, and I don't think there's anyone up there. We never met anyone coming down – it's like no one was there, but you know who was there, don't you? Or you will, in time."

They reached the parking lot. The building had been gutted by flames, carving a great black teardrop into the mountainside. "That fire must have been hotter than Hell itself," the fireman marveled. "I don't know if we drowned it or if it just burned itself out."

What at first looked like the remains of fallen trees, Vetta saw, were actually the splayed-out bodies of ten giant wolves, sprawled across the debris that had vomited from the restaurant, each blackened to a crisp. Their very bones were dark as night. The firemen whispered in awe to each other, picking through the scene, and Vetta was able to break away from them and search through the remains herself.

She found what she presumed to be Lugal, tangled up in the molten spiral staircase, its rails snarled around his enormous limbs, his jaw wide open, belching smoke even now. His dead, cooked eye looked up at her. She tugged it out and went to throw it, but then the orange tabby emerged from the brush beyond. It looked expectantly at her.

She saw the bite marks on Lugal's corpse. She saw the gaping voids where the cats had feasted, after he'd been broiled in the collapsing building. And she saw the heads of cats poking from the woods, each eyeing her, as if to say: we never really wanted to leave. We miss him too.

The tabby made a gesture with its forepaw. She tossed the eyeball to it. It grabbed the treasure and trotted away.

David Dunwoody's *first novel, a zombie epic titled Empire, is due out this year from Permuted Press. Other Permuted publications include appearances in volumes 1-4 of the Undead series and History is Dead. Dunwoody's fiction also appears in Fried! From Graveside Tales Press and Read by Dawn 2 from Bloody Books. He writes reviews for The Hacker's Source magazine and Oh-The-Horror.com from his home in Utah.*

MOSQUITO
by Brandon Berntson

Dennis Ketchum thought it funny how a brisk, cool touch pervaded the morning air despite an August in Eastern Texas.

Sometimes you win, he thought. Sometimes you lose.

He smiled, thankful it was that time of year again. One month. One long, relaxing month away from the stress of the job and time alone with his family. Vacation's first day of the year! Dennis relished it like a good book.

Every summer, he took the entire month of August to vacation with his wife and daughter. The yellow Buick station wagon was already packed and waiting in the driveway. Alison and Elsey were just as anxious to indulge in summer's festivities. These vacations were always memorable, sometimes perfect, Dennis thought. He hoped it would be the same this year.

They lived in a tan brick one-story house in a densely forested town called Nacogdoches, near the Louisiana border. The air, during that summer in 2007, was as thick as a quilt and obnoxiously humid. The Atlantic would be worth the wait.

Dennis tolerated the humid, painful summers. He was originally from Idaho. He didn't complain about the weather when Texans had been tolerating it their whole lives. The management position at Docks Outlet had transferred him from Idaho to Texas with an impressive boost in pay. The Ketchums had been in Nacogdoches for three years now, and Dennis—though he often missed the white Christmases of Idaho—was thankful for the warmth and the humid regions of alligator country. Despite how uncomfortable it was, it was a nice change. "Summer" was not a misnomer. It was a different adventure, he often said to his wife and daughter, more thrilling and dangerous. You didn't have to watch out for scorpions, moccasins, and copperheads in Idaho like you did in the south. Have fun playing outside, kids.

As he waited in the driveway for Alison (to finish whatever she was doing) on that slightly brisk morning, Dennis felt a surge of love for his wife and daughter. For reasons he couldn't explain, the feeling surprised him.

Eight-year-old Elsey sat in the back seat of the station wagon, bobbing along to modern pop songs on her headset. She wore a cool yellow and white summer skirt and top, a Houston Astros baseball cap turned backwards. Her feet were bare. She wore Dennis' sunglasses, giving her a colossal, bug-eyed look.

Dennis had changed the oil in the car yesterday, checked the tires, and finished it all off with a good wash, buff, and wax. Suitcases, sleeping bags, toiletries, and various snacks for the road overloaded the car. The tent was strapped onto the roof. You always forget something, though, Dennis thought. That was the law of travel, vacation's first maxim. Whatever they forgot, they'd have to live without. He wanted to get going, back the wagon into the street, put the car in drive, and go go go!

Hit somebody's BMW on the way, and suddenly everyone's vacation is cut short, he thought, with wry humor.

What was taking Alison so long? He thought about calling for her, but resisted.

From town, he'd steer the Buick onto Highway 63, loop onto Interstate 10, and head across Louisiana, Mississippi, part of Georgia, and into northern Florida.

The Ketchums were campers. It saved money and made for robust Christmases later. Camping along California's coastlines had been the tradition before this particular summer. They'd agreed on a change. This year, it would be the Atlantic instead of the Pacific. They'd see Florida for the first time. Elsey would play on the beach and make sand castles. Alison would lounge and swim, basking in the summer rays, and Dennis would therapeutically bury his toes in the hot sand, wrap himself in a good book, and forget about life for a while.

Alison, despite how much Dennis loved her, wasn't a big fan of driving. She'd read US Weekly magazines for most of the way, bounce restlessly in her seat, and ask (at least as many times as Elsey), "Are we there yet?" She'd take pictures for the scrapbook.

For Dennis, driving was half the fun, half the trip, the part that made burying his toes in the sand worth the wait. Dennis thrived on the taming that driving instilled. For him, it was one of the more enjoyable aspects of a vacation. Something about the drone of the tires on the open road, he thought. Very relaxing.

Not that he had to worry about the job now. He'd been waiting anxiously through the summer for this very moment. He'd hardly gotten any sleep the night before, he'd been so excited.

Now, however, he could forget. Let someone else have the headaches and the stress from the managerial position. It wasn't his problem now.

Elsey, he thought, was at an age where she would remember and, hopefully, appreciate the experiences these vacations provided, the sights they'd see.

Thanks, daddy, she'd say when it was all done.

"Don't get sappy," Dennis told himself, still waiting for Alison. Surprising himself once again, he shivered with the strange morning chill.

Dennis grinned. He looked at Elsey, still bobbing along to some song, throwing her arms over her head in time to what was probably an offbeat remake more terrible than the original. At least Alison wasn't around to see Dennis talking to himself.

He looked to the front door where his wife finally emerged, lithe and tall. She wore white summer shorts and a pink tank top, her auburn hair in a ponytail. She was as excited as he was, he saw; her bright green eyes glowed. It was going to be a good vacation.

"That's everything," she said, with relief in her voice.

"I hope," he told her.

She returned his smile, and they got in the car. Dennis shut the door after him and buckled in.

Dennis turned to Elsey. "Ready, princess?"

Alison buckled into the passenger's seat. Elsey silently mouthed the words to some song Dennis didn't know, put a hand behind her head, and pointed at him. She nodded. At him or the song, he didn't know.

Dennis shook his head dramatically and started the Buick, put it in reverse, then backed into the street. They made a quick, last-minute stop for ice and various goodies, and were soon on the highway, heading east.

"The beginning of a vacation is all about relaxation," Dennis told them with emphasis, his hands on the wheel. Other drivers passed them on Interstate 63. "So, sit back, get comfortable, and enjoy the ride. Elsey? Can daddy have his sunglasses?"

Elsey didn't reply. She smiled, bobbed her head, and continued to dance, pointing at him.

"I thought the whole vacation was about relaxation," Alison said.

"I thought the whole vacation was about being in Disney World and having Daddy buy me all kinds of cool stuff," Elsey said, tuning in from the back seat. She smiled.

Dennis raised his eyebrows. Alison did the same and shook her head.

"Your cool stuff is in the cooler," Alison said. "Where it belongs."

Elsey stuck her tongue out, turned up the volume on her headset, and continued to bob her head, ignoring them.

Dennis finally retrieved his sunglasses. The morning sun warmed quickly, and he turned the air conditioner on. Elsey was enthralled in her compact discs, seldom asking questions or stating the fact that she was hungry. The conversation throughout the morning was light but anxious. For Dennis, he felt better already just being on the road.

Throughout the day, they stopped again for gas, to eat, relieve bladders, take pictures, and revel in the first day of their vacation. They joked on and off as they drove. Alison and Elsey took long naps.

When the light faded to dusk, the Ketchums had made it through a virtually hassle-free, eleven-hour drive. They stopped to camp at a KOA campground in Mississippi. The night was still and warm.

With the tent set up, after some awkward labor, Dennis made a quick run for burgers and fries. He returned to camp, dispersing the necessities, and built a fire in the dark. Other campers hid among the thick trees and talked idly or loudly depending on how much they'd had to drink. Dennis found several sticks and shaped them into spears with a pocketknife. Raccoons twittered and made noises in the nearby trees. The position at Docks Outlet felt light years away.

The stars came out one by one, spreading a vast, nebulous array of light across the sky. The moon was almost full. Dennis resisted mimicking a werewolf to keep his family entertained. The fire kept the bugs away. They toasted marshmallows with spears Dennis made and sucked on their sticky fingers.

Why do I do this, labor boy, for what, Dennis thought. What is relaxation good for if you can't enjoy it? That's an eleven-to-one ratio. Not good odds. Why the hell am I doing this to myself?

"Because I love my family," Dennis said aloud, not realizing, for the second time that day, he was talking to himself. Alison raised her eyebrows. Elsey looked slightly repulsed.

"That's sweet," Alison said. "But why?"

Dennis smiled, but didn't reply. He gazed into the fire and let his marshmallow sizzle in the bright orange flames. In the next instant, it dropped into the coals. He smiled and reached for the bag beside his daughter.

"That's your fourth one already, dad," Elsey said.

"Ninth, actually. I had a few when you weren't looking."

Docks Outlet did demand a lot; that was true, but Dennis felt the toil of the job lift in a way previous vacations failed to do. He didn't work a simple eight hours like his fellow employees. He worked ten to twelve hours a day, sometimes six days a week. It definitely made August worth the wait and more enjoyable. One of these days, he thought, he'd have to find something that didn't demand as many headaches, more quality time with his family, and less time outside of home.

But that's not why you're here, he thought.

He knew that, too. He didn't get the opportunities to spend with Elsey as he would've liked. He wasn't getting the time he wanted with his wife, either, making memories, something he could steal from the night sky and put in his pocket. He was trying to make up for the eleven months of being so tiresomely busy. So…gone.

"This is your time, not mine," Dennis wanted to tell them. "It's important you have a good time now, better than any other time of year. That's what you have to remember. This is what I want to give you as long as you take it, keep it, and put it in your pocket."

Yes, he thought. Time away with them. Forever away without bills and gas and groceries and paychecks and toys that'll eventually break on the staircase when you step on them.

Dennis plopped a perfectly browned marshmallow into his mouth.

"Mmmm," he said, through a mouthful. "Good."

Alison grinned. Elsey chuckled.

No more thoughts of the job, Dennis thought. Not for the rest of the night, not for the rest of this trip. You're here with family now, and that's what you've got to savor. The month will go by too fast as it is. Every second counts, comrade.

Dennis thought this, watching the flames cackle. Sparks popped in the air and disappeared above the fire.

Elsey dropped a marshmallow into the flames, reached for it before realizing the consequences, then snatched her hand back.

"Maybe I'll just get a new darn marshmallow," she said, grabbing one from the bag. "Dad keeps eating them and I have to catch up."

"It's a race you can't win," Dennis said, grabbing another marshmallow. "At this rate," Alison interjected, "I'll be towing home the Pillsbury Dough Boy and his cream-filled daughter."

"Looks like you got some catching up to do," Dennis said.

"Did we bring any strawberry syrup?" Alison said, grabbing the marshmallows before Dennis and Elsey could snatch them.

"Strawberry syrup?" Elsey said. "On a marshmallow?"

"Strawberry syrup, baby-cake," Alison said, "goes on everything. Especially roasted marshmallows."

The night was not fit for sleeping. Dennis contributed his decent rest to a long day of driving and the air mattress. When he awoke, the Mississippi sun warmed the tent, making him anxious for another day closer to their destination.

When Elsey went into the showers, she quickly exited, dry and paler and more wide-eyed than when she went inside. Dennis quickly corralled her.

"What's the problem?" he asked.

"I'm not taking a shower in there," she said.

"Why not?"

"Let's just say one day without a shower isn't going to kill me, if that's what you want to know, Buster Brown."

He'd seen the same thing in the men's washrooms. Spiders the size of his palm covered every square inch of the shower stalls. Was it the humidity or just the South? Dennis braved the showers anyway, despite the revulsion he felt, knowing all those tiny eyes were staring at his naked body. Alison decided a day without a shower wasn't going to make her grow gills either. She was eager to hit the road again. Elsey and Alison instead washed up by the cold faucets at the campground.

"You actually showered in there?" Alison said, when Dennis returned to camp. The morning sun was bright and intense in a cloudless blue sky. She wiped her face with an oversized blue Tweety Bird towel.

"It's not as bad as you think," Dennis told her. "They've just got big hairy legs is all. Puts hair on your chest. I thought they were kind of cute."

Alison shuddered.

"You're not quite right," she said, tapping her head. "Up here. You know that, don't you?"

"You're easy to disturb," he replied.

"I'm gonna have nightmares for weeks," Alison said, rubbing the towel through her hair.

After a quick breakfast of cold cereal, they packed the car, rolled up the tent, and steered the Buick onto the highway again.

Clouds moved in. Before Florida's border, a pelting, driving rain hit the interstate. Traffic became congested. The rain sounded like thundering golf balls on the roof of the car. The wiper blades were useless. Dennis found it difficult to think with the noise of the storm and the traffic.

"Good Lord," Alison said, raising her voice over the downpour. "I never thought a rain storm could be so scary."

"Do you mind?" said Dennis. "There is a child present."

"Oh, I forgot."

"Good Lord, mom," Elsey said, daringly. "What the hell's the matter with you?"

Alison's mouth gaped. She stared at her husband. Dennis raised his eyebrows. He knew he shouldn't encourage Elsey's language, but he couldn't help laughing.

"Lucky for you, young lady, we're on vacation," Alison said, turning to face her daughter. "Otherwise you'd have to paint the shed, garage, and our bedroom, clean up the dog poop, scour the toilet bowl, and make other forms of restitution with the neighbors."

"Uh," Elsey said, dramatically. "Duh! We don't have a dog."

"What are you teaching our daughter?" Alison asked Dennis.

"Yes," Dennis said, looking in the rearview mirror. "You know what parent you like best, don't you, princess?"

"I'm still debating," Elsey said.

"Ouch," Alison said. "That's gotta sting."

Dennis shrugged.

They came into Florida soon after mid-day, and the storm finally passed. Elsey was asleep in the back seat. Alison flipped absentmindedly through her US Weekly magazine. Dennis' back was one dull throb from driving. He couldn't wait to stretch out on the beach and run his toes through the sand.

"Are we there yet?" Elsey said, waking from her two-hour nap. Her hair was an auburn mess of swirls and corkscrews sticking to her sweaty face.

"Yeah, we're there," Alison told her.

"Good," Elsey said, relieved. Out of sorts, she reached for the door handle, unaware they were still driving and not parked at the beach. The door was unlocked and unchildproofed, and when Elsey opened it, the loud, rushing sound of wheels over the highway filled the Buick.

Alison screamed. She turned and reached for Elsey, pulling her away from the open door, the blurring road.

"In Jacksonville, baby, not at the beach," Alison said. She crawled halfway over the seat and pulled the door shut. She locked it with emphasis and let out a terrified breath. "Jeez, angel, don't do that to me again," she said. She put a hand to her heart and took a deep breath. Her eyes were wide, looking at her husband.

"Are you okay?" Dennis asked, frowning and checking on Elsey in the rearview mirror. Humorously, she leaned over and closed her eyes, unfazed by the episode.

"Wake me up when we get there, will ya?" Elsey said.

Alison looked at Dennis, her forehead perspiring. She shook her head.

"'Wake me up when we get there,'" Alison repeated. "If there's ever a problem, just wake her up when we get there, okay? Dragged like a dog on the asphalt is no big deal because we'll just wake her up when we get there."

"She's definitely like her mother," Dennis said, slightly calmer after the scare.

"Yeah, she'll change the course of history." Alison finally relaxed, catching her breath.

"She'll throw the entire defense off course," Dennis said, searching for a game to play to pass the time.

"You sound pretty sure of yourself," Alison said, taken aback. She, too, was acting.

"It's something to pass the time," Dennis said.

"How's it hanging behind the zipper?" Alison said, with a devilish smile.

"Hey! There's a little girl back there!" Dennis said, feigning shock.

"She's asleep," Alison said.

"Am not," Elsey said.

"See," said Dennis.

"Damn," Alison muttered. She shook her head.

"You made it happen," Dennis said.

"You're no fun," Alison said, folding her arms. "I don't know why I come on these blasted, hot, sticky trips."

"You're our comic relief," Dennis said. "Vacations wouldn't be the same without someone to pick on."

Alison rolled her eyes.

"If I didn't tease you, it'd mean I didn't like you," Dennis told her.

"That's reassuring," she said.

"Can I come up there and sit with you guys?" Elsey said.

"Depends on if your mother can behave herself," Dennis said. "I don't like the way she's acting lately."

Alison gave in with a grin, and they continued to drive.

Sometime after 7:00 p.m., they found an endless stretch of white uninhabited beach, a subtle shoreline to their right. The sun, although, in the opposite direction, provided a soft orange-red light to the blue Florida sky.

"Well," Dennis said. "I guess we'll have to enjoy it while we can. Take a good long look, guys. Maybe we can pretend to know what it feels like."

"What are you talking about?" Alison asked, frowning.

"Well, we're not really gonna camp," Dennis lied. "I just wanted to show you what the Atlantic looked like." He sighed and shook his head. "Man, it's gonna be a long drive back to Texas."

"No!" Elsey said from the back, easily outwitted. "That's not fair!"

"Well, I was just hoping you wanted to see the ocean, baby, not actually swim in it," Dennis said. "I didn't really have as much time off as I thought. They only gave me a few days. We're all used up. Isn't this just as good? I'll make it up to you at Christmas. I promise."

"Daddy, that's not fair!"

"Just stare at it for a long time, sweetie," he said. "Imagine how warm that water must be. They'll believe you at school when you tell them. The ocean's overrated anyway. Don't believe everything you hear."

"Dad!"

Dennis giggled.

"Not as sharp as we thought," he said. "Okay. Okay. Just joking. We'll stay the night, but we definitely have to go back tomorrow morning."

"Dad!"

Dennis giggled with immaturity, then finally gave in. "All right, all right. We can stay."

"I don't think you're very funny." Elsey pouted, folding her arms.

"Your mom's laughing," he said. "Look at her. She's frickin' crying!"

"Mom! It's not funny!" Elsey said.

"You believed him," Alison said, pointing a finger at Elsey. "You believed him. Ho ho ho."

"You guys are kinda cruel, you know that," Elsey said. She tried looking offended, but she was a good sport. She, also—despite being the butt of the joke—thought the episode amusing. "Mean and nasty!"

"We're sorry, baby," Dennis said, trying to be serious. "We're just trying to have a little fun."

Elsey stared rebelliously at the ocean, white caps folding and unfolding on the wet sand.

Dennis paid a nightly fee to a sickly-looking man in a booth who granted them access to the beach. The man smiled, showing a toothless grin. His white hair was sparse and erratic. Maybe it was the fluorescent lights from inside the booth, Dennis thought, but his eyes looked almost black. His skin was a clammy, blue-veined white.

"Thank'ee, sir," the man said. "Have yourselves a good stay."

Dennis tried to ignore it. The man left him with creepy sensation. He shook his head and forgot about it. He steered the car slowly along the asphalt drive through the empty beach. He couldn't believe they had this endless stretch of sand and shore to themselves. He found a place farther along where they were could set up the tent.

This is perfect, he thought. Absolutely perfect.

Dennis was excited, grinning from ear to ear. He pulled the car to a stop at the far end of a narrow drive. He stepped out and into the warm Florida night, stretched his legs, put his hands on the small of his back, and stretched. He yawned and then surveyed the surroundings with a boyish smile. Campsites surrounded them, situated in large squares made from railroad ties along the sand. The entire stretch of beach, however, was empty. Strange, he thought. Summer vacation, and they were the only ones here. They had the entire Atlantic to themselves. In the morning, the sun would rise over the ocean. He couldn't wait to get up and watch it.

"I can't believe we're the only ones here," Alison said, stepping out of the Buick. Elsey stepped out of the car as well.

"Man, I wouldn't complain," Dennis said. "As nice as it is. This is as good a spot as any, don't you think?"

"It's perfect," Alison said. She stepped around the car and wrapped her arms around Dennis' waist. She planted a hard kiss on his lips. Dennis was surprised.

"Thanks," he said. "I needed that."

"Would you guys stop?" Elsey said. "Jeez! That's all I ever get to see. I'm sick of it."   "We can drive you back home?" Dennis said.

"Kitchen needs a coat of paint," Alison said.

Elsey ran around the car and hugged Dennis around the waist.

"I love you so much, daddy!" Elsey said, squeezing with all her might.

"Only when you want to get your way," Dennis said, feigning disinterest.

"Daddy!"

"What do you say we get everything set up and get to a burger joint," he said. "I'm starved."

"Sounds great," Alison said.

"I love you, daddy," Elsey apologized, frowning.

"That's nice, dear," Dennis said, hiding his smile.

* * *

After dinner, they returned to camp and sat in fold-up chairs in the evening dark, listening to the waves. Dennis had purchased a bundle of wood and made a fire in the pit provided by the campsite. The moon wasn't quite full, but the circle of incandescence was a white bulb in the sky. The ocean was as black as ink in the dark, with its white foam illuminated under the light and the stars. It was a warm, intoxicating night. Dennis sank his toes into the sand.

The ultimate relaxation, Dennis thought, closing his eyes, savoring the moment.

It felt good after the long drive, feeling the ocean breeze, smelling seawater. Dennis kept his eyes closed and breathed it all in. It was too good to be true, he thought. It was virtually too perfect.

"What do you guys want to do tomorrow?" he asked, opening his eyes and looking up into the night sky.

"Let's just relax in the sun," Alison said. "Swim and play in the ocean."

"Elsey?"

"Sounds cool to me, dad," she said. "I'm easy."

"Nah, that's your mother," Dennis said.

Alison gawked.

"What?" Elsey raised her eyebrows.

"Nothing," Dennis said.

Alison, not participating, slapped her forearm.

Dennis raised his head and looked at her, a question in his eyes.

"What's your problem?" he asked.

"Mosquito," Alison said.

* * *

The following day was hot, blue, and lavish. Alison prepared bacon and eggs on the small gas stove they'd brought along. The ocean was intensely blue, a tropical postcard under the clear, cloudless sky. The sand was bright and warm under their naked feet. They rubbed each other down with suntan lotion, played practical jokes, and laughed in the Florida sun. Elsey played along the shore with a plastic red bucket. Alison and Dennis tried to "drown" each other in the warm Atlantic waves. Dennis donned the snorkel gear, but it was difficult getting out past the current. Elsey spent most of the afternoon building a sandcastle and then asked her dad to come look at it.

"That's incredible, Elsey," Dennis said. "It looks like a palace." He was impressed, not humoring. The castle had spires, a moat, and a drawbridge.

"You and mom wanna help me destroy it?" Elsey asked, hopping up and down. She clapped her hands together.

"We'd love to, sweetheart," Dennis said. "Hold on, I'll go get her."

When they were through stomping on the castle, they cleaned up, got in the car, and headed into town to see the sights. They bought souvenirs in local shops, ate a late lunch in town, and headed back to camp in the afternoon.

"Well," Dennis said. "Maybe a few more days here and we'll start heading south. I've always wanted to read a Travis McGee novel on the beach. Then, we'll see what Disney World is like."

Elsey looked at him with eyes the size of softballs. She had the bucket in her hand, ready to play in the sand some more.

"What did you just say?" she asked.

"Disney World?" he said, playing dumb. "Did I forget to mention Disney World? Of course, we don't have to go to Disney World if you don't want to. We could spend the rest of the vacation fishing, I suppose."

"Dad, that's not funny," Elsey said. "Are we really going to Disney World?"

Dennis shrugged, playing again. "It's up to you. If you—"

Elsey yipped excitedly, throwing the bucket into the air. She jumped up and down.

"I think you made her very happy," Alison said.

"I have a way with the ladies," he said. "You can calm down now, Elsey."

"Yee-haw!" she cried. "Disney World! Dad, you are the coolest!"

"It's been said," he told her.

Dennis and Alison, amused, continued to watch their daughter.

Dennis suggested they make hot dogs for dinner, sip a six-pack on the beach. He'd have to go into town for the beer, but they'd packed the supplies for hot dogs in the cooler. Alison agreed it was a good idea.

I'll stay here, and we'll get the stuff ready," Alison said. "And when you come back, you'll have a warm hot dog waiting."

Dennis thought about saying something to this, but resisted. Alison was waiting for a reply as well, it seemed. Sometimes the jokes went a little too far, he thought.

Alison studied him, reading his mind. He blushed.

"Maybe I'll go find that beer," he said, awkwardly.

Dennis waved good-bye, got in the car, and drove down the road until he came to the first convenient store he saw, a place called the Gas-n-Grub on the east side of the road. He parked the Buick in front of the store. He took the keys from the ignition, opened the door, and stepped outside. Damn, it was hot!

It's August in Florida for God's sake! You should be used to this.

He opened the door to the Gas-n-Grub, a ding! registering his entrance. It was hot in the store, too, he realized. Didn't they believe in air conditioning?

Dennis stepped around the aisles. He stopped at the cooler, grabbing a six-pack of Moosehead in bottles. He wasn't sure Alison had brought buns for the hot dogs, so he grabbed a package of these as well.

"Anything yer lookin' fer in partik'l'r, sir?"

A moment of déjà-vu surged over Dennis. Where had he heard that voice before? No, that was strange… It wasn't the man from the booth the night before, was it?

Dennis turned and saw the most abhorrent creature he'd ever seen in his life. He realized then… Yes, the glimpse he received of the man yesterday. He was looking at the same person now, his twin brother perhaps. Something about them…

It's not a man at all, Dennis thought. Men don't come in packages like this.

He tried keeping his revulsion at bay.

Keep your eyes from going wide, he thought. Keep your mouth from hanging open. Don't stutter or stumble over your words. This is a real person. He may not look real, but he is. He is very real.

The man looked like…

A mosquito?

The nose was long and pointed, a hook resembling an exaggerated beak. The man looked fit for the grave.

No, he looks older than that. He looks nine hundred and eighty years fit for the grave.

Dark brown spots covered the man's flesh. They weren't liver spots. His teeth were tiny black stumps, as if he'd just drunk a quart of motor oil.

Baby teeth, Dennis thought.

A thin, white T-shirt revealed pale blue, transparent skin.

It, Dennis thought. Refer to It as It. This is not a person. This is a one-hundred-and-ten pound insect. So, be nice.

The old man's hair was thin and white, exactly like that of the man in the booth the night before. His mouth was lipless. He wore long, baggy black pants that covered his feet. Dennis wondered if the man had claws for toes.

Of course, he doesn't have regular feet, Dennis thought. Some other alien appendage is keeping him up. He doesn't have real feet, not human feet.

Dennis resisted the urge to laugh. When he looked at the man's eyes, nothing comical came to mind. Something was terribly wrong here. He'd seen it in movies, read about it in books, but he'd never experienced it because he didn't think it was real. He didn't think it was possible.

It was possible, though, because it was right here in front of him. The man's eyes were enormous. They were enormous and solid black. No white was visible in the man's eyes at all. Two solid black shiny orbs stared at Dennis Ketchum. He could see his reflection in them, like in a pool of black ink.

Dennis went cold all over. He shivered and rubbed his eyes. He wasn't thinking about hiding his disgust then. He just wanted out of the goddamn store.

Do you have any idea how creepy you are? he thought.

"Excuse me?" He remembered: The man asked if he was looking for anything "in pertik'l'r."

"Oh!" Dennis said, trying to regain his composure. "Uh... I think I have everything I need, thanks." He tried to sound normal. Wanting to get out of the Gas-n-Grub as quickly as possible, Dennis hurried to the register.

"Aye, that's well," the insect-man said. "Cause I know where everything is, I do! Can get you anything you need reeeaal quick-like." The old man snapped his fingers with a sound like whip-whip..

"I'm sure you can," Dennis said, setting the items on the counter. "You have the store so finely laid out, I didn't need any help."

"Aye-aye," said the old man like a pirate.

Another man, not half as abhorrent as the one ringing up his groceries, sat in a chair to the right of the register. This man wore a solid brown suit, a brown fedora, and shoes to match. He had a thick black mustache and wore black horn-rimmed glasses. The man did not look at Dennis. He was absorbed in a Penthouse magazine.

The old man was pushing at the buttons on the old-fashioned register with all his might, it seemed.

I'm gonna tell my wife all about you, about how creepy you are, Dennis thought. And she isn't gonna want to touch those hot dog buns. I'll be lucky to get the beer down her throat.

"That'll be eight-seven-ty-seven," the man said.

Dennis handed the creature a ten and waited for his change. When he received it, he tried not to touch the old man's skin, but it was inevitable. The man's fingers were like wet clay. Dennis closed his eyes for a second, trying to catch his breath. The man put his items in a small plastic bag. He found himself looking closely to see if the man left an unctuous film on the beer and hot dog buns.

"Thank'ee fer stoppin' by, sir," the man hissed, putting the bag on the counter. "Will there be anything else, sir?"

The quickest way out? Dennis thought.

"No, thank you," he said.

Dennis forced a smile, the best he could muster. It was harder than he realized. The same familiar ding! sounded above him when he opened the door on his way out. He took the bag and stepped outside into the unsettling Florida heat. When Dennis looked behind him, the creepy old man smiled and waved at him through the window. A chill quivered the length of Dennis' spine.

Not wanting to think about the man, Dennis carried his items to the car. He put the groceries on the passenger's seat, shut the door, and started the Buick. He was sweating. The same frigid shiver traveled down his spine again. He stared through the window at the Gas-n-Grub. He thought about the man in the booth the night before. Did the creature have a brother?

Dennis tried laughing it off as he drove, but a part of him couldn't shake the sudden feeling of dread. What was he thinking? It was only an old man. Maybe the Florida sunshine wasn't as healthy as people claimed. Maybe they should have gone to California this year, too.

He finally managed to laugh about it as he pulled into camp. Once he saw the ocean, the long sandy stretch of beach, he was more his old self. He forgot about how frightening the experience had been. The old man's eyes hadn't been solid black at all, he told himself. It was only the intensity of the lights in the store.

Fancy lights, he thought, bringing the Buick to a stop.

The gas stove, next to the tent, billowed smoke. Dennis shut the car off, grabbing the buns and the beer. He stepped outside, shutting the door behind him.

Did Alison burn the dogs? he thought. Dennis preferred his dogs virtually burnt, but not crunchy.

"I leave that girl alone for one minute—" he said, jokingly.

Alison and Elsey were nowhere in sight. Dennis walked over to the tent, frowning, and set the buns and beer a foot away from the stove.

"Yo!" he called. "What's this all about? Did you fall asleep?"

He peeked inside the tent, but it was empty. He turned back to the stove and lifted the lid. A cloud of hot dog smoke swallowed his face, making him gag. Dennis winced, looked at the black, wrinkled dogs, and turned the propane off. He set the lid on the sand, stood up, and scanned the beach in both directions, his hand shading his eyes.

"Hey! Yo! What gives! Hello! Anybody there! You burned my damn dog!"

He'd been gone how long, twenty minutes? No longer than half an hour. Alison was a goof, but she wasn't careless. Looking at the charred dogs, Dennis' previous dread returned. He looked in both directions down the beach again, moving away from the tent and closer to the shore. Did they take a run or a quick swim, he thought, forgetting about the hot dogs?"What the hell?" he said.

They couldn't have gone far, he thought. The beach stretched for endless miles. They'd be visible for hundreds of yards in either direction. They must've taken a swim.

Ocean waves crashed, rumbling to the sand several yards in front of him. Dennis looked out into the water.

Don't panic, he thought. Perfect reason. Everything happens for a reason.

"Alison!" Dennis cried, putting his hands to his mouth. "Elsey!"

He walked closer to the waves, shading his brow with his hand again. He couldn't make out anything other than the blue waters of the Atlantic. He looked back to the tent, quiet and lonesome. Dreadful silence welcomed him. It was too quiet, except for the crashing waves. He squinted and scanned the south end of the beach. Dennis looked to the north. He put his hands on his hips. "Where in the hell are you guys?" he said.

Had Alison said something about her and Elsey going somewhere else until he got back? Dennis couldn't remember. He looked at the tent again. He stared at the charred dogs, which were still smoking. He couldn't take his eyes off them. Something about them...

Nothing went wrong when you went on vacation, he knew: another of vacation's maxims. The reason you took a vacation was to distance yourself from the stress of home and the job. What he felt, though, contradicted everything he knew: the man in the booth, the trip to the convenient store, how he felt when he was there, the charred hot dogs...

Horrible things happen only to everyone else. Not the Ketchums, Dennis thought. The trip to Florida would prove no different. They still had to visit Disney World. He was supposed to read Travis McGee on the beach.

Despite how impossible it seemed, he panicked. The dread he felt was very real. Dennis' heart picked up speed, beating at a terrible rhythm. He frowned, on the verge of tears suddenly. No, he thought. Not now. Not this. Not my family. Not to us! Oh, dear, God, please let them be okay!

"Where in the hell are you?" he shouted. His palms were wet with heat and perspiration. Or was it fear? His ears and neck were warm from the afternoon sun.

They'd taken a walk, he told himself. They were okay. Maybe they'd tried to follow him to the store to remind him to get ice cream or something.

No excuse, no matter how outlandish, made him feel better. Something terrible had happened. Something horrible. They had somehow—as impossible as it seemed—disappeared.

Minutes passed. He waited for them to walk up the beach, two lone figures walking hand in hand.

But the longer he waited, the more the silence, the aloneness consumed him. Feeling like an imbecile, Dennis cried in frustration.

They were playing a trick. The burned hot dogs were only a ruse. The look on his face would be worth the burned dogs when they jumped from hiding yelling, "Surprise!"

His panic turned to full-fledged terror. He cried and shouted their names, trying to convince himself they were fine, knowing they weren't fine, that everything wasn't fine, that something beyond the most nightmarish imaginings had happened while he was gone.

Dennis Ketchum had lost his wife and daughter to the sea. He didn't know how that was possible. They'd gone for a swim. The tide had pulled them under.

A claw ripped the insides of his stomach apart. Tears streamed down his eyes.

Disney World would not be. Someone else would have the headaches of the department store.

Dennis imagined the worst. Watching the crashing waves, he knew, somehow, they'd taken a short swim before he returned. They'd drowned while the insect-man asked him if he needed anything "in pertik'l'r."

Dennis walked beyond the shore and into the waves. The foaming water curled around his ankles. Tears blurred his vision. Dennis trudged, battling the waves, and beyond. Soon, he was up to his waist in the water.

"ALISON!" Dennis screamed. "ELSEY!"

He couldn't see them. They were gone. The antics, the games they played—all of it—for nothing. His wife and daughter had disappeared, and they weren't coming back.

You're back home in bed is all. That's it. You haven't taken this vacation yet. You're back in bed, dreaming an awful dream. You'll wake up soon. Just force yourself to wake up. People do it all the time.

Dennis continued to cry. It wasn't panic and fear he felt then. It was cold, abandoned horror.

He continued to fight the waves. Something brushed against his waist. Dennis looked down, his sight blurred by tears. Was that a shark, a jellyfish?

He wiped tears from his eyes. It was not a shark, he realized once his vision cleared. Unless sharks had human hands...

But those aren't human hands, either. Human hands do not look like that.

It wasn't his wife, he told himself. Something awful, something horrible in the worst possible way had happened while he went into town.

The thing in the water wasn't his wife. It was a corpse, a lolling, emaciated figure sapped of every life-giving essence. The thing had no substance, no form. It was a skeleton with shriveled skin.

Auburn hair spread across the water. Her fingers were thin and skeletal; her wedding band had slipped off. Alison's body rolled in the waves, long dark hair encircling a wan face, thin neck and arms. He recognized the light blue shorts and white shirt.

Dennis' lungs collapsed. His horror was profound; nothing came from his throat, no sound at all. His eyes stared wide, unblinking, unable to grasp this sudden, nightmarish reality. He'd been longing for this vacation for months. Now his wife was dead.

Dennis did everything to hold onto his sanity.

He sensed the slip, felt it click. It moved at full throttle. From a black, cold abyss, leprous tentacles encircled his throat. If he lived, he'd be a changed man from now on. He would never be the same.

Something had drained Alison's body of every ounce of blood. Something had sucked the life out of her. He was looking at an ancient relic, nourished by the salty waters of the sea. She was a corpse, rotting for years in the grave, only recently unearthed.

Dennis was too horrified to scream, but he was—if only for an instant—able to speak: "Dear God," he said. "Oh, dear God. No."

He said this quietly, as if he were an outside observer looking in. He told himself it wasn't happening to him, but to someone else. He was still in bed, tossing fitfully from one end of the mattress to the other.

Reaching out, Dennis pushed the body aside, but it attached itself to him, refusing to part.

You're going to look like this very soon. That is what you're going to be.

Dennis screamed. He screamed loud and painfully, wailing into the cruel Florida sky. When he couldn't scream anymore, he hung his head in defeat and cried. Where in God's name was Elsey? What had happened to his little princess?

As if in answer, the drone of a titanic engine filled his ears. Looking up from the body of his wife, Dennis wiped his eyes. He frowned as the sky darkened with a million pinpricks of black.

In seconds, they were on him, swarming, crawling into his ears with maddening propulsion. How many did it take to cloud the sky, to bury the horizon, to cloak his vision? Millions? Billions? More?

They crawled up his nose. Tiny needles drilled his eyes. They covered his arms and hands, the space between his fingers. His hide was inches thick with them suddenly, a miracle in and of itself. Streaks of blood ran across his arm when he tried to brush them off. A dry, sandy texture filled his throat as they crawled into his lungs.

They had weight, he realized. Of course, more than a billion were bound to have weight, and he felt them, a leaden mantle pushing him down into the water. Thinking about them, he would've never thought it possible.

Dennis spared a thought for his daughter. They hadn't gotten her, he thought. Elsey was somewhere safe. She'd outrun this horror, he told himself.

He tried coughing them up, but too many forced him to gag instead. He heard them whining inside his chest. His eyes swelled shut. Soon, he felt an intolerable itch. It was everywhere…

Dennis reached up, trying to scratch his ears, the space at his neck. He couldn't get to the itch. A spot on his back was impossible to reach, the space between his shoulder blades…

He fell into the water, submerged. Perhaps that would teach them, or at least make the itch stop, but the little bloodsuckers followed him into the water. He could not drown them.

Dennis tried comprehending how they'd swarmed in such numbers. Didn't this kind of thing happen only in foreign countries, distant lands, fairy tales?

The waters of the Atlantic came together above his head. Water filled his mouth and nose. Could they swim, he thought? Could they follow him into the dark of the Atlantic?

He thought about his wife slapping her arm the night before, what she'd said. He would've never thought, never believed, never imagined...

The darkness was thick and heavy. Maybe that was only his blood leaving him...

Dennis had enough sense to realize his wife was somewhere beside him. He reached for her hand, but clutched empty water instead.

* * *

Ocean dark surrounded him. Night had fallen. He was, somehow, still alive. How that was possible, he didn't know. Then again, how was any of this possible?

They hadn't drained him completely. He had enough blood in his bones for volition, for drive.

Hunger propelled him, a feeling of being incessantly parched. The thought, miraculously, made him smile.

Dennis found the shore. He pulled himself from the ocean water and onto the wet sand. He didn't think he had enough strength to stand, let alone walk. He was confined to all fours, crawling across the beach, a pale, hungry predator. He wanted more. He had to have more.

He put his nose to the air and sniffed. He could've avoided this, he realized. In the cool, summer night, he detected the scent of leprous skin, huge black eyes, an insect who spoke like an Irishman.

Dennis dragged himself across the sand. He could get to his feet with nourishment, but only then. A second chance had been awarded because he was still alive. He was willing to take it.

It was early in the morning, well after midnight. No one was visible as he pulled himself across the road. Not a single car passed.

Strange, because it was summer. Dennis thought the streets should be teeming with people, despite how late it was. Didn't everybody have the month of August free to share with their families?

You know what happened anyway, he thought. It's the same. No one makes it to sundown. It's all over. No one has enough time to warn anybody else. No one cares.

He crawled for a long time. It seemed forever, but eventually, the lights from the Gas-n-Grub emerged just ahead.

He'd forgotten how to read. Messages eluded him. He didn't have to know how to read, however, because the smell was strong: oily, dead skin, blood, the rot of decaying teeth.

He crawled across the warm asphalt until he made it to the door. Feebly, he reached out, pushing it open—the ding!—registering his entrance. The floor was cold. It felt good after carrying himself across the warm sand and asphalt.

He didn't see anything at first, only the aisles of various products. Apparently, the store was open 24 hours.

Something moved to his left, someone hurriedly coming into view from behind the counter. The old man stopped directly in front of him. Had the sonofabitch been waiting for him?

He tried to smile. Instead, his cheeks split, cracking his face open. What little blood he had left spilled to his chin. He wondered who the real monster was here.

"So, you've come back here all on yer own, 'ave ya?" the old man said. "I've got cans of bug spray 'at'll do you in."

Surprising Dennis, the man grabbed a can of Raid from behind the counter, aiming the bug spray at him. A large, toxic cloud issued into Dennis' mummified face. The bug spray, however, was harmless. The incident would've proved comical in his previous life. Now, it only drove him deeper into undead madness.

Smiling, Dennis dragged himself across the floor on his hands. The man threw the bug spray at him. It missed by several feet. It clanked against the window and rattled to the floor.

"What 'ave you come back here for anyway?" the insect-man said. "You'll be better off, you'll see. There's no avoidin' it."

Dennis wasn't listening. He wasn't sure he understood. What did it matter? It was the dryness in his throat. He needed something to quench that dryness, not water or milk, but something richer, something with more substance, something…sustaining...

The old man stepped backwards. He'd trapped himself in front of a display of chocolate pies and cupcakes.

"Ant'ony!" the old man cried, looking to his left. "Ant'ony, get in here!"

Dennis smiled wider, furthering the cracks in his face. He didn't wait for Anthony, the man in the brown suit, apparently.

Dennis lunged himself at the old man. The surge of strength and speed surprised him. The rack of cupcakes and chocolate pies spilled across the floor. The old man screamed and fell under Dennis' weight. He grabbed the man's shirt collar, crawling toward his throat.

How had he gained this newfound strength? Was it a need that sustained him, knowing he must wet his palate?

The old man struggled underneath him, clawing, kicking, and screaming like a schoolgirl. Dennis opened his mouth. He clamped his teeth onto the old man's neck, tearing away a shimmering chunk of oily flesh. Blood splashed between his lips, but it was bitter. Blood spilled into his mouth, over his tongue, and down his throat. Bitter or not, it quenched his abominable hunger.

Dennis drove his face deeper into the old man's neck, gnawing at the tissue underneath, his jaws working in mechanical motions. Using suction, Dennis sucked in mouthfuls of blood, and drank it all down. He felt the blood moving through him like alcohol, warming every fiber and nerve ending. He began to see with more clarity. It was beautiful.

He felt better, more alive. He felt strong. He felt like running his toes through the sand.

Love and light. Love and song. I wonder if this is how Dracula felt?

Blood circulated through him, making everything vivid, electric, and warm. He was starting to see; he was starting to feel.

Under him, the old man quivered, convulsed, and was still.

Dennis nodded a single time. He closed his eyes, relishing the moment, blood dripping from his ashen face. He realized he had strength in his legs to move now. Feeling spread through every nerve ending, tissue, and bone.

Anthony, the Penthouse man in the brown suit, stood in front of him after a time-consuming trip to the men's room. Dennis hadn't noticed. For all he knew, Anthony was still human. At least, he looked human. The thought made Dennis smile, blood spilling down his cheeks again.

Anthony took a step backward, shock and horror on his face. Dennis blocked the man's only escape route. Unless there was an exit at the back of the store, Anthony had trapped himself like the old man had done. He shook his head, holding his arms out. He couldn't speak. His mouth gaped.

Dennis pushed himself off the floor. He forced his legs to work for him. He didn't have to worry about his legs, he knew, only the strength in his jaws, what his teeth could do...

The love for all undead things encompassed him, clutched him in a loving embrace. Maybe it was vice-versa. It didn't really matter, he supposed. Dennis pined to speak, to talk to them. He had a lot to learn. He was a part of them now.

It is up to me now to share this cold isolation, this permeating dehydration. The sea is my timeless castle, my palace from the rigmarole, a place to slake my quiet suffering.

Dennis awoke to a newer and more complete understanding.

For the dead, he thought. For Dracula.

The thought gave him added strength, and he smiled. Anthony was too terrified to move. Dennis lunged at him, burying his teeth (fangs?) into the man's face. He didn't have to limit himself to throats, he realized. He was anxious to go beyond layers of skin to the warm blood underneath.

Anthony screamed and fought, but he wasn't strong enough. Dennis overpowered him, tore flesh away from his face and drank.

The sound of blood rushed loudly through him. He wasn't as thirsty now. The drink was for his ancestors, for rotting corpses the world over. It had nothing to do with hunger, he realized.

He drank for Alison and Elsey.

Anthony went limp. Dennis sucked him dry. He drank until he was full, until the blood gave him the capability to see even more clearly than before, to stand, to move without having to crawl.

He surveyed the carnage. Blood was everywhere. The dead men on the ground were barely recognizable. Glistening pools of blood were smeared across the white tile. The smell was thick and fresh, wet as amphibious flesh.

They weren't human to begin with.

The thought made Dennis want to laugh.

It's your old self coming through. Good to have you back.

Despite this optimism, a feeling of sadness overwhelmed him.

What about my family? he thought.

How could he bring life to them? How could he have them in his loving, dead arms again? Would things ever be remotely the same?

Dennis didn't know. He felt a new perspective, however, coming through. He wanted to find out, no matter what the cost. He'd promised his daughter the amusement park, hadn't he? He still wanted to read Travis McGee on the beach. He wondered if he still had the chance to reclaim his status as husband, his fatherhood. He'd made promises. He was a man of his word, and by God, he would keep it.

Strength found its way into his legs. Dennis stood up. He lurched from the store and into the silent Florida night. Before he knew it, he was running. Yes, he had strength in his legs all right, and it was perfect!

He passed streetlights, empty, vacant storefronts. It felt good, the cool night air whipping through his thin hair.

Eventually, he reached the quiet beach, the lonely, deserted camp where the station wagon and tent now sat as mere relics from a time long ago.

Dennis stopped running. For a minute, he looked longingly at the sea—a look of quiet desperation—the dark waters under the night sky.

His family was out there somewhere in all that ocean dark. If he were any kind of father at all—any kind of husband—he would find them. He'd bring them something special, even if it wasn't what they had before. Something was worth salvaging in all this, he thought, something worth fighting for, something to live for...

Sand kicked up under his naked feet as he began to run. It felt good between his toes. He was surprised how much strength he had despite being dead.

The late tide rolled, easing back from the shore. The moon was a full, massive eye in the clear night sky.

It was funny, he thought. Life suddenly made more sense to him now than it ever had.

We can feed on things of the sea, he thought.

It was worth a shot, he realized. After all, with immortality, he had all the time in the world.

A second chance...

Dennis ran out beyond the waves, determined to resurrect his family, and dove headfirst into the warm black waters of the Atlantic.

Brandon Berntson *lives in Boulder, Colorado and has been writing speculative fiction for almost twenty years. His influences include: Poe, Hawthorne, Dickens, London, Ernest Hemingway, Peter Straub, Clive Barker, Jonathan Carroll, Ramsey Campbell, and that dude from Maine.*

"I am no man's servant, nor do I act without my best interests in mind..."

"I love no one, and no one loves me. This inalienable fact affords me great peaceful slumber..."

"I do not question the existence of God for I have witnessed the devastation He has wrought; moreover, a cordial of fine absinthe is proof enough..."

"The Webley MK VI may be an old revolver, but it will cleanly take the head off of a festering animated corpse..."

"Nothing sickens me more than the grotesque banality of suburbia; while nothing excites me more than thick black eyeliner on a nineteen-year-old girl with fresh piercings and healing tattoos..."

"I am no man's servant, I am Hiram Grange, your last—and ultimately unreliable—hope against the sickness and scourge of the Abyss..."

WWW.HIRAMGRANGE.COM

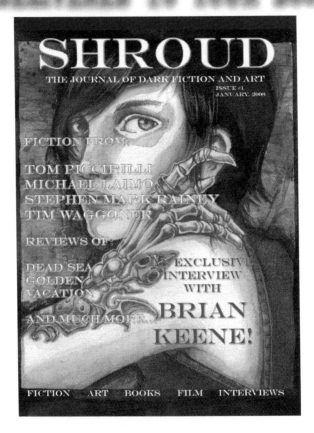

Horrifying New Tales!

Made in the USA
Lexington, KY
28 February 2013